Stealing Phoenix

Joss Stirling

OXFORD
UNIVERSITY PRESS

OXFORD
UNIVERSITY PRESS

Great Clarendon Street, Oxford OX2 6DP
Oxford University Press is a department of the University of Oxford.
It furthers the University's objective of excellence in research, scholarship,
and education by publishing worldwide in

Oxford   New York

Auckland   Cape Town   Dar es Salaam   Hong Kong   Karachi
Kuala Lumpur   Madrid   Melbourne   Mexico City   Nairobi
New Delhi   Shanghai   Taipei   Toronto

With offices in

Argentina   Austria   Brazil   Chile   Czech Republic   France   Greece
Guatemala   Hungary   Italy   Japan   Poland   Portugal   Singapore
South Korea   Switzerland   Thailand   Turkey   Ukraine   Vietnam

Oxford is a registered trade mark of Oxford University Press
in the UK and in certain other countries

British Library Cataloguing in Publication Data
Data available

ISBN: 978-0-19-275658-9

3 5 7 9 10 8 6 4 2

Printed in Great Britain

Paper used in the production of this book is a natural,
recyclable product made from wood grown in sustainable forests.
The manufacturing process conforms to the environmental
regulations of the country of origin.

Stealing Phoenix

For Rachel Pearson

The boy seemed the perfect target. He stood at the back of a group taking the tour of the London Olympic stadium, attention on the construction vehicles beetling up the huge ramp to the athletes' entrance, not on the thief watching him. The building was nearly finished and to my mind resembled a giant soup plate stuck in a wire salad shaker on a green tablecloth. All that was left to do was the last-minute landscaping and put in place the final touches before the world arrived for the games. Others from the Community worked on the site and had taught me where to get in past the tight security. I'd been in a couple of times before because tourists like these students made easy pickings. I had plenty of time to scope out my victim and not many people around to mess up my approach. If I got a good haul I could relax for the rest of the day, head off for my favourite haunt of the local library, and not have to worry about the repercussions of coming home empty-handed.

Crouching behind a parked JCB loader, I studied my target. It had to be the one I was meant to hit: no one else was tall enough and he fitted the photo I'd been shown. With jet black hair, tanned skin, confident stance, he looked as if he wouldn't

1

miss a mobile phone or wallet. Probably had insurance or parents to step in and make up the loss immediately. That made me feel better, because stealing stuff wasn't something I did by choice; it was a means of survival. I couldn't see his face full on, but he had the distracted air of someone whose thoughts were often elsewhere, feet shifting about, not looking where the others did as the guide pointed out the features of the Olympic Park. I guessed that was good news as dreamers made excellent marks, reacting too slowly to a snatch. He was wearing knee-length khaki shorts and a T-shirt with 'Wrickenridge White Water Rafting' running across his broad shoulders. He looked like he worked out so I'd have to get this right. I probably wouldn't be able to outrun him if he chased after me. I retied the shoelaces on my ratty pair of Keds, hoping they'd hold out.

So where were his valuables? Shifting slightly, I saw that he had a backpack slung over one shoulder. Had to be in there.

I edged out from my hiding place, hoping I blended in to the group with my cut-off jeans and tank top—my best and newest clothes which I had nicked from Top Shop the week before. One of the downsides of my ability is that, to make a successful strike, I have to be close to the group I'm working on. That was always the riskiest part. I had prepared by bringing a canvas bag I'd taken from a boutique in Covent Garden, the kind foreign visitors buy as a souvenir with 'London Calling' scrawled on it in arty graffiti. I was fairly confident I could pass myself off as a rich visitor like them if they took the scruffy shoes as a deliberate fashion statement, but I wasn't sure I could pull off looking intelligent enough to belong to their party. According to my source, they had come in from London University and were attending a conference on Environmental Science or some such geeky stuff. I'd barely been to school, educating myself in informal lessons from others in the Community and what I'd read on my own in libraries, so I couldn't speak Science Student if anyone challenged me.

Pulling my hair out of its elastic band, I brushed a couple of long, dark strands forward to flop over my face, the better to hide me from the CCTV camera on the wall ten metres away. I sidled up to two girls standing a metre or so from my target. They were dressed in shorts and tanks like me, though from the pallor of the blonde one's skin she had spent way more time indoors this summer than I had. The other had three piercings in her ear, which I hoped made my five a bit less noticeable. They gave me a sideways look then a cautious smile.

'Hi, sorry I'm late,' I whispered. I had been briefed that none of them knew each other well, having only arrived for their conference the night before. 'Have I missed anything good?'

The one with the earrings grinned at me. 'If you like wild-flower meadows. They've seeded the place with weeds, at least that's what my grandaddy would call them.' She had an accent from America's deep south, dripping with sugar and magnolia. Her hair was braided in tight cornrows that made me think 'ouch' just looking at them.

The fair-haired one bent close. 'Don't listen to her. It's fascinating.' She also had an accent—Scandinavian maybe. 'They're using a light polymer-based membrane for the roof. I played about with the formula for that in the lab last semester: it will be interesting to see how well it holds up.'

'Oh yeah, like that's really . . . um . . . cool.' I was intimidated by them already: they were clearly geniuses and still managed to look good.

The guide beckoned the group forward and we walked up the ramp into the stadium itself. Despite my reasons for being there, I couldn't help feeling the thrill of treading in the same path as the Olympic torch. Not that I'd ever have the chance of being there for the real thing; my dreams of following any kind of sport had never got off the starting blocks. Unless, that was, the Olympic Committee decided to go wild and introduce a medal for thieves—then I might stand a chance. I knew the exhilaration of making a successful steal, the elegant sweep-in and clean get-away; surely that took as much skill as running in circles round some dumb track? Yeah, I was a gold medallist in my discipline.

As the cheerful female guide waved her parasol to encourage us to follow her, we entered into the great oval space of the stadium. Wow. I'd never got this far before on my other excursions on to the site. I could hear in my head the echoes of the cheering crowd. Rows and rows of empty seats filled with shadows of their occupants-to-be. I hadn't realized the future held ghosts as well as the past, but I could sense them clearly. The energy rippled through time even to this quiet Wednesday morning in July.

Reminding myself to keep focused on the job, I eased my way nearer to the boy. I could now see him in profile: he had the kind of face you saw in girls' magazines next to some model as gorgeous as him. He had got the whole deal in the genetic department: chiselled nose, casual-cut ink-black hair that looked good no matter how rumpled it was, dark brows, cheek bones to die for; I couldn't see his eyes because he was wearing shades but I would bet they were huge and a soulful chocolate brown—oh yeah, he was too good to be true and I hated him for it.

I caught myself before I glowered at him, surprised by my response to the guy. Why was I reacting that way? I didn't normally feel anything for my victims, apart from a twinge of guilt that I'd singled them out. I always tried to find people who wouldn't notice the loss that much, a bit like Robin Hood. I enjoyed outwitting my rich targets, but I didn't want to think anyone really suffered from what I did. The Sheriff of Nottingham had his ill-gotten taxes; these days people had insurance from big multi-nationals, and they were the ones who really ripped off the poor. It wasn't as if I were like them, robbing widows and orphans, was it? They got compensation eventually. At least that was what I told myself as I planned how to pick his pocket. This job was a bit different as I was acting under orders; it was fairly rare for me to be asked to steal from a particular mark, but I was relieved the target looked like the sort to be insured up to the eyebrows. Neither he nor I had chosen this so it wasn't rational to turn against him. He'd done nothing to earn it but stand there, looking so sorted, clean and kind of centred whereas I was such a hopeless mess.

The guide wittered on about how the seating had been constructed to be removable. As if I cared about Olympic legacy; I was never convinced I'd see next month, let alone ten years away. A plane rumbled overhead on the Heathrow flight path, scarring the summer sky with its white trail. As the boy looked up, I made my move.

Reach for their mental patterns . . .

They were whirring away like so many beautiful kaleidoscopes, ever shifting. Then . . .

I stopped time.

Well, not exactly, but that's what it feels like to be on the receiving end of my power. What I really do is freeze perceptions so that no one notices time passing—that's why I need small groups in enclosed spaces. Other people might just notice if a bunch of people suddenly went into Madame Tussaud mode. It's a bit like the sensation of passing out under anaesthetic and then jolting awake again, or so I've been told when I've tried my ability out on others in the Community—that's my sort-of-home, though often it felt more like a zoo.

All of us are Savants in the Community: people with extra sensory perceptions and powers. Savants exist because every now and then a human is born with a gift, a special dimension to their brain that allows them to do what others can only dream of doing. There are some of us who can move stuff with their minds—telekinesis; I've met a few who can tell if you are using thought-speak, or telepathy; and there's one person who can mess with your head and force you to do his will. The ways the Savant powers develop are many and varied, but no one else has a gift exactly like mine. I preferred it like that; it made me feel special.

The little group of ten students and their guide all stopped in their tracks, the Scandinavian girl with her hand halfway through her hair, an Asian boy mid-sneeze—the 'aah' never reaching the 'choo'.

Go me: I can even stop the common cold.

I quickly rifled through my target's backpack and struck gold: he had an iPad and an iPhone. That was brilliant news as both are easy to conceal and have a high resale value, almost as much as the original shop-bought items. I felt the familiar rush of victory and had to resist the temptation of taking a picture with the phone of them all standing there, eighteen year olds caught playing Musical Statues. Experience told me that I would pay for indulging my winner's celebration with a crashing headache if I held them for more than twenty or thirty seconds. Stuffing the goods in my canvas tote, I settled the backpack on his shoulders exactly how it had been—I'm good at the details. But now I was standing so close, almost embracing him, and I could see his eyes down the side of his glasses. My heart stopped when I caught sight of his expression. It wasn't the dull glazed look my victims usually wore; he was somehow aware of what was happening, fury burning in his eyes.

He couldn't be fighting my power, could he? No one had ever managed that, not even the strongest Savants in the Community had managed to throw off my freeze-frame attack. I quickly shifted focus to use my other power to check his mind-pattern with my inner sight. I see brainwaves like a corona around the sun, a little as if the person is standing before an ever-changing circular stained-glass window of their souls. You can tell a lot about a person from the colours and patterns, even glimpse their preoccupations. His wasn't stopped in the last arrangement before I struck—that had been an abstract halo of blues entwined with numbers and letters; his brain was still moving, more slowly but definitely alert. The corona drifted into the red spectrum and my face now danced in the flames.

Oh, that really sucked.

Abandoning my attempt to do the zip of the backpack up all the way, I legged it for the stadium exit. I could feel the strength of my hold on them slipping free like sand running out of the bottom of a split sack, far faster than normal. Part of me was screaming that this couldn't happen: I was good at nothing except this; my power to freeze minds was the one thing that had remained totally reliable through all the other madness that was my life. I felt scared to death that somehow that too was failing me. If it did, I'd be washed up. Finished.

My left shoe slapped my heel as I ran out of the stadium—the frigging lace had broken. I headed for the JCB I had originally hidden behind. If I could get that far, I would be able to duck down out of sight and lie in the wild-flower meadow grass. From there I could go on my belly to the concrete culvert that I had used to conceal my entry to the site.

My sole slipped on a rough patch and I lost the Ked by the ramp but I was too panicked to retrieve it. I never made these kinds of mistakes. I always went in and out of a steal leaving no trace. I reached the loader, my heart pounding against my ribs like an amplifier with bass notes booming. The connection snapped and I knew the rest of the students would be aware again. But had he managed to shake off my freeze attack already and track my exit route?

The sounds of the construction work carried on without interruption. No shouts or whistles. I sneaked a peek around the wheel of the JCB. The boy was standing at the top of the ramp, quartering the Olympic Park with his gaze. He wasn't raising the dust, demanding a search be carried out, or calling for the police: he simply looked. That made me even more scared. It just wasn't normal.

No time to think. I retreated to the long grass and found the path I'd already made in the meadow. That should lead me directly back to safety. There were fewer security cameras fitted on this part of the site and several blind spots if you knew where they were to be found, so I should be difficult to locate. I could still get away.

Lying on my stomach, I cast the bag to one side and sagged against the earth for a moment, adrenalin still thundering through my veins like a runaway tube train. I felt sick—disgusted at myself for my unprofessional panic and terrified of what had just happened. There was no time to get my head round it; I still had to escape into the streets and get rid of the stuff I'd stolen.

Reminded that I was now in possession of two very expensive bits of kit, I checked my bag. It felt warm—no, hot. I stuck my hand inside to see what was wrong—so stupid.

The phone and tablet burst into flame.

Swearing foully, I pulled my hand back and pushed the bag away. My fingers stung like hell and it looked as though my whole hand was burnt. Shaking away the agony, I couldn't stop to see how bad it was because my tote was now on fire, sending up a smoke signal of exactly where the thief was. I stumbled to my feet and ran blindly for the fence, gasping with pain. I had to get my hand in water. I no longer cared if anyone saw me; I had to get out.

More by luck than judgement, I found the concrete channel and the gap in the perimeter fence. Wriggling through the wire, my hair got caught and I had to pull hard to get free, adding another injury to my growing list. Then, limping and cradling my hand to my chest, I headed across the waste ground for Stratford Station to get lost in the crowds on the platform.

Chapter 2

'Tony, Tony, let me in!' I beat with my uninjured fist on the battered fire door at the back of the Community; it was the kind with the push-bar on the inside so I had to wait for someone to take pity on me before I could enter.

As I'd guessed, Tony was the only one on duty this early in the day. The others were out and about 'gathering' the Community's wealth. I could hear him shuffling to the entrance, his bad leg dragging with every other stride. With a thump, he fell against the bar and forced it open. The bottom scraped on the broken concrete paving.

'Phee, what are you doing home so soon?' He stood back to let me past and then dragged the door closed. 'Where's your bag—did you stash it somewhere?' A little guy with pepper-and-salt hair, bronzed skin and eyes like a hedgerow bird always on the lookout for a predator, Tony was the closest I had here to a friend. Two years ago, he had come out worst in an argument with a truck he was trying to jack in a lay-by near Walthamstow, not realizing the driver was asleep in the cabin. The man had taken off when he heard Tony's telekinetic powers at work on the door locks, not looking to see the cause.

Tony had gone under the wheels and nearly died. Since then, he'd only had the use of one good arm and leg, the others crushed and never properly healed despite everything I tried to do for him. Community members aren't allowed to use emergency services. We have to fly under the radar, according to our leader.

'You shouldn't be back.' Undecided, Tony hovered in the entrance, not knowing if he should kick me out or shut the door.

'I'm hurt.'

He gave a nervous glance over his shoulder. 'But you're still walking, Phee—you know the rules.'

Having had enough of struggling along, my eyes filled with tears that I could not afford to shed. 'I know the effing rules, Tony. My bag went up in smoke, OK? And I got burned.' I held up my blistered palm. For once, I wanted some sympathy, not to be told my duty. 'It really hurts.'

'Oh, *dashur*, that looks ugly.' His shoulders curved in defeat for a second as he contemplated the consequences, then he stood up straight. 'I shouldn't let you back in but so what? Come with me and I'll sort you out.'

'Thanks, Tony. You're a star.' His kindness helped more than he knew.

Closing the door, he waved off my appreciation. 'You and I both know this won't be the end of the matter, not when our *kommandant* gets to hear of it.' He gave a hopeless shrug. 'But for the moment let's deal with your injury. I expect we'll both regret it.'

I mopped my tears with the back of my hand. 'I'm sorry.'

'Yes, yes.' With his back to me, he made a dismissive gesture with his fingers, a flick of defiance at the onset of trouble. 'We're all sorry—sorry all the time.' He shuffled on ahead down the ill-smelling corridor, part basement, part service tunnel. The Community was squatting on an empty council estate slated for demolition. I think the Local Authority had had dreams that the Olympic development would swallow up this ugly bit of their housing stock but the recession had cut those dreams off at the knees. They'd emptied the low-rise blocks, thinking that the benefit-claiming inhabitants would be replaced by tax-paying city workers, but no one had moved in with bulldozers to build the fancy apartments they had speculated would replace the concrete boxes. Instead, six months ago, we had crept in and established our own little colony. It wasn't as bad as some of the places we'd been in as it still had water, even if the electricity had been cut off. The police had been persuaded with a well-placed bribe or two to look the other way as we broke in to the boarded-up flats. The area tough guys who would've used it for dealing had soon been scared off by our guards. If there was any bad stuff going down in this place, our leader wanted to make sure he was the one benefiting. So we were left to ourselves, a group of about sixty Savants and one dominant Seer, him being our equivalent of a queen bee and us the workers.

'In you go.' Tony ushered me into the little cupboard of a room he had been allocated. Forced by his injuries off active duty, he was only allowed to stay through the 'goodness' of our leader's heart. That goodness only stretched to this hole. I, by contrast, had been granted a proper bedroom on the top floor—the equivalent of a commendation. And, being the best at my craft, I'd never failed the Seer, until today that was.

'How bad?' I asked cautiously as I held out my arm to the grimy window. I could see a white blister forming in the centre of my palm and angry red skin all over my arm up to the elbow.

Tony sucked in a breath. 'Perhaps you should've gone to Casualty, Phee.'

'You know I can't.'

He got a tube of salve out of his holdall, which lay on the mattress. None of us ever unpacked as we always had to be ready to move at a moment's notice. He squeezed a little on to my skin then looked at me through his lashes. 'Not unless you weren't planning to come back.'

'I . . . I have nowhere else to go, you know that.' Was he testing me? The Seer often checked our loyalty by putting us up against each other and we all realized there were spies in our midst.

'Really? A young girl like you should be able to find a better life than this.' He rummaged through his pack and came up with a roll of cling film, our answer to a surgical dressing. We lived like soldiers in enemy territory, self-sufficient, our own first aiders. 'This should keep it clean.'

I bit my lip against the pain as he wound the film around the affected hand and arm, watching the salve squash between burn and covering. 'Is there anything else, Tony? I've never been outside the Community. The Seer says people like us aren't welcome.'

Tony snorted. 'Yes, and *he* knows everything.'

He had always seemed to as far back as I could remember. 'So why do you stay?' If I was being tested, I could at least return the favour.

'I really do have nowhere else to go and no money. I'm not here legally, *dashur*. If they ship me back home, I'd end up in Albania a washed-up ex-car-jacker with no means of support. And I didn't leave my family in the best of circumstances; they'd probably shoot me on sight.'

Most of us in the Community were like Tony, stateless drifters. It was just one layer in the trap in which we found ourselves snared. 'I'm not legal either. I've no birth certificate, nothing. I'm not even sure where I was born.'

'I was there.' He snapped off the last length of film. 'I think we were in Newcastle.'

'We were? So far north?' I hadn't realized Tony had been with us that long so was absurdly pleased to have a little of the blank filled in. 'Do you remember my mother?'

Tony shrugged. 'Yes, she was one of the Seer's companions at the time. Pretty thing, bit like you to look at. Don't you have any memories of her?'

I nodded. 'Not from then—from later, when she wasn't in good shape.' She'd died of cancer when I was eight after a year battling the disease and all I could recall clearly was a painfully thin woman with a fierce hug. Fortunately I'd been old enough to take over her gathering duties so we'd kept a roof over our heads for the last days of her illness. Even facing a death sentence, she couldn't go to hospital—the Seer hadn't allowed it. He'd told me that doctors weren't able to help when his own healing powers had not managed to kill off the tumour. I'd believed him then, but nine years later and a lot wiser to his ways, I wondered. His healing powers had never seemed to me much more than mind over matter. My mum proved that you can't believe yourself better and ignore the pain, as he told us to do, when your body gave out.

'That should do the trick.' Tony dropped the medical supplies back into his bag. 'Are you going to tell me how you got that?'

I swallowed and then nodded. I'd have to tell the Seer later so I might as well see how the story struck a friend. 'I was on the site as I was ordered last night.'

Tony sat down on his mattress. He knew that part already, having been at the meeting where our duties had been divided up as usual. Our colony was living off an area of east London that took in the financial riches of the City and the new Olympic developments on the Lee Valley, sucking up the wealth like a parasite on a healthy animal.

'It was going fine—I lifted an iPhone and an iPad from this student's backpack—a sweet, clean steal.'

Tony whistled in appreciation.

'I'd nearly got away when they . . . um . . . well, they exploded.'

Tony shook his head. 'Phee, those things don't just blow up.'

I held out my hand as evidence. 'They do now. It was like the guy had put fireworks inside them or something. I guess he'd rigged them.' A thought struck me. 'Jeez, you don't think he was a terrorist planning a hit, do you?'

'If only your fingers got burned, then no. Sounds more like an electrical fire than a bomb.' Tony frowned.

My expression mirrored his. 'I did read something about laptops going up in flames a few years back—something wrong with the batteries.'

'Yes, but to do so when you had just stolen them—that can't be coincidence.'

I'd concluded as much myself.

Tony scratched his chin, patches of bristle in the wrinkles making a rasping noise against the rough skin of his palm. 'But he shouldn't have even known you'd taken them, not if you were still on the site.' Tony was shrewd; he knew how my gift worked and had spotted the oddest thing in my story.

I curled up on the foot of the bed, weary to the bone. 'I know. That part really freaked me out. He was aware of me—I swear it. I could see my face in his thoughts as I stole from him—he wasn't completely under, fighting off my freeze attack.'

'Phee!' Tony struggled up to his feet, finally as shaken as I was by the whole sequence of events. 'You can't tell the Seer that! He'll kill you if he thinks someone knows who you are.'

My throat went dry. 'He . . . he wouldn't, would he?'

Tony gave a strangled laugh. 'Where do you think Mitch

went last year after he got arrested and released on bail?'

I didn't want to hear this—I really didn't. 'He went to Spain, didn't he? On a job for the Seer.'

'*Spain*? That's one word for it. He went into a shallow grave in Epping Forest, *dashur*. The Seer got very, very angry with him.'

I wrapped my good arm around my waist and leaned back against the wall. It felt cold and slimy to my bare shoulders. Part of me had sensed the horror that existed just below the surface of life with the Seer, but I wished I could pretend ignorance a bit longer. I was afraid that fear would rob me of what little independence and pride I managed to maintain in the Community.

Tony sighed when he saw my expression. 'Phee, you can only get out of the Community in two ways—you die or disappear.'

'I thought we could leave if we found our soulfinder—our other half,' I said in a quiet voice.

Tony grimaced. 'Who's been feeding you those fairytales?'

My mother, but I wasn't going to tell him that. She had kept on hoping that she would be saved from this living hell by stumbling across her perfect match in one of the cities we'd passed through. According to her, every one of us with a gift had a counterpart, conceived at the same time as us somewhere in the world. Born within a few days or weeks of each other, our lives were a search to find the Savant who could complete us. The hope of meeting my soulfinder had been the story that had warmed my childhood, my mother whispering that I had my own personal Prince Charming waiting somewhere for me. And if my mother had found hers first, then we would have left the Community and I would've had a father, someone to cherish me as a daughter. Of these two stories of hers, I wasn't sure which I'd wished for most. But then my mother had died.

Slowly the dream of a soulfinder—a special person to care for and love me, a relationship more intense than any normal love affair—had died with her. In fact, now I thought about it, it had always been too good to be true.

'I no longer believe such a thing exists.' Echoing my thoughts, Tony squeezed his working hand into a fist. 'It's too cruel to carry on hoping. And even if you did find yours, the Seer would never let you go.'

I closed my eyes briefly, indulging for the last time in the sweet dream that I had a lifeline outside the Community, someone I could stay with for ever. Savants without their soulfinders never commit to another—they can't; they shift from one partner to the next as my mother had. I had never wanted that kind of existence but that was the one I was going to have to live. It was a child's wish to believe someone was waiting to save me. I had to let it go.

'So you have two choices, Phee: death or disappearance,' Tony continued. 'Please, please think about the second; I don't want to be there if the Seer chooses the first for you.' Tony closed the distance between us and placed his mangled hand on my cheek, fingers curled against his palm. 'You deserve better than this. And don't tell him what you told me.'

'He'll know. He always knows.' That was the reason he ruled us: the Seer could smell a lie at a hundred paces. His gifts were strong. He could switch machinery on and off with his brain, manipulate electricity and enter the mind, flipping your private switches to make you do what he wanted, even to the point of killing yourself if that was his wish. Mitch had probably dug his own grave and then thrown himself in on the Seer's orders. Our leader was also a shrewd reader of character, knowing a disloyal thought even before you had a chance to act on it. We had reason for our willingness to serve him.

Tony dropped his hand. 'He'll only bother to check if he doesn't believe you, so make your story convincing. Practise your shields.'

'I've never been able to hold one up against him.' I'd always been too scared to try anything so defiant.

'The Seer likes you; he won't look for flaws if you don't show him any. You need another story.' Tony rubbed his forehead. 'I know, why not say the tour party was a no-show? If you hide your burn, you could claim that there was a change in plan. I'll have a word with Sean—he was on site today but he won't say anything if you make up the loss tomorrow.' Sean was our man on the inside, working security at the Olympic stadium.

'So what was I doing all day?'

Tony paced the small space of his room. 'You . . . you went in search of your targets when they didn't come—it was some conference, right, at Queen Mary College?'

I nodded.

'And you figured out when to hit them tomorrow to get a haul worth at least two days' work—make the Seer drool for all those laptops, foreign currency and phones. He'll give you a day to prove yourself to him.'

I brushed my upper arm above the burn. My skin had goosebumps. 'But he wanted me to hit a particular target and that guy saw me. It's asking for trouble to go after the same person twice.'

'Yeah well, you'll have to do something about that too.' Tony was no longer looking at me, but at the cracked plasterwork above my head.

'What do you mean, "do something"?'

'I guess I mean you need to make sure your iPad boy isn't thinking about someone stealing from him by giving him something bigger to worry about.'

'Like what?'

'For seer's sake, Phee, use your imagination. Freeze him and throw him down a flight of stairs; give him concussion; bash his hand with a hammer—you can come up with something. So far you've only used your gift to steal, but surely you're not too dumb to realize it gives you a chance to do a lot more than that!'

'But he'd get hurt!'

'Go to the top of the class.' Tony turned away, disgusted with me. 'I'm not telling you to kill him—just give him something to occupy him. If he's busy dealing with doctors, he won't be worrying about the case of the exploding iPad, will he? Make him go home.'

'I . . . I can't.'

Tony flung the door open, his patience worn out. 'You forget, Phee, you dragged me into this when I let you in without any haul for the Seer. You need to make sure this ends well and that we are back to normal tomorrow—either that or you make yourself disappear so it doesn't come back on me that way.' He practically threw me out, getting spooked by how many rules we had just broken together. 'Go hide and get your story sorted for your report. I can't help you make those decisions—it's on you.'

I had just run into one of those barriers in the way of real friendship that are part of life in the Community. I took my leave with a brief word of thanks. All of us were trying to survive and a sense of loyalty to another only went so far. Praying for better luck than normal, hoping not to meet anyone, I took the stairs up to my flat as quickly as I could. The light and smell got better the higher up you were. I had one small room on the fifth floor; the rest of this level was occupied by the Seer and his small band of bodyguards and favourites. They would be the only other people at home at this time but I had to trust that they were occupied with their own business and not patrolling the stairwells. The Seer had made his own lodgings fairly luxurious, complete with private generator that was parked outside my door so that all my evenings were spent to the accompaniment of the engine drone and diesel fumes. I didn't mind because it drowned out the noise of his parties. Bad things happened at those and so far I had managed to keep out of them. I wondered for how much longer: I had noticed recently that the Seer had begun looking at me oddly. Having been one of the few children raised in the Community, I'd been protected by the long shadow of childhood; now I was seventeen that had begun to fade. I did not want to be dragged into the light for the Seer to use and cast aside as he had so many other women.

Like my mother.

I made it back to my flat without being spotted. Once inside, I put the flimsy chain across, not because it would stop anyone, but because it made me feel better. The art of living in the Community was to make the most of the small concessions the Seer gave us—privacy one of the most prized. The flat was used as storage for Community goods: stolen electronics, cases of wine, packing cases of leather jackets. It smelt like a department store, not a home. I'd been allowed a bedroom and even a bedstead, a definite mark of favour when most slept on mattresses on the floor. The only others given this privilege were the bodyguards and two other younger members of the Community, both boys, Unicorn and Dragon. Weird names, but then I was called Phoenix so who was I to talk? They were close to the Seer so their special treatment made sense; my privileges were less easy to explain, though I suppose our leader found my gift useful and unique.

That was if it still worked. The Seer would not like to know that there was an exception to my influence. Before the steal, I'd been mentally crowing about being a gold medallist, now I felt like a runner coming in a disgraceful last place. Whatever else I did to the boy, I had to make sure no one else learned that he had been able to resist me.

chapter 3

Nine o'clock at night: my least favourite time of day. Come rain or shine, the Community gathered in the vandalized playground in the centre of the housing complex to report to the Seer. Like the Pope on Easter Sunday, he would emerge on to the balcony above us, watching while his men fetched the haul from each worker. The next day's schedule was then announced, and then, if all was well, we would split up, either back to our rooms or off on another job.

If all was well.

If not, then the offender would be taken up to the Seer's room to speak to the man himself. I knew that was what I was likely facing: no goods to hand over definitely required his personal attention.

I prepared for the meeting by putting a long-sleeved top over my burn and tying a bandage round my palm so it would appear that I'd just cut myself—a frequent hazard of breaking and entering so unlikely to raise any eyebrows. I checked my appearance in the shard of mirror still hanging over the sink in my bathroom. My tan made my dark blue eyes look lighter than normal; my shoulder length hair had been rough cut by me a week ago and now fell in unequal wisps about my face, flipping up at the ends. It looked better than it should do after the hatchet job I'd performed on it with nail scissors. With no make-up and a row of modest studs in my ears, I looked younger than seventeen—which I hoped would count in my favour.

My alarm beeped on my bedside clock, warning me that it was only a minute to go until roll call. I left my room at a jog and joined the others running down the stairs to the playground. No one spoke: the tension at this point was always too high; after the ordeal had been survived, that was when we would stop to talk. I slid into my usual spot by the roundabout and sat on the edge, picking at the paint. I could see Tony lurking over by the swings, as usual keeping a low profile.

At nine o'clock precisely, with a touch of the Seer's mind, the floodlights went on, driving away the dusk. A door opened on the top floor and the white-suited form of our leader came to the rail.

The Seer, real name unknown. Black hair slicked back, face pillowed by double chins, puffy fingers stuffed with rings: he was a heart-attack waiting to happen, but sadly he had never had so much as a twinge. I'd sometimes fantasized how it would be if he did keel over: would we all disperse like escapees from a prison break or would some other bully step into his shoes? He had been grooming Dragon and Unicorn for the top job for a couple of years now, amusing himself with their rivalry. If any of us was going to take over it would be one of them. Dragon's power was to move things by mind alone—I'd seen him shift a car once that way; Unicorn could make things age—fruit ripen, plants bloom and die—that kind of stuff. Of the two, I'd prefer to be attacked by Dragon: being chucked across a room held many more attractions than losing years of my life.

The Seer's men were spreading out through the rest of us to do the collecting. They had adopted a uniform of black T-shirts, leather jackets and trousers, the negative to the Seer's white suit. I kept my eyes on my fingernails, picking off the blue gloss, hoping that by some miracle they'd pass me by. I had plenty of time to think myself into a depression. What was it about us Savants? Why with these gifts were we reduced to living such a shitty life? I'd watched enough television to know that most people my age had families, went to school, had normal settled lives in nice streets. Why was I here in this dump? I'd love to be somewhere where the people under the roof outnumbered the rats. Being a Savant should mean we'd drawn the long straw in the genetic lottery, as by a quirk of nature we'd been given extra, but somehow it had worked out to mean we were twice condemned. Firstly, we were separated from the everyday world by a gift others couldn't know about or they'd dissect us in a lab or kill us out of fear; secondly, we were destined to be alone as we had been given by the Fates a partner we would probably never meet. We were like Lego kits with half the bits scattered on the other side of the world.

'So, Phee, what have you got today?'

Great, my luck was really holding in the 'consistently bad' zone: it was Unicorn who had stopped in front of me. Tall and gangly with a generous nose, he reminded me of a stretched Mr Bean with the personality appeal of Hitler. He enjoyed inflicting punishment on weaker members of the Community; all of us kept our distance when we could.

'Oh, hi, Unicorn. I had a no-show today at the site. But I found out where they'd be at the college tomorrow so I'm planning to hit them then.' Did that sound as reasonable as I'd planned?

He rubbed the bridge of his beaklike nose. 'What are you saying? Does that mean you've got nothing now?'

I didn't have to look up to know that attention was now turning to our little conversation. Any pause in the gathering was never good news.

'Not today. But I'm expecting a really big haul tomorrow, though.'

'Oh, Phoenix, you know tomorrow's no good to the Seer.' His voice was mock sorrowful.

A big chunk of blue paint chipped off. 'I . . . I thought it'd be OK, you know, this once. Just this once.'

He hauled me up by the elbow—my good elbow, thankfully. 'Come on. Let's go tell the Seer.'

No one met my eyes as I was towed across the playground; disgrace has its own repelling force field.

'How did you get back in?' Unicorn asked coolly as he kicked open the waist-high gate.

I didn't want to land my only friend in trouble. 'I twisted Tony's arm. He really didn't want to let me past but I told him about my plan for tomorrow.'

'You could've nicked some other stuff to make up, saved yourself the heat for this.' He pushed me to go up the stairs first.

I shook my head as if surprised by the notion. 'But I thought we had to do the mission we were given—not strike out on our own.' That was one of the Community rules.

'Yeah, but there are times to play by the book, and times to go a little off piste, you get me?' He shoved me in the small of the back as I wasn't going fast enough for his long legs. 'With your gift, I'd have you travelling by tube all day, freezing commuters in the tunnels. Don't know why the Seer wants to waste your gift on small fry like the tourists at the site.' He cleared his throat, realizing what he said sounded too much like rebellion. 'But I'm sure he had his reasons.'

Footsteps climbed the stairs to catch us up.

'Hey, Corn-boy, where you taking Phee?' It was Dragon,

puffing with the unaccustomed exercise. A redhead with freckles, he looked friendlier than he was—a jovial rugby player but with a vicious bite like his namesake.

Unicorn enjoyed his moment of tale-telling. 'She didn't bring anything in.'

'What, nothing?'

'Zero. Nada. Zilch.'

'Phee, you gone mental or what?'

I hung my head, trying for the confused kid look. 'It was no good at the site today so I thought I'd do the job tomorrow at the college—that's if the Seer still wants this group hit.'

Unicorn prodded me back into motion. 'Yeah, he does. He really wants the gear off that one he told you to single out.'

'But I can get lots of stuff off all of them—they each have a laptop at least. Foreign currency too.'

He shrugged. 'Whatever. Tell your excuses to the Seer, not to us.'

Dragon held him back for a second. 'But it's Phee we're talking about. What if he makes her punish herself?'

I was surprised Dragon had any pity for me. Sure, we'd grown up together but that made us more like crabs in a sack, clawing at each other, not allies.

'Not really our problem, is it?' Unicorn hurried me out on to the balcony on the fifth floor. 'I doubt he'd take it too far, not with her. Blood counts for something.'

Blood?

'You're right.' Dragon gave a huff of relief. 'He's not got rid of any of us kids so far.'

I came to a dead stop and swung round to face them. '*Kids?*'

I'd halted so quickly that Unicorn collided with me, pushing me to the floor. He stumbled over my body, treading on my hand. 'Keep moving, you fricking idiot! You can't make it worse by making him wait.'

I clutched my hands to my chest—now both were injured but my shock numbed the pain. 'You said "kids".' I didn't want to get up, not without answers.

'So? Don't say you didn't suspect. The Seer does not keep children in the Community unless he thinks we're his.'

Oh God. 'I'm going to be sick.' I twisted on to my knees to retch but nothing came up but bile. I'd not eaten since the day before so was running on empty.

Dragon seized me by the back of my shirt and pulled me to my feet. 'Get a grip, Phee. The Seer's your daddy and he gave you your powers so you should be grateful to him.'

'He's not my father.' My mother had always said my dad was someone wonderful that she'd met on a romantic holiday in Greece just before she hooked up with the Community. He had been tall, dark blue eyes like me, and handsome—the perfect man, but not a Savant so not her soulfinder.

Dragon shook me. 'I don't give a flying freak who you think your daddy is but I don't want to see you hurting yourself, so stop acting like a fool and do this right. You have to explain yourself to the Seer, not have a mental breakdown on the floor.'

His words were rough but he was speaking sense. Whatever was the truth, I had to box it away, stuff it in the attic and deal with it later, like so many things in life here. 'OK, OK, just give me a moment.' I took a deep breath. A sensible girl would try and make the best of the news, not go into a spin. 'So, if you are . . . you know . . . does that make you, like, my brothers?'

Unicorn snorted. 'Half-brothers, but that's not much more than a biological coincidence, so don't go making more of it than it deserves.'

'Yeah, and have you seen how baby birds behave in a nest?' Dragon grinned, showing his uneven teeth. 'We'd have you up and over the side if you get in the way.' He slapped me on the back, making me stagger into a walk.

OK, so that was clear enough: my may- or may-not-be brothers were only slightly interested in my future, mostly because if something bad happened to me, it could happen to them too. Nothing much had changed.

We reached the Seer standing outside his front door. The other Savants were still gathered down in the playground, held there by his gaze, which was more painful than staring straight at the floodlights. Hearing our footsteps, he turned to us, bringing his pale blue eyes, tiny jewels in a shiny cushion of a face, to rest on me. I immediately felt the prickle of his search through my mind for my excuses. In defence, I flooded my mind with my distress at just learning he might be my father, something that should be enough to distract even him. He broke the contact with a small smile, the sort Dracula has before he sinks his teeth in a vein.

'Unicorn, hand out the schedule for tomorrow.' The Seer's voice was a whisper, as though he was being perpetually strangled. 'Dragon, bring Phoenix inside.'

The one place in the estate where any work had been done was this apartment. The Seer's men had knocked out a couple of walls in complete disregard of structural considerations to make a large lounge-come-party space. The gleaming expanse of floor was oak, stolen from a DIY store and laid by us before the Seer moved in. Three huge leather sofas corralled the massive TV at one end of the room. The Seer's current girlfriends were draped decoratively over the cushions sipping improbable looking cocktails. I always thought it weird that he was pretending he was in a Manhattan penthouse when outside we were in scraggy old Mile End. The effect was about as convincing as a knocked-off designer Rolex selling at the market for fifty quid. The Seer loved his fantasies and this was a cheap version, an approximation of the kind of life he watched on the screen.

The Seer plumped his fat butt down in the centre of the middle sofa, a space already concave to his shape as he sat there most of the day. He wriggled his fingers—a sign that I was to approach. 'Phoenix, explain.'

I stood before him, pausing at the edge of the fluffy white rug as I was afraid I'd get it dirty if I trod on it and so increase his desire to punish me. My story sounded frail even to me as I trotted it out again. Dragon had positioned himself immediately behind the Seer and I could tell from his glum expression that he didn't think it was going well.

I'd wound down to an unimpressive close when the Seer held up his finger. 'You saw the boy I told you to steal from?'

I'd been given a photograph of the target the day before, a copy of his passport mugshot. 'Yes, from a distance. He was easy to spot. I saw him . . . um . . .' think of a plausible place, 'going into a lecture room with the others. He's tall.'

'And you think you can do the job tomorrow—get his valuables as I asked?'

No, because his stuff was a pile of melted circuit boards. 'I'm sure.'

Really? The Seer had switched to using telepathy. I hated the feeling of him crawling around inside my brain.

Yes, I'm certain. I replied in the same way, trying to keep my thoughts fixed on the single thought 'daddy'.

He smiled again and beckoned me closer. I took that as an invitation to sully the rug with my feet. Pointing at a spot immediately in front of him, he waited. What now? I glanced up at Dragon. He was making 'get down' gestures. My knees folded and I sank to the floor at the Seer's feet. A heavily ringed hand patted my head.

'You look very much like Sadie did at your age. I'll have to find you a partner in the Community soon—someone worthy of being tied to my bloodline.'

Ice ran down my spine. I did not want to hear him reminiscing about my mother—or his plans for my future.

'I wondered when you would realize your relationship to me. Your mother filled your head with a lot of lies and it's taken you a long while to come to your senses. I think it's about time you joined Unicorn and Dragon as part of my dynasty.' He paused, clearly expecting me to fill the gap with profuse thanks when I really wanted to run a mile in the opposite direction.

'I . . . um . . . don't know what to say.' That was true at least.

He cupped my chin, squeezing a touch too hard. 'Get the American boy's stuff, Phoenix. I need it. Then we'll see about your future.'

I still had one? 'I will, I promise.'

He let go and I mistook that as my signal to rise. 'Wait. Your punishment.'

I sank back on my knees. The room fell silent; the women not daring to move on the sofas, no ice clinking in cocktail glasses.

A little worm crept into my brain and began sliming its message across my mind.

'You will not eat or drink until you've done this. You won't be able to.' He spoke the words as he imprinted them on my mind telepathically.

Dragon let out his breath, obviously fearing something far worse. The women relaxed; one took a nibble of the olives on the glass-topped coffee table.

The Seer released me. 'Do you understand, Phoenix?'

I nodded, hand pressed to my throat. I could already feel the revulsion to the thought of taking any refreshment planted by his power over my mind.

'Then you'd better make an early start. You wouldn't want to miss breakfast, now, would you?' He chuckled, the great rolls of his belly heaving up and down like a little island undergoing an earthquake. 'Run along, my petal.' He glanced at the blank screen behind me and the television blared into life.

I got up and hurried from the room, leaving the Seer surrounded by his cronies. It didn't take a genius to work out that those not already related by blood were jockeying for position to gain the chance of being the partner he would choose for me, yet another rival for Unicorn and Dragon to worry about. My two 'brothers' would be no friends to this scheme.

Tony hovered in the shadows of the landing, braving the fifth floor when he should have been in the basement. 'Everything OK, Phee?'

I nodded, though I should have shaken my head if I was being truthful. I didn't really have that evil man's DNA, did I?

'You not tell them about me?' So that was why he was here.

'Unicorn knows, but he didn't make a fuss about it. I said nothing to the Seer because it didn't come up.'

Tony scratched his chin then gave a satisfied nod. 'All right. It's all sorted with Sean too, he won't say what went down at the site. You just make sure you come back with lots of stuff tomorrow, deal?'

'Yeah, deal.'

He gave me a brief grin. 'For once, the little guys win a round, hey?'

I wouldn't call it that but he could have his illusory victory. 'Yeah.'

'Goodnight.' He waved farewell as he shuffled off to the stairs.

I couldn't bring myself to reply: there was nothing good about this night. I was going to be hungry and thirsty but unable to do anything about it, but the sickening revelation about my father was the thing that was really going to rob me of sleep. If I had had a star to wish on just then, I would have asked never to have been born.

I was about to retreat into my flat when Unicorn appeared

out of nowhere. He pulled me up short and pushed me against the wall, hand on my neck. 'What did Tony mean?'

'That I . . . I didn't get punished much—that I was given a second chance,' I said quickly, too terrified to struggle against his grip. This was turning into the second worst day of my life—the first place going to the day my mum died.

Unicorn leaned in to me, tightening his grip. 'And the Seer still wants you to go after that boy?'

'Yes.' I closed my eyes against the pain. Was there an inch on me that wasn't going to end up hurting tonight?

'Why?'

How was I expected to know? But then Unicorn wasn't really talking to me, the question hanging in the air between us. He released his hold on my neck and stepped back.

'Tony let you in.'

I'd already told him that. 'Yes.'

'You care about Tony?'

Loaded question. I answered with a shrug.

'I know you do. If you want Tony to be kept out of this, you bring me what you steal from the boy first, OK? *Before* you take it to the Seer.'

That was not in the rules. We were supposed to hand everything over in public at the gathering, not make private exchanges behind the Seer's back.

My expression must have told him I was not happy with this suggestion. He put his hand back on my throat, this time stroking the bruise. 'Does Tony mean so little to you? I thought he was your friend.' He said the word as if it were a synonym for 'cockroach'.

'OK, I'll find you first. Just don't do anything to Tony, please?'

He lifted his hand away and smiled. 'As if I would.'

chapter 4

Infiltrating the Queen Mary College campus was much easier than I anticipated. I was the right age for a student; had made an effort to look as though I was meant to be there, equipping myself with a couple of brochures from the foyer, so no one even challenged me as I pushed through the front doors.

'Can I help you?' the woman on the conference reception asked as I walked up to her. I hope she didn't notice the shadows under my eyes or my unease as I mustered a smile for her benefit. She had a pile of folders and plastic badges arranged alphabetically in front of her. I let my eye drift across the selection, settling on 'Ann Peters'. I glanced quickly over my shoulder to check no one else was behind me who might give me away.

'Hi, I'm Ann Peters.'

She gave me a warm smile in return and handed me the badge and conference material without another word. Then again, who in their right mind would break into a meeting about—I checked the title—*Modelling Climate Change*? I suppressed a snort as I had an image of a bunch of science geeks floating down the catwalk wearing a range of raincoats and sunglasses.

'The first session doesn't start for an hour but you are welcome to go to the café or visit the exhibition in the college library.'

'OK, thanks.' I liked libraries; they'd always been a haven to me. Tucking the pack under my arm, I hurried off in the direction she had pointed. I was trusting that she wouldn't remember that I'd already taken the Ann Peters badge and put the fact that it was missing down to a mistake, but just in case I worked on changing my appearance. I ducked into the Ladies and tied my hair up with a dull brown scarf. Then I put on my favourite pair of clear glass specs which gave me a studious air with their thick black frames. I'd made sure I looked very different from the day before, choosing a long-sleeved white shirt, cardigan and frumpy skirt. No earrings and thick-soled shoes completed the fashion-disaster look. As a final touch, I turned the name card round—didn't want to bump into the real Ann with her name around my neck like an albatross. I wrote 'Wendy Barrie' in the slot, the first name that came to mind, following on the tail of Peters. Inspecting myself in the mirror, I thought I'd pass as a completely different person: Wendy, the ugly sister of the Cinderella who had lost her shoe.

Still, the make-up would have to go. Removing the glasses and running the water in the sink, I washed it off and dabbed my face dry with a hand towel, leaving my skin bare. Even I could see that no mascara or eyeliner made me look vulnerable and tired. I'd not slept in twenty-four hours or had so much as a sip of water for twelve. If I didn't get this done quickly, I was going to be in no fit state to try again. I already knew the Seer was going to be disappointed with me; my target would not have had time to replace his stuff and all I could get from him today would be a wallet and a passport—that's if I was lucky. My confidence had taken a battering. I couldn't forget that the boy had resisted me yesterday; now he knew what to expect perhaps I'd not even get those few seconds of time-freeze. But unless I successfully stole something from him I'd die of thirst—that focused my mind like nothing else could.

Taking a deep breath to steady my fluttering nerves, I consulted the map at the front of the conference programme and headed for the library. I had no intention of looking at the exhibition but had decided it would be the best and least conspicuous place to spy on conference-goers. Finding a quiet corner in the environmental law section, I pulled a book off the shelf and propped it up in front of me, a barrier against the rest of the world. I had a good view—I could see the courtyard where the café was doing a good trade in early coffees and croissants, as well as the exhibition they were all supposed to be taking in.

My stomach rumbled, telling me I was hungry but a stranglehold on my throat warned me not to eat.

What would it be like, I wondered as I watched the students gather in the sunshine, to have such opportunities—travel, friendship, education? The couple of girls I'd spoken to on the site crossed my line of vision like gazelles on the veldt, slim and elegant. They were another species from me, superior beings unaware of just how lucky they were. There were a number of elephants too, lumbering boys who didn't know what to do with their limbs, or how to juggle their stacks of books; I felt a bit less intimidated by them. A short Asian boy stalked through the crowd, a wading bird at the waterhole, picking up choice bits here and there. And then came the leopard, prowling into their midst with the fluid motion of the big cat, shrugging out of his backpack with a ripple of shoulders. I let out the breath I hadn't realized I was holding. My target. He sat next to the gazelles, accepting a bite of croissant from the fair one. They chatted and laughed together, completely at ease in each other's company. How did people become friends so quickly? Didn't they know you couldn't trust anyone? I watched from the sidelines, envious of that comfortable companionship but also suspicious. Nobody I knew behaved like that.

Coffee drunk, the three of them rose and headed in my direction, my leopard pausing briefly to say something to the wading bird. I shrank behind my book. It would be perfect if they came in here—I could get the job done with no fuss. Peeking over the top, I saw that he had left his bag behind in the charge of the Asian student. I felt a snap of annoyance; it was as if he did it on purpose to thwart me. So you aren't making this easy for me then, big guy.

They were talking as they came in, their voices carrying in the hushed atmosphere of the library. I had already noticed that it was deserted out of term time, normal students already on holiday, and none of the others attending the conference were showing much interest in coming in from the sunshine.

My three targets circled the display boards.

'Yves, have you rung your parents about your iPad yet?' the dark gazelle asked, patting his arm.

Yves. So that was his name. Like Yves Saint Laurent, the fashion designer, pronounced 'Eave', though it was spelt with a 'Y'.

'Last night. But it's OK, Jo—fortunately, it was a freebie. I'd been given it by Apple to test—the next generation.' He had a great voice, what I thought of as a hot-chocolate tone. I could listen to him for hours, even if he were just reciting the phone book.

'Wow.' She gazed adoringly up at him. I had a bizarre urge to slap her out of her worshipful daze.

'Yeah, it was supposed to be a secret.' He shifted a step away, a little embarrassed by her full attention being on him. 'As it got destroyed rather than stolen, that won't bother the company so much as if the thief had gotten away with it. They might be annoyed, but not at me.'

At least that explained why the Seer might be so insistent on getting his hands on this guy's stuff: a new model of anything by Apple would be worth a fortune.

The Scandinavian girl stopped in front of a photo of melting icebergs. 'It was so mean of that thief—why run off with your bag and then burn it—that's just spiteful.'

He shrugged. 'No telling what makes someone do that. Probably on drugs, high as a kite.'

Never. I had enough problems without adding a habit to the heap.

Jo scowled. 'But she was good at it—I didn't even see her make the snatch. Did you, Ingrid?'

'No. It was all very strange. Hey, look at this.' She tugged them away to the display board at the far end. With their backs to me, I took advantage of their distraction and got up to leave, hoping I could get at his bag while he was inside.

I wandered out into the sunshine, assessing the café to see if it was suitable for one of my strikes. It didn't take me long to decide that there were too many people and the place was overlooked by hundreds of offices. Would the old-fashioned thief method of walk-up-and-grab work? Headphones in ears, head back to enjoy the sunlight, the Asian boy was sitting over the bag like a hen on an egg. I could just imagine the hue and cry that would hound me and I was too far from the exit to be sure of making it out of the campus. I'd have to wait until they got into a more confined space. Flipping through the timetable, I spotted that they had seminars at eleven in something called 'break-out' rooms. I hadn't ever had the chance to go to college but I guessed from watching TV and films that seminars were smaller than lectures. My power worked on a maximum of thirty at any one time, so that sounded my best chance.

Confident that my disguise had no one connecting me with the thief of the day before, I trailed after the conference students and sat through their introductory lecture. Sitting in the back row was a bit like being on the top deck of a bus gazing down on the people below, not really hearing what was said but enjoying the experience of nosing into other lives. The two teachers down the front spoke enthusiastically, clicking their way through a slide presentation like confidence tricksters drawing a crowd in by their spiel. I wouldn't have been surprised if they had concluded by inviting us all to shell out to buy a bit of a timeshare in Tenerife but they finished without selling us anything. A wasted opportunity in my view; any member of the Community would have had the students digging deep in their wallets by now.

The audience filed out of the room discussing which groups they were going to go to next.

'I'm going to "Scientific Evidence",' declared Gazelle Jo pertly. 'How about you guys? Ingrid?'

'I'm thinking of "Human Impacts".' Ingrid turned hopeful eyes on Yves who had replaced his shades with a cute pair of rimless glasses.

Cute? Get a grip, Phee!

'I'm down for "Ecosystem Impact" so see you both later, OK?' He turned left at the corridor junction. Both girls looked upset by their wrong guesses. I nearly laughed; they were so transparent in their desire to shadow the fittest boy at the conference. Yves, for his part, didn't seem sorry to be free for a time of their rather obvious attempts to snag him as their conference romance; I concluded that he wasn't sure how to handle such blatant signals of female interest. Poor big good-looking guy, I smirked, as I set off on his trail.

Us Ecosystem Impacters (I had just elected myself to the group) took our places in a small room in one of the older buildings of the campus. I sat behind my target near the window. We were on the first floor with a balcony overlooking a lawn and white clock tower—a bit of nineteenth century posh on the Mile End Road. I had the reassuring glimpse of my world—that of the cars, taxis, and pedestrians—just the other side of a low white wall. I couldn't make my move until everyone was gathered in case I was interrupted, so I slowly counted the numbers coming through the door, getting worried when we reached twenty-five. Sweat began to trickle down my spine. I had to allow for a speaker yet and we were almost at my maximum.

And then he decided to be nice.

Yves turned round and smiled. He had probably decided I was a safe female as I'd not yet asked him for his telephone number like every other girl he met.

'Hi, um . . . ' he peered at my label, 'Wendy. You just arrived today, am I right?' A gentle, humour-filled sound that made something inside me want to purr like a contented cat.

'Yes.' My voice was a whisper—not my fault as I hadn't had anything to drink for ages.

'Any relation?'

'Sorry?'

He flicked a pencil at my name. 'To J. M. Barrie. You know, *Peter Pan and Wendy?*'

He knew that? This science genius knew that the book had first been published with both names in the title? I thought only rejects like me who haunted the obscurer corners of public libraries took an interest such arcane stuff. But he needed an answer. I couldn't keep on gaping at him like a stranded fish.

'Er . . . no. I wish.'

'What school are you from?' He was looking at me now as if he thought we'd met but he couldn't quite place me.

I grabbed at the first place that came to mind. 'Newcastle . . . um . . . School for Girls.'

'Newcastle. That's in northern England, isn't it?'

'Yeah.' Wendy wouldn't say 'yeah'. 'Yes, not far from the border with Scotland.'

'Never been there.' That was a relief. The way my luck was going he would have had close family in my birthplace. 'Going to college up there too?'

'Um . . . yes.' I grappled to think of a place he wouldn't know. 'Aberdeen.'

'Oh, cool. They've a great Geoscience department which is doing really cutting edge stuff on petroleum extraction. Have you read their recent paper on CO_2 storage?'

No. 'Well of course. That's why I applied. Me, Miss Geoscience. Petroleum . . . um . . . attraction is so fascinating.' Shut up, Phee.

Yves gave me a sceptical look. '*Extraction*, you mean.'

'Sorry, slip of the tongue. Extraction.'

He still looked dubious. 'So what's your course?'

'Geoscience.' Duh, he couldn't catch me out that way.

'Yeah, but within that you have to specialize, don't you?'

I did? 'Well, I thought I'd concentrate on the Geo bit to start with.' That sounded dumb. 'I mean, Geography.' Was that a geoscience? I didn't know.

My answer seemed to satisfy him. I felt like someone who just avoided a car crash by a last-minute braking, tyres still screeching in my head.

'I'm taking Environmental Sciences at Berkeley in the fall, but I'll be dipping into the Geography programme too. So we have lots in common, then.' He turned back to face front as the teacher came in.

We did? 'Er . . . yes, that's really interesting. Berkeley.'

He glanced over his shoulder. 'California.'

From his expectant expression I guessed I was meant to know that. 'Absolutely. I've heard of it. Of course I have.'

There: I'd confirmed him in the impression that Wendy was an idiot who really shouldn't be taking Geography as she didn't know where to find Berkeley.

The lecturer, a young Indian woman, came to the front of the room and held up her hand, mesmerizing me with her clinking rows of bracelets. I never wore things like that because they got in the way of stealing.

'Hello, everyone. My name is Dr Sharma. I cannot tell you how delighted I am to see so many of you have chosen this option.'

Not me: by my count, we were on thirty-two in the room. I'd never tried to hold so many at once.

'You've all been chosen as you are the top science students from your colleges and schools—our brightest stars who we hope will shine for the next few decades at least. And, as you all know, Ecosystem Impacts is where the action is really going to be for any innovative scientists. Let's start by doing a table round and finding out a little about each other.'

Let's not. I had to stop this before she asked me. Closing my eyes, I reached out for their mental patterns. Most whirred away in cool blues and greens, images of mountains and rivers flicking through; a couple of girls had Yves's face dreamily floating in their meadows; my target was stuck in a black and white zone, my appearance yesterday crossing with how I looked today.

Bloody hell, he was working it out, suspicion fracturing the black and white with orange flames.

'Girl at the back—sorry, I don't know your name—are you all right?'

I opened my eyes to find Dr Sharma was addressing me. The carefully gathered patterns scattered like sheep escaping from a fold. I nodded.

41

'Good, because I usually expect to send my students to sleep after I've spoken for a bit, not before I even get started.'

Her audience laughed politely.

'Yes . . . er . . . sorry,' I said hesitantly.

'Shall we begin then? Perhaps the student in the seat in front of you would like to introduce himself?'

Yves jolted out of his own thoughts. 'Yes, Dr Sharma, I'd be happy to.'

I would've liked to listen to him but I had to do this. Stretch my mind out to gather in the threads of their thoughts, reel them in, and then . . .

Stop.

It worked—for a second. Someone was pushing back hard, trying to untangle himself from my trap and I didn't have to look to find out who that was. There was no time to search his stuff; I just grabbed his bag and ran, stumbling over the legs of the boy opposite stretched out in the aisle.

How can you? The protest sliced into my mind like an ice pick. I crashed into the door, holding my head in my hands. My whole body was ringing with the telepathic message, un-like anything I'd experienced before. It was as though he had found my private wavelength and was playing at full bone-tingling volume a song specially written for me, so enticing and haunting that I couldn't shut it out. I wanted to answer, felt myself yearning to respond but how could I? I was stealing from him, wasn't I?

My connection to the mental patterns in the room fractured and everyone snapped into awareness and saw me crouched at the exit.

'How did . . . ?' Dr Sharma swung her head between my chair and the door in confusion. To her senses it would have appeared that I leapt the gap like some superhero.

Yves did not bother to gape like the rest. He vaulted over

his desk in pursuit. Shocked back into motion, I slammed out of the room and sprinted down the corridor. What had just happened? I couldn't outrun him so I would have to do something he wouldn't. Darting into the next empty class, I made for the window. Only first floor. My world just a fifty metre dash away if I could get down without breaking an ankle. I ripped the window open and climbed on to the balcony, his bag slung over my shoulder. Not quick enough. A hand grabbed my calf.

Who are you? What do you want with me?

His thought-speech shivered through me. I couldn't get my brain in gear. *Go away. Just go away!*

He went still, then his grip tightened on my leg as he tried to haul me back into the room. *How do you do that? You . . . you're different. Speak to me again.*

Bugger off.

He had the gall to laugh, his whole demeanour changing from fury to a weird exhilaration. *It's you—I know it's you!*

I didn't know who he thought I was but I wasn't planning on staying to find out. This strange intimacy of our thought-speech was freaking me out. I kicked hard, thanking Wendy and her thick soles when I managed to get a connection with his stomach, but the bloody Yank wouldn't let go.

Uh-uh, none of that, Wendy. He tumbled me to the floor by the window and solved the problem of me struggling by sitting on my back. 'I'll take that, thanks.'

He removed his bag from my shoulder and chucked it out of my reach. This wasn't good. This smacked of police and prison. I lay still, defeated for the moment. Grimly, I realized that as I'd not done what I'd been told, I wouldn't last long in a cell in any case. Probably be dead by the end of tomorrow if I couldn't drink.

'Please let me steal something from you.' That sounded pathetic, but I was reduced to begging.

'We'll get to that later.' Yves placed a hand on my head, cupping it gently. He was showing far more presence of mind than I was at this moment. 'Who would think my soulfinder would turn out to be a thief?'

I went very still. *Soulfinder?* He had to be joking. That was a fairytale.

'You know what that means, then?' He brushed my neck, sending shivers down my spine. My body recognized him though my mind was still shrieking that I had to get the hell out of here. 'I thought, maybe, you didn't. My brother's soulfinder didn't know. You're a Savant?'

I could hear sounds out in the corridor as the rest of the seminar group went in search of the two errant members. I nodded.

Someone was approaching our room. 'If I let you up, shall we tell them it was a joke?'

I nodded again, planning to dive out of the window as soon as he eased off me.

'But you have to promise not to do anything stupid like *try to escape me.*'

Damn. 'OK.' At least, if we could pass this off as a trick, I bought myself a bit more time.

He slid his hand down to take mine, encountering my bandage.

'I did this?'

I didn't answer.

'Sorry. I couldn't let you take that stuff—it wasn't mine for you to steal. But I admit I lost control. I have to keep a lid on my emotions or my gift gets out of hand. You really pissed me off yesterday.'

And he hadn't been enjoying setting fire to me much? I'd seen his mind-patterns; I knew he'd liked outwitting the sly thief.

Taking my elbow, he helped me to my feet just as the door banged open.

'What's going on here?' Dr Sharma stood in the entrance looking exasperated.

Yves stepped in front of me protectively. 'Please accept our apologies, doctor. Wendy and I are old friends and have this deal going where she teases me by taking my bag.' He shrugged. 'Started with stealing Twinkies at grade school, now progressed to whole backpacks. Really juvenile, I know.'

'I'm disappointed in the pair of you. This conference is not for children but young adults—act your age.'

Feeling me weave on my feet, Yves moved his hand to my waist, holding me up. 'Absolutely. We hear you loud and clear. Please accept our apologies.'

'Then get back in the seminar so we can do some work.' She flounced away with a waft of her loose-cut turquoise jacket.

'I can't go back in there,' I hissed as Yves propelled me along.

'Yes, you can. There's a break at twelve; we can sort everything out then.'

'I know nothing about that stuff you're doing.'

He smirked, clearly finding the whole situation delightful rather than the nightmare I was experiencing. 'Yes, I guessed, Miss Geoscience.'

Black edges appeared to my vision. I shook my head.

'You OK?'

No, I wasn't. Thief. Soulfinder. Mess. I was so thirsty I couldn't think straight. I licked my parched lips.

Yves marched me back into the seminar room, laughing off the comments about his abrupt departure. He distributed apologies like a benevolent lord scattering gold coins to the masses—generous handfuls. He pulled me into the seat next to him, not releasing his hold on my arm.

'Got any handcuffs?' he muttered under his breath, expecting me to share the joke.

I put my head on the desk as Dr Sharma resumed teaching. Fortunately, she'd abandoned the idea of a table round after that disturbing display of high spirits.

A bottle of water appeared in front of my nose. *Drink.*

Can't.

Why not? I haven't even opened it.

Please let me steal something from you.

Keeping his eyes on mine, Yves put the water back in his bag and then nodded to me. *That's my water. Whatever you do, don't take it from me.*

I reached down and snagged the bottle. Twisting the lid, I took a gulp. It felt wonderful, so good I drained the whole thing.

Watching the pantomime, Yves shook his head. *You're strange.*

I crushed the empty bottle. *And you're not?*

Chapter 5

Yves did not get up at the end of the seminar when everyone else left so I stayed in my place too. Dr Sharma departed first, calling out something about the panini in the canteen not being bad if you got there early. We sat there silently, watching the rest crowd through the door, their thoughts on lunch.

So were mine. Underneath everything else I was hungry. And tired, so very, very tired. I had just discovered that the fairytale was true. Soulfinders existed—and this one was mine. I'd always imagined the discovery would give me an amazing lift, like winning the National Lottery, but instead I just felt empty and sad. I knew that I couldn't have him even if I wanted him more than anything I'd wanted in my life before. I was the kid with no money in her pocket with her nose pressed up against the sweetshop window. Face the facts: I was a criminal who had never been to school; he was top of his class, everything about him wholesome and squeaky clean. He lived in the States and I lived in a forgettable succession of squats. He was decent and had a future; I had ties back at the Community, ones that would be hard to break, and a newly discovered sort-of-father who had his claws in me. The Seer had this way of knowing things; it was no simple matter of saying 'I quit'. Tony may have told me I could disappear but I didn't have the first clue how to go about doing it. Staying anywhere near the last target I had been told to hit would be incredibly stupid. Anyone looking for me would start with my last known job and that would lead the Seer right to Yves.

I just didn't deserve him and couldn't drag him into my troubles.

'Shall we start with our names?' Yves asked softly. He took my bandaged right hand in his. 'I'm Yves Benedict. I come from Wrickenridge in Colorado.' He paused but I didn't fill the gap. 'That's in America. In the Rockies.' Still nothing. 'I've seven brothers and I'm number six. My younger brother, Zed, found his soulfinder a few months ago.'

That sounded nice. A big family. Brothers. He had a good life. I was happy for him. He could go back to that.

'And what about you? Is Wendy your real name?'

I tugged the badge off. Not much point in my disguise any more. I couldn't see the words I'd printed as my eyes were swimming.

'Hey, hey, what's the matter?' He pulled my head to rest on his shoulder—it felt so good. 'Finding you is the best thing that's ever happened to me, don't you understand? Aren't you pleased that it's me, not even a tiny bit?'

Sweet of him to think that I was upset because my soul-finder had turned out to be the kindest, best-looking guy I'd ever seen. I liked the fact that he didn't realize just how attrac-tive he was to girls, didn't take it for granted that I'd find him perfect. This wouldn't be so painful if he had turned out to be a spotty-faced wimp with the personality of a postage stamp.

'Look, I know it's a lot to take in, but give it time. I realize I come across a bit geeky—you know, correcting you about petroleum extraction and everything.'

As if that even mattered. I didn't care about him making fun of me—I deserved that for pretending to be like him and the other students.

His hand rubbed the back of my neck. 'We didn't get off to the best start, I admit.'

I gave a choking laugh at that. 'You mean because I stole your stuff?'

He didn't stop running his hand over the sensitive skin of my nape. 'Well, yes, but I also hurt you when I blew up my gear. I'm really sorry about that. What did the doctor say?'

I couldn't give in to this weakness—had to stand on my own feet or I'd never be able to leave. Pushing off his chest, I sat up and mopped my eyes with the bandage. 'It's fine.'

He pulled my wrist towards him and spotted the cling film. 'You didn't go to a doctor, did you?' His tone darkened; his mental pattern was whirling back into reds and oranges, my melted tote spinning in the flames like a kebab over a barbecue, flickering swear words, ones he was too polite ever to say out loud.

'People like me don't go to doctors.' I tried to retrieve my hand.

'They do now.' He got up, dragging me with him. Unluckily for my escape plans, his shyness and uncertainty about girls disappeared when he had a rescue mission to run. 'Come on, I'll find out where the nearest emergency room is. I'll never forgive myself if that scars.'

'I'm not going. I can't.'

He turned to face me, a muscle in his jaw twitching as he tried to control his temper. It made me wonder if he was going to set something on fire; he'd warned me his gift could get away from him when angry. 'Wendy, don't make a mistake. I'm ready to forgive you for trying to steal from me—twice, wasn't it?—but if you won't get yourself medical attention then I'll have no choice but to turn you in to the police and let them make sure you're seen by a qualified practitioner.'

Just listen to him! Didn't he have a mouth full of long words, all declaring that he was better educated than me? I pushed my chair back roughly. 'Get the hell away from me. You don't know the first thing about me and my life and already you're ordering me around!'

He tapped the centre of my chest, looming over me, six feet of angry male. I should have felt scared but gut instinct told me that he wouldn't hurt me. Something might get singed but it wouldn't be my hand this time. 'You're completely wrong. I do know the first thing about you: you're my soulfinder. That fact now takes first, second, and third place in my life. What about in yours?'

I covered my face with my hands, wanting to scream with frustration. 'Just . . . just go away!'

I must have really riled him because his temper was escaping him like steam from an overheated car radiator. A pile of papers on the desk beside his right hand began to smoulder. 'I can't go away. You're being foolish—reckless with your own health.' He noticed the fire and quickly smothered it with a book from his bag. 'Goddamn it, look what you made me do!'

'Me? The fire thing is your business, not mine.'

He took a deep breath, clearly deciding a slanging match would be unproductive right now. 'Look, I've got to stick with you—that's the deal with soulfinders, you know that. Do you think I'm pleased to find mine is a thief—a sneak who uses her gift to rip people off?' I flinched but he didn't see, too busy parading his disappointment in his fate. 'Hell no! I'd dreamed about this moment—but it involved, I don't know, moonlight and roses or something, not a kick in the stomach and a thousand dollars of property up in smoke! So the least you can do is see to that burn if I tell you you should!'

I didn't need a marching band to blare it out, or even him shouting at me. Of course he would despise me. I despised myself. I should never have let his kindness fool me into thinking anything else.

Gathering my shredded dignity, I stood up.

'I've seen to my injury as best I can. You needn't worry about it.'

My tone was flat as my brain moved on to what was going to happen next. I'd say goodbye, slip away somehow, and go back to the Community to report that the target only had a bottle of water on him, his valuables having met with a freak accident. That would go down well. I'd face my next punishment and then . . . and then . . . My imagination failed at that point. The Seer would either kill me or hand me over to one of his supporters in some kind of arranged marriage. I'd not protest, not say anything. That way no one would ever suspect I'd found my soulfinder; it was the only way to protect him. Yves could get back on his plane and go and be a successful scientist or whatever, perhaps not as happy as he would've been if I had turned out to be a gazelle rather than a scavenging rat, but at least he'd have a life worth living.

He folded his arms, standing between me and the door. 'Not good enough, Wendy. I made my gear explode, and that hurt you, so I am responsible for clean-up.'

'Not this time. I'm not your mess to clean up.'

He smiled grimly. 'That's exactly what you are.'

I changed my mind. He wasn't kind; he was a dick. 'Well, thanks for that. Nice meeting you. Really must be going.' I headed for the exit.

'You can't leave.'

I stood staring at the fire notice on the back of the door. 'What are you going to do? Wrestle me to the floor? Oh, I forgot, you did that already.'

The door opened before I could reach it. I took a step back. Jo and Ingrid put their heads round the gap.

'Yves, what's keeping you?' asked Jo. Her expression soured when she saw me. 'Oh hi, sorry, did we interrupt something?'

Yves picked up his bag and hooked it over his shoulder. 'Wendy's burned her hand. I was just offering to take her to a doctor to get it dressed properly.'

Ingrid wrinkled her nose at my do-it-yourself job. 'That looks painful. The poor thing. Do you want us to come?' In her mental patterns, I could see that my presence was about as welcome as a third dog in a fight over a bone.

Yves wouldn't let me even open my mouth to answer before he swooped in. 'No need, just let the conference organizers know where we've gone if they ask. See you later.' Yves took my arm and marched me away. He was really annoying me now: it was as if my protests were nothing more than snowflakes melting in his ocean of certainty. I was hurt—he knew the cure. I was his soulfinder—he demanded I obey him. Were all his family arrogant jerks or had I just pulled the short straw?

We reached the reception. I only went with him because he was finally taking me nearer the exit. Already I was plotting my escape.

'Excuse me.' Yves turned his devastating, earnest smile on the lady with the folders. 'My friend here burned herself yesterday and I really think she needs to get it looked at by a doctor. Is there a hospital nearby?'

The lady—way too old for him so really should have known better—fluttered and preened until she found her emergency list. 'The Royal London, Whitechapel Road. A stop on the tube—that's the subway to you.' She giggled—she actually giggled. 'Or you can walk if she is well enough to do so.' She drew a big circle on the handout map; I wouldn't have been surprised if she had scribbled her phone number on the reverse.

He blushed, disturbed by her overeager response to him. 'Thanks. We'll jump in a cab.' He continued to frogmarch me off the premises.

Waiting until we were outside, I shoved him away from me. 'That's enough. What part of "I'm not going to hospital" don't you understand?'

'The "not" part.' He bit down on a smile that I had no intention of joining in. 'Look, Wendy, what harm can a little trip to the ER do you? You guys don't even have to pay, so it can't be the money or insurance problems.'

I gazed longingly at the traffic streaming east, out of town, away from him. So close. 'It's not that I'm stupid. I just can't.'

He shoved a hand through his hair in frustration. 'Wendy, why do I get the impression that you are about to sprinkle your fairy dust and fly away from me?'

I shook my head, folding my arms around my waist. He was wrong; he was the one offering fairy dust, Peter Pan volunteering to carry me off to the Neverland of soulfinders and happily ever after. But he was too late. Last night, I had had to grow up and I now knew that such dreams did not exist; real life was more like living with Captain Hook's mercenary pirates than playing happy families in a treehouse.

A finger under my chin tipped my head up. 'Wendy, talk to me. Let me help you. I'm sorry I said that stuff inside, but I was angry. I act like an idiot when my gift gets loose—just ask my brothers. It annoys the hell out of me that even after all these years of discipline and practice, I'm not in full control of my emotions.' He gave a rueful smile. 'Don't suppose you'll give me a pass for it being the day I met my soulfinder, hey?'

I nodded, not wanting to respond to his coaxing tone but unable to help myself. Everything inside me was yearning to reach out to this guy despite the warning from my common sense.

'Wendy, I can't bear to see you in pain when we can do something about it.'

And I couldn't bear to have him calling me by that fake name any longer. 'Phee. My name's Phee.'

He smiled, brown eyes warming for the first time since we quit the classroom. 'Just Phee?'

'Short for Phoenix.'

'Any other names?'

I never used it, but I supposed I should take my mother's surname. I didn't want to sound so shabby as not even to have a proper name. 'Corrigan.'

'So, Phoenix Corrigan, you have an allergy to hospitals?' He shifted his weight on to his other leg, waiting for an answer.

It was a good enough explanation. I nodded.

'Doctor's clinic?'

'Same deal.' Was he really backing down? All it had taken was one little concession from me and he suddenly became more reasonable?

He took out his phone. 'I've an idea. Don't move.' Selecting a contact from the home screen, he lifted it to his ear. I tensed, ready to bolt if necessary. 'Hey, Xav, got a minute? Where are you? I've got a bit of a situation here. Can you meet me back at the apartment in half an hour? OK. Yeah, I know, I'm a pain in the butt. Tell her you'll call her later. Uh-huh. But trust me, you'll want to be part of this.' He ended the call and grinned. 'Problem solved.'

'Who were you just talking to?' I rubbed my forearms, feeling the prickle of suspicion that I was being watched. Glancing around, I couldn't see anyone but there were lots of places to hide, doorways, bus shelters . . . Tony? He'd be worried I wouldn't come through with my part of the deal. Unicorn or Dragon, checking up on me? I hadn't earned the Seer's trust with my failure yesterday so I wouldn't put it past him to have me under guard today.

'My brother, Xav, he's in London with me.'

'Xav?' I made myself concentrate on what Yves was telling me.

'Yeah, my mom and dad had this alphabetical thing going with us, starting with Trace and ending with Zed. Xavier, he's the next one up from me. We told them they should've started with "A" and then we could all have been things like Alan, David, and Ben, but they thought that was too boring. Mom and Dad can be like that—you know, different to make a point.' He paused, realizing he was drifting off message. 'Xav's a healer, not that you'd guess that, terrible bedside manner. I'm taking you to see him. You won't have to put a foot in a medical practice.' Stopping at the kerb, he hailed a taxi. One cruised up to us immediately—such was this boy's luck. 'Take us to the Barbican, please.'

Reassured, I got into the taxi without a fuss. I knew the Barbican well: a concrete maze of arts centre, walkways, tunnels and posh flats, good for picking the pockets of late-night theatre and concert-goers. If I could have some attention paid to my burn, I still stood a good chance of getting away from him there.

Yves stretched his legs into the wide space in front of the rear seat. I'd never been in a taxi before; it felt really decadent, the kind of thing only rich people did. A cyclist flashed by in lemon sherbet shorts, zipping through the traffic like a stone skipping on the sea.

'He's really annoyed with me,' Yves continued, making conversation when I clearly wouldn't. 'He's spent all morning chatting up a guide at the Globe Theatre and now he's having to dump her just when things were looking promising.'

'He shouldn't—not for me.'

'Course he should. You're mine, so that makes you family. Our need is greater than his.' Yves put his arm around my shoulders. Something inside me broke a little and craving for his warmth seeped out. I tried to ignore it, holding myself stiff against the seat back. 'Don't you have brothers or sisters?'

Everything was so easy for him. You took a complete stranger and called her one of your inner circle, all because, by a quirk of nature, we were matched at some genetic level. The only things he knew about me were bad, but still I deserved to be helped. I folded a little deeper into myself, a rock pool sea anemone refusing to be poked into emerging by his prodding questions.

'I wish Sky was here,' he murmured to himself, looking out of the window at the traffic slowly forcing its way into the City. 'She'd be able to help.'

I'd vowed not to speak but my curiosity (or was it jealousy?) got the better of me. 'Who's Sky?'

He pulled me closer to his side, hoping I'd relax against him but I kept the steel in my spine. 'My youngest brother's soulfinder. She's British.'

'Oh.' Probably one of those pretty English rose types that I saw at Liverpool Street station going to music festivals in their wellies, rucksacks, and denim shorts, looking so unbearably pleased to be young and alive. With one glance, she'd know what a skank I was.

'She sees people's emotions. Makes her really intuitive. And she's come from a rough place. I think she'd understand you better than any of us.'

Yeah right. 'But she's not here?'

'No, she's on vacation with Zed and her parents.'

There you go: Sky had parents. That made her housetrained; I was feral.

The cab pulled up in one of the underpasses below the Barbican Centre.

The driver held out a hand. 'We're here, mate. That's six pounds forty.'

Yves pulled a tenner out of his wallet and handed it over, barely paying attention to the exchange. 'Will you tell me something about yourself, Phee? I want to know where you're coming from.'

I couldn't believe it: he was getting out of the cab without waiting for his change. I pulled him back and shoved my hand in the little gap to collect the coins. The driver gave a snort of disgust as I pressed the lot in Yves's palm. 'You can't give him three-sixty as a tip.'

Yves tipped the coins back into the plastic tray. 'Yeah I can. Leave it, Phee—it's not a big deal.'

Still spluttering at the careless waste of money, I stumbled out on to the pavement. Cars whizzed by, the noise reverberating in the tunnel so that any further protests would be lost. Our disagreement about the tip only served to highlight just how different we were. What was I doing with him?

Follow me. Yves held out a hand, expecting me to take it.

I had had enough of being pushed about, towed here, shoved there. *Lead the way, O master.*

He raised an eyebrow at my sarcasm. *Glad to see you have seen the light. I only want what's best for you.*

Mr Arrogant or what?

I don't mean it like that. He shook his head, telling himself off. *I just want to make this right but I seem to be doing it all wrong.*

Then let me go.

That would be a tragedy. Give me a chance here. Please. His uncertainty around girls had returned; he was no longer taking my agreement for granted, and that, more than anything, made me relent.

OK. *Until my hand is seen to. Then we'll go from there.*

Digging a key out of his jacket pocket, he guided me up a short flight of steps to the bottom of the Shakespeare tower, a great, brutal razorblade of a skyscraper. Looking up made me feel sick, as if the whole thing was going to fall on us. He called the lift then fitted the key in the residents' slot to allow us to go up to the twentieth floor.

'I thought you lived in America?' I asked.

'Borrowed the apartment off a friend of one of my brothers.' He tapped the wall restlessly as the numbers flashed past.

'Which one? Wilbur? Walt?'

He smiled. 'Not a bad guess. Victor. I don't have a brother called Wilbur or Walt—just Will. You'll like him.'

'If I ever have kids,' which I wouldn't, 'I'm going to call them really simple things like that. Names that are so normal no one will blink when they answer the register at school or . . . or get a library card.'

He laughed a little awkwardly. 'Yeah, I know what you mean. I got teased for having a girl's name—you know, Eve—by morons in my first grade. My mom and dad plucked names from their ancestors all over the world for their sons—most Savant families are really international—and I had to suffer for it. Phoenix must have been a burden at school until, I suppose, it became cool to be different.'

I shrugged. 'I wouldn't know. Never went to school that I can remember.'

The doors 'ting'-ed open, a bright sound like the bell at the end of a round in a boxing match.

'How . . . but surely you have to go to school in England? Everyone does.' He led the way into the carpeted corridor.

'Hmm.' That's how much he knew about those of us off the map.

'But you know things—you've read *Peter Pan*.'

'*And Wendy*. I didn't say I didn't have lessons. You can learn a lot if you want to.' If you were starved of knowledge, desperate to join the normal world. Mum had taught me all the basics before she died. After she'd gone, if I finished my job for the day, I would sneak into the children's section of the city library, using my gift to freeze my way past the women on the desk, and read my way through from beginning to the end of the shelves. These days I could go into the adult section without anyone questioning my right to be there. I got a fair bit of random stuff into my skull that way.

'I suppose you can.' He put the key in the lock of the last door in the corridor and entered. The flat was one of those all-white places that look good in magazines but must be horrible for real people to live in: white carpet, white furniture, black highlights of African carvings and an expensive sound system. 'Hey, Xav, we're back!'

The fact that he knew his brother was already there suggested he had been talking telepathically to him since we came in range. Xav came out of the room on our right, drying his hands on a black towel. His resemblance to his brother was immediately apparent, though his hair was longer, more surfer-casual as it hung past his collar, than Yves's neater crop. He was also thinner, rangy, a long-legged thoroughbred to the leopard. Nothing of the geek about him, but I didn't make the mistake of underestimating his intelligence. I sensed I was sandwiched between two very bright and formidable Savants. 'Hi, Phee. I've set up in here. Bring the patient in, Nurse.'

'You told him about me?' I hissed, refusing to enter the bathroom until I knew exactly what I was walking into.

'Only your name and that you got burned by one of my fires.' Yves gently prodded me between my shoulder blades. 'Didn't want to distract him with the rest until he's seen to your hand. Let's not keep the doctor waiting.'

Xav had put a stool in front of the sink for me to sit on. Yves hovered at my shoulder as his brother carefully pushed up my sleeve and unwrapped my bandage. Xav didn't say anything for a few moments as he turned my arm over to inspect the ugly yellow-white blister on my palm.

'Sheesh, Yves, I thought you grew out of playing with fire.'

'Don't rub it in. You know I try.' Yves's temper was simmering again.

'This needs a hospital.' Xav glared at his brother.

'She won't go.'

The glare now turned on me. 'You're an idiot, do you know that? I can help but I can't see how deep this has gone. Does it hurt?' His touch was soothing.

I bit my lip and nodded.

'Don't take this the wrong way, but that's good.' Xav winked at me, softening the 'idiot' remark. 'If it was really deep then no pain is a danger signal.' He covered my hand with his. Not trusting what he was doing, I searched his mind patterns; I watched them shift to a soothing blue. I could see my arm in his thoughts, layer by layer, bone, nerves, muscle and skin, like an illustration in Gray's *Anatomy*. He really was trying to heal me. I wondered what it was going to cost.

Yves moved around behind us quietly, disappearing into the kitchen, muttering something about making drinks for us and putting together a round of sandwiches. The calm after the confusion of the past twenty-four hours was a welcome oasis. I found some of my tension untwisting like a tie-dye T-shirt coming out of the wash to reveal a new pattern on the surface. I had a soulfinder. I'd been in such a panic about discovering this that I'd not really stopped to think. I'd been acting like someone carrying the plague trying to cut themselves off from the healthy. That was still probably the right thing to do, but I had to consider this more slowly, work out what was the next best step. I'd only had an hour or so with him, but already it felt so good to be close to Yves that even when he was in the kitchen I was missing him. Though he irritated the hell out of me, I kind of liked it. The sparks of attraction flew between us even when we were yelling at each other. Maybe even more so then.

'Does that feel any better?' Xav released my arm.

The blister had shrivelled up to lie flat against the new skin forming underneath. The redness had faded. I flexed my fingers to find that the tight pain I'd had since yesterday was almost completely dulled. 'That's amazing.'

'Happy to help.' He took out a dressing from a first-aid kit. 'I'll put this on your blister but I think the rest of the arm will be OK.' He fastened it with tape then stood back, rubbing his temples.

'Are you OK, Doctor?'

He laughed. 'Bad headache. Get them when I push my gift.'

'So do I.' It slipped out before I realized what I'd said.

Xav didn't seem surprised that I was another Savant. 'What do you do? Not put out fires obviously.'

I pretended to examine my new dressing. 'This and that.'

'She stops time—or slows it.' Yves had appeared in the door to see if we were done.

'Neat.' Xav chucked the old bandage in the bin. 'Useful.'

'Yeah, allows her to be one of the sharpest thieves I've ever seen in action.'

'Shut up!' I hissed, outraged that he would share this about me.

'Oh yes, and she's my soulfinder. Lunch is served.' After dropping that bombshell, Yves headed back to the kitchen.

Xav was speechless. He stared at me as if I'd just crash-landed from a flying saucer.

'Phee, Xav, hurry up or I'll eat it all,' shouted the jerk from the kitchen.

Xav patted me awkwardly on the shoulder. 'You have my commiserations. He may act like a twit sometimes, but he's the nice one in our family, so it could've been worse.'

chapter 6

I locked the door after Xav, saying I needed a moment, then sank to the floor, head on my knees. Not even hunger was going to drive me out of here. If I had Yves's power, I'd blow up that plate of sandwiches and make sure it splattered all over his face. But all I had was a gift that didn't work too well on him, not even giving me enough time to escape.

A tap on the door. 'Phee, are you OK in there?' Yves.

I banged my head softly on the wood behind me.

'Look, sorry I came out with it like that. I tell my brothers everything—we're really close. I should've thought what you might think.'

Yeah, you should've.

'He won't mind if I don't mind—about the stealing thing.'

Well done him. God, I was so tired of all this. Yves had clearly not smoothed out his rough edges when it came to handling girls if he thought this excuse for an apology would sweeten my sour mood. A trickle of flame poured under the door then spun to form a little ball of fire. Was he trying to burn me out? I yelped and scurried backwards, but then saw that the carpet was not even singed.

'For you,' said Yves quietly.

The ball began to spin faster, then split into three different spheres, flame-yellow, white-hot, and blue like a gas ring—three little planets revolving around each other. Suddenly, they flared open, forming into the shape of flowers in bloom. They came to rest at my feet like lilies on a pool before snuffing out of existence, leaving only a faint smell of smoke behind. Nothing was damaged; not even a soot mark on the floor where they had been.

I was stunned: no one had ever given me flowers before. That had been awesome; I'd never thought to create something beautiful out of my powers but Yves must have spent a long time honing his skill to do so.

'Come out when you're ready,' he said, retreating to the kitchen.

I sat for a few more minutes, brushing my hand over the spot on the carpet in front of me. Staying locked in Yves's bathroom wasn't really a good plan: I'd have to emerge eventually. The longer I left it, the harder it would be. I quietly opened the door and went into the corridor.

The entrance to the kitchen was diagonally across from the bathroom. I could hear the boys talking but they couldn't see me. I had no qualms about eavesdropping—I had to know what they really thought of me before I decided my next move.

'All I can say, little brother, is that, after years of faultless living, when you get into trouble you do it properly.' Xav poured himself a glass of water from the dispenser on the spaceship-sized refrigerator. Ice clunked into his glass with the noisy whirr of some machine in the enormous door. 'If it had been Zed, Trace, or Vick, I'd've understood, but you!'

'We don't choose our soulfinders.' Yves sounded more distant; I guessed he must be at the far side of the room.

'Are you sure it's her? I mean, she doesn't look a likely match for you, not like Zed and Sky.'

'Come on, there was nothing obvious about them at first either—they grew together.' Yves's tone was doubly defensive. 'That's how it'll be for us.'

'You hope. You didn't say if you were sure. I mean, don't take offence, Yves, but I know you haven't dated that many girls and I thought, maybe, you were, like, getting mixed up.' Something went 'bang' and I heard Xav swear as he put out some flames. 'Holy cow, that was my doughnut you just nuked!'

'Back off, Xav! Just because I'm not the Super Bowl champion in serial dating like you! I know what I feel when I'm seeing a girl and I'm telling you, this is completely different—another orbit entirely. When she answered me telepathically, it all kind of clicked. More than that—my whole centre of gravity shifted to her, you know?'

'No, I don't know—I've not found mine, have I?'

'Sorry.' A cupboard door snapped shut.

'No problem, I'm not offended. Hey, I think I might be the lucky one today. She's . . . she's not what I expected. Weird looking—those funny glasses and clothes like something our grandma would wear. I thought there'd be some kind of chemistry, you know, with a soulfinder.'

'I guess.' A chair scraped on the floor. 'She didn't look like that yesterday—I'm not sure what's the real her at all. I think I'm in over my head. She's got issues—and issues under those issues. She won't tell me much about herself: all I've got so far is a name and the fact that she's never been to school.'

'And that she's a professional thief—don't forget that choice bit of information. If you keep in mind the other reason why we're here, don't you think it odd that she zeroed in on you as her target?'

Other reason? I shrank back against the wall.

'Yes, I know: we'll have to ask her about that. I will, but it's all so complicated at the moment. She doesn't trust me. What time is Vick getting back from his meeting at Scotland Yard?'

'About six. You've got five hours to work out if she is going to be a security risk or not, then we'll have to turn her over to him to check out.'

'She's not going to like that.'

Too right. *She* definitely didn't like the sound of that. *She* had decided she was out of the front door on the first mention of the police. I crept backwards, hoping the sound of my footfalls would be absorbed by the carpet. The front door was locked and bolted. I could undo all the locks but the very top one, which was out of my reach. I looked around for something to stand on but this arty flat didn't run to normal bits of furniture, only glass shelving that was fixed to the wall.

'Going somewhere?' Yves appeared at the kitchen entrance, watching my increasingly desperate attempts to reach the top bolt.

He had no right to keep me prisoner. 'Yes. Home.' I jumped, my fingers brushing the bolt but not moving it.

Yves walked calmly towards me. 'And where is home? I don't think you said.'

'That's right: I didn't say.' I kicked the door, leaving a black scuff mark on the pristine gloss.

'You've not had lunch yet.' Yves reached over my head and undid the bolt.

'Not hungry.' I couldn't believe he was letting me go.

That's a lie.

What? You're a mind-reader now? I wrinkled my nose in disdain; I was the one with that kind of gift. He didn't have a clue what I was really thinking or he wouldn't be so calm.

No, I sense energy and yours is dangerously low. Everyone has a different and unique energy signature; yours is telling me you have no gas in the tank. When did you last eat?

I shrugged. A lifetime ago. 'I'll get something on the way back.'

He turned away and returned to the kitchen, saying over his shoulder, 'You need a key for the lift.'

'I'll take the stairs then.' Twenty floors—thanks a lot, mate.

'Need a key for them too unless you want to set off the fire alarms,' his disembodied voice called.

I stalked into the kitchen and held out my hand to the two boys sitting at the kitchen counter. 'Can I have the key please?'

Yves slapped a sandwich into my palm. 'Eat.'

My stomach churned at the pink rim of ham. 'I'm vegetarian.'

Xav whisked the sandwich away as Yves replaced it with a cheese and tomato on granary. '*Please* eat.'

Resentful of their manipulation, I moved to the window and perched on the radiator, taking small bites of the sandwich. Thankfully, they left me alone while I demolished it; not that I was flattered: they acted like zookeepers of a dangerous animal, not wanting to provoke the beast any further. Angry, I gave them my back. It was a good job I had a head for heights because the view was amazing: I could see all the way to the Olympic stadium and the visitor park. It looked pretty from up here: a patch of green and white in the tired urban jungle of east London and the snaking lianas of roads and railways. If I looked carefully, I could even make out the housing estate where we were living at the moment—a biscuit-coloured stack of termite hills. I hesitated to call it home but I'd have to go back, wouldn't I?

I finished the sandwich and brushed off my hands. 'Are you going to return to the conference?'

Yves shook his head. 'Got more important things to sort out now.'

'Jo and Ingrid are going to be disappointed.'

'Jo *and* Ingrid?' laughed Xav. 'And here was I thinking these conferences were all for guys who looked like Brains out of *Thunderbirds*. I got you all wrong, bro. I should've paid more attention in class.'

'There is no inverse correlation between beauty and intelligence,' Yves threw back at him.

'Ooo, long words.' Xav chucked a crisp at him. 'Sorry, a dumbo like me needs a translation.'

Yves rolled his eyes. 'Pretty girls can be clever too. In fact, they often are.'

'So why didn't you say that first time?'

This was stupid: they were teasing each other as if nothing extraordinary was going on. Hello: there's a stranger in the room with you.

'Another sandwich?' Yves offered me the plate.

'No, I'm done.'

'You're still hungry.'

'Just . . .' I held up my hands between us. 'Just give me a break, OK? I've got to go now.'

Yves glanced at his brother. 'Make us a coffee, will you? Phee and I need to talk. We'll be in the lounge.'

'No, *Phee and I* won't. Phee will be heading out of here. Key please.' I cupped my palm, wiggling my fingers in a 'hand-it-over' gesture.

'Maybe you prefer tea?' suggested Xav calmly.

'Screw. You.' I went to the counter and upended the tray of loose change and odds and ends, searching for the key.

'Before you ransack the house, Phee, I think you should know we only have one key each and they are in our pockets.' Yves walked out on me again, heading for the lounge.

'If you're going to hurt someone,' said Xav as he filled the kettle, 'I'd really prefer it to be my brother.'

They were playing with me and I hated it. Boiling with rage,

I stamped after Yves. No sooner had I got into the lounge and filled my lungs to yell at him than he pounced on me from behind the door and tumbled me back on to the sofa, pinning my hands at my sides with his body. A traitorous part of me wanted to link my arms around his neck and pull him into a kiss, but the indignant majority was screaming to escape.

Yves squashed any rebellion by the simple method of letting me bear his full weight. 'OK, this seems to be the only way to get you to listen to me, so I'm good with that.'

I closed my eyes but I'd already seen his mental pattern which must've matched mine in its hot intensity. In his mind, he wasn't pulling some kind of weird dating move, just worked out that logically this was the quickest way of ending my attempts to escape. The fact that the full body contact was turning into something else had taken him by surprise. He lifted his weight on his forearms, embarrassed but determined.

'You can either have a coffee with me like a civilized person while we sort this out, or we do it the hard way.'

'Hard way?' I couldn't help cringing. Living with the Seer I had too much experience of what that meant. I knew Yves was too good to be true. Scratch anyone deep enough and the monster emerged. 'Please, I . . . I'll talk to you. Don't hurt me.'

The tension left his body as he dropped his forehead against mine. 'Phee, I'm not going to hurt you. Don't even think that.' He scooted back, letting me sit up. 'I just meant we'd wait for Vick to get home. He's the second eldest in my family and he's good at getting answers out of people—that's his power. But none of us would harm you; we only want to help you.'

I hunched over my curled legs. 'Yeah, right.'

Yves shoved his fingers through his hair, a gesture I was beginning to recognize as characteristic of him when he reached the end of his tether. I was pushing him there a lot.

'I'm sorry,' I whispered.

He took his glasses off and pinched the bridge of his nose. Without the specs to enforce the intellectual look, he appeared vulnerable and younger—a bit like me without my make-up.

'Look, I know I'm making mistakes with you but if you won't tell me anything, that's bound to happen. I want you to believe that you can trust me. It's obvious you've come from a difficult background: won't you share a little of what's going on? What about your parents? Will they be a problem? Don't they know about soulfinders?'

I picked at a loose thread in my horrible skirt. 'My mum died nine years ago.'

'I'm sorry to hear that.' He cleared his throat. 'So who do you live with? Your dad?'

I gave a grating laugh. 'Maybe.' I didn't elaborate.

'Phee . . .'

'OK, OK. Look, I live in a sort of group of Savants. We don't stay anywhere long.'

'Who looks after you? I mean after your mum died and everything.'

'You're joking, right?' People did not take in other people's kids in my experience. 'I looked after myself of course. With my gift, I was able to keep my place.'

'What does "keep your place" mean?'

'I have to bring in what I'm told to take. Kind of like a rent.'

He took my hand but I pulled it back. 'OK, Oliver, I think I'm getting the picture. So who's your Fagin?'

I snorted at the *Oliver Twist* reference: we were far from a merry band of singing orphans. 'More like Bill Sykes, you mean.' Rats, I hadn't said that, had I?

But Yves had set his trap cleverly and leapt on my admission. 'So you're scared of someone—he's making you do this for him?'

Yes—and no. Of course I was scared: I couldn't remember

a day when I hadn't lived in fear of the Seer, but neither was I the fresh-faced Oliver shocked when he saw his friends nicking a handkerchief. I knew what I was doing when I stole and I very often enjoyed it—that would shock him to the core. 'Yves, just accept that my world is not yours. You won't understand how it is for me.'

'Not if you don't tell me.'

Xav entered, bearing two mugs of coffee on a tray with milk and sugar on the side. 'I'll be in the kitchen if you need me,' he murmured, more for his brother's sake than mine, I'm sure.

'Thanks, Xav.' He handed me a mug and then the milk. I poured until the coffee turned caramel coloured and then shovelled in some sugar. If my energy levels were down, I'd have to replace some of it quickly to keep my wits about me. 'Phee, I have to know why you sought me out in particular yesterday and today. It could be important.'

'Oh, yeah, have I told you I'm sorry about that? You were just a job, you know, nothing personal.'

'What kind of job?'

Would it hurt to explain how it had been set up? Not if I didn't mention names. 'I was shown your photo and told to get your valuables. I suppose someone wanted that next-generation iPad of yours.'

He narrowed his eyes, his wariness disappearing. He was all business now. 'How did you know about that? It looked just the same as the usual model.'

'Heard you telling Jo-Grid this morning. If it was a secret, you really shouldn't go shooting your mouth off in public.'

'It's not a secret—not now at any rate as all that's left is an interesting modern sculpture of tortured Apple technology.' He gestured to a grey hunk of junk marring the blond wood sideboard. Oops.

'I'd say I'd pay you back but I can't. I don't have that kind of money.' Or any money unless I picked a pocket.

'You can pay me back by answering my questions.'

I took a sip of coffee, considering my options. 'Do we have to do this now? I'm really tired and I don't like talking about myself.'

'I would never have guessed.' He gave me an ironic flick of a smile. Oh lord, he was beautiful: face like an angry angel, a St Michael slaying the dragon, sleek black hair and eyes that shone with intelligence and curiosity. His frameless glasses added to the very correct impression that here was a boy not to be underestimated.

'Yeah, I'm sorry.' Exhaustion was creeping up on me. I yawned, trying to work out how long I had. The brother called Vick was due back at six. I could sleep for a couple of hours, give some vague answers, and still get away before he returned. My gift would be stronger if I wasn't so run down and I'd need it to get the key and flee. 'Would you mind if I curled up here for a bit? You can still ask me questions.' And I'd sleep through them.

'Be my guest.' He seemed happy to continue the interrogation in more relaxed mode, perhaps hoping to get more answers out of me that way.

I put my coffee back on the tray, then swung my legs round.

Yves put a cushion on his lap. 'You'll be more comfortable this way round.' He patted the pillow.

Looked good to me. I took off my glasses and swivelled so I could put my head down. 'Fire away.'

He laughed, making the pillow jiggle under my cheek. 'You shouldn't say that to me—I'll take it as an invitation to flex my power. Three fire incidents in two days—you are hell on my control.' He didn't ask any questions, just let me lie there, his hand resting on my hair. He unravelled a few strands from the scarf. Fed up with the pull on my scalp, I tugged the scarf off.

'Better? He shifted through the uneven locks.

'Hmm.'

'Did you know you've got really soft hair?'

That sounded nice.

'But you should sue your hairdresser.'

I smiled into his denim clad thigh. 'I'll tell her you said so when I wake up.'

Chapter 7

It was four in the afternoon when I surfaced from my sleep. Yves hadn't moved but was sitting with his hand resting on my shoulder, reading a thick book on climate change. It sprawled on his spread palm like a grounded fat pigeon with limp wings and must have been very uncomfortable to hold like that for any length of time. I lay still for a moment, able to see the page he was studying without him knowing I was awake. I liked his fingers: long and tanned on the back; dark hairs on his arm as far as his wrist, then a pale palm etched with lines. It felt good to know such tiny details about him, how his tendons bunched as he carefully turned a page so as not to disturb me, how he had a scar on the heel of his hand. If I bunched my fist, I was sure he would be able to fold it in his much larger palm, but unlike with Dragon, the thought that he was bigger and stronger than me did not intimidate. I was sure now that he would not hurt me intentionally; the fact that he had let me sleep when he wanted to interrogate me proved that. It was even more amazing that I had trusted him enough to let down my guard; I wondered if my traitorous DNA was overruling my brain in the presence of my soulfinder.

I shifted my head, feeling the damp patch under my cheek where my mouth had been partly open. I hadn't been dribbling in my sleep, had I? How humiliating.

'Awake, Sleeping Beauty?' Yves put the book on the glass-topped coffee table, squashing the photo of polar bears against the ice surface.

I sat up quickly and wiped my arm across my mouth. 'Thanks. I needed that.'

He got up and stretched, shaking out cramp from his legs. 'Ready for another drink? A soda?'

I followed him into the space-age kitchen, units gun-metal grey. It smelt of ground coffee and a sharp lemon spray. Xav was tapping away at a computer keyboard and just smiled briefly at me before returning to his task.

'What flavour is "soda"? I only know it as something you use for cleaning drains or baking.'

'A fizzy drink in British English.' He got out a large bottle of lemonade. 'Or perhaps you'd prefer a juice?'

'Yes, orange if you have it.'

'Something to eat?'

I shook my head.

Yves put two juices and a packet of biscuits on a tray and led me back to the sofa. Used to taking my own decisions, I felt more than a bit pathetic trailing after him but for the moment I could only wait and see what he had in mind. He cracked open the packet and offered me one. Bang went my no-food resolution—they were chocolate and this girl only has so much self-restraint. I took one.

He still didn't say anything, just sat back and sipped his drink, gazing out of the window at the seagulls circling the tower. His silence was beginning to unnerve me. Had he changed his mind about me while I slept? Had he decided to go for the 'hard way' after all?

'So . . . um . . . what do you want to know?'

'Why you came back today would be a good start,' he said quietly. 'You knew my stuff was trashed, but you still followed me and tried to steal from me again. That doesn't make sense if, as you said, you were after the new Apple technology.'

I swallowed and nodded. I was going to have to tell him enough to satisfy his curiosity without giving anything important away. 'Yes, I see how that looks weird to you. The . . . um . . . thing is I didn't tell my Fagin, as you called him, that the iPad exploded—he wouldn't believe me or he would've punished me and . . . and . . . someone else I care about.'

Yves's brow furrowed, eyes narrowing with suspicion. 'And who's that—the person you care for?'

Now he was jealous. I found that oddly reassuring. 'A man in my group who's been kind to me. He was badly crippled and I helped nurse him. I went to him when I needed someone to bandage my arm.' I dusted the arm of the sofa with a tassel on a big white satin cushion. 'No one you need worry about.'

He flashed me a grin. 'So transparent, am I? OK, so what about your Fagin?'

I scrunched the pillow to my chest. 'He's not a nice man.'

Yves sighed. 'I guessed that.'

'He's really powerful—you have to take him seriously.' I could tell Yves didn't get it; no one 'got' the Seer until they'd had the misfortune of crossing paths with him. 'Anyway, he was really set on stealing from you but didn't tell me exactly what he wanted. When I messed up the first time, I thought I could get a result to keep him happy today—a passport or wallet or something. I didn't know that iPad and phone were special until I heard you telling Ingrid and Jo.'

He rubbed his chin, sorting through my words. 'But why take the risk of coming back to me? If you thought I was just an ordinary tourist, you could have stolen all sorts of things with your gift and said they were mine. Who would've known?'

'Yeah, that did cross my mind, but the Seer . . .'

'The who?'

Damn, damn, damn. Hot tears pricked my eyes. I thought I could play this 'Any Answers' game without tripping up and I'd failed almost instantly. I got up, grabbed my Wendy glasses from the table and stuffed them in my pocket.

'I can't do this, Yves. I'm sorry. Too many people will get hurt and I'm in enough trouble as it is.' Oh God, the Seer would kill me if he found I'd mentioned him to anyone outside the Community.

'Sit down, Phee.'

'No, I have to go. You've got to let me go!' I scrambled round him to the door.

'Xav!' shouted Yves.

'I'm there.' His bloody brother was in the hallway blocking the door.

Yves guarded the way through to the kitchen. 'You're not going anywhere. I thought you understood that.'

I hung between them like a person stuck halfway down a zip wire, dangling with no way of getting the motion to go on. 'No, no, it's you who doesn't understand. He'll hurt me.'

Yves held out a hand to me. 'Phee, I won't let anyone hurt you.'

I stood poised for flight by the coffee table, my reflection in the wall mirror telling me I looked like a demented pixie, hair sticking out every which way. No wonder they weren't taking me seriously. 'You don't know the Seer. It's not that simple. If I hadn't stolen the water from you today I'd be pretty much dead—he'd made it so I couldn't eat or drink until I did the job. He . . . he does stuff to your mind, makes you obey. If he catches me, he could tell me to murder you . . . or . . . or jump off a bridge . . . and I'd do it, too.'

Yves flinched, not so confident now that he had the answer to everything. He looked to his brother, seeking reassurance.

'I've told Vick to get back as soon as possible,' Xav confirmed. *They were using telepathy, keeping me out of the loop.*

'Just stop it—how do you think I feel knowing you're talking behind my back!' I grabbed a stack of magazines and chucked them at Yves, flipping them like Frisbees.

'Calm down. You're free of him, Phee, this Seer person. You're staying with me.' Batting away the missiles, Yves used a soothing tone that right now only wound me up. *This was not the moment for being cool and reasonable!*

'Shove that: what about Tony?' I threw a cushion at him.

Yves caught it. 'Tony?'

'My friend! You can't keep him safe too, can you? If I'm not back by nine then he'll get so hurt and I promised—I promised him I'd keep my side of the deal. Oh God, oh God.' Strength giving out, I folded in on myself and hunched in the doorway.

'Xav?' Yves rushed to me.

'I'm on it.' Xav placed a warm hand on my back and flooded me with his sedative touch. 'She's exhausted and run down, Yves. We've got to be very careful with her; she won't be able to take much more. She's so strung out, more pressure could make her snap.'

'I've got to go back,' I whispered.

'No, you don't.' Yves gathered me to his chest and lifted me up. 'Your Seer might be strong, but three Benedicts far outweigh one Fagin. You, Phoenix Corrigan, are going to go to bed and let us deal with this. When Vick gets here, you tell him where to find this Tony and we'll sort out something to stop him getting harmed.'

'I think we need Sky and Zed,' Xav murmured.

'Yeah, let's see if they can break off their vacation. Mom

and Dad too.' Yves laid me down on a bed, then pulled off my shoes.

Xav gave a dry chuckle. 'Why not get the whole tribe here—great idea. Call Trace, Will, and Uri while you are at it.'

'She's my soulfinder, Xav. Nothing's too much.' He covered me with a duvet.

'Yeah, I know, bro. I don't mean to needle you. Mom and Dad are a good idea. We're going to have to get to work on some serious paperwork to get her out of here.'

There they went: sorting my life out as if I had not a grain of sense. They were treating me like someone just checking into a secure ward in a mental hospital. Next they'd be cutting up my food and spoon-feeding me.

I threw the duvet off. 'You don't understand. They'll work out I'm with you. I can't stay. Just can't.'

Yves pulled the cover back up. 'Don't worry about that, Phee. We'll make sure no one gets to you.'

They were leaving me no choice, smothering me with well-meant but impossible concern. I couldn't think past nine o'clock. I'd have to freeze them, but I stood a better chance of getting away if they didn't think to check on me immediately. They would have to believe I was cooperating.

I clutched his hand. 'Promise?'

'Yeah.'

I pretended that was good enough. 'OK, I'll get some rest.' I snuggled under the duvet, trying to look the good little girl who didn't have escape on her brain.

'Thanks.' Yves pulled the curtains, leaving the room in half-light. 'Trust us, Phee, we'll get everything straightened out.'

Trust? In the Community, I'd learned not to trust anyone.

The two Benedicts left the room. I counted to three hundred but they didn't return—they trusted me to rest more than they should. I couldn't wait any longer as there was the mysterious Vick on his way home: he was one Benedict I had no intention of meeting. Slipping back into my shoes, I tiptoed to the door and eased it open. They were talking in soft voices in the kitchen. Perfect. Creeping to the entrance, I peered round and reached for their mental patterns. Away from the aggravation of my presence, Yves's had shifted to a calm, more abstract intertwining of greys, greens, and blues like a filigree pattern of ivy on a marble column. His formidable intellect was sorting through options, how to get me a passport and take me with him when he left for the USA, what to do when we got there; he had absolutely no doubt that our future lay together. If only. Xav's was more volatile, a zany stream of thoughts and images—ski slopes, mountains, a pretty girl at the Globe theatre, all on the backdrop of a rainbow window.

Go easy, like wriggling into a pair of tight jeans, inch by inch. Take them and . . . hold.

My nap on the sofa had restored something like my usual strength. Unaware that they were being set on by a stealth attack, they drifted into freeze mode. I couldn't risk destroying this delicate balance by rifling their pockets; I went straight for the front door. Yves had left it unbolted so I was able to slip out without further delays.

And let go . . . I released my grip on their minds gently, like breathing out; if I was lucky, they would not have even noticed their few seconds of absent-mindedness.

Trying to look as if I had every reason to be there, I headed for the lift, guessing that the stairs would be nearby. When I triggered the alarm by opening the fire door without a key, my departure would be announced, but I was hoping to have enough of a head start still to beat them down. My plan was to summon the lift on the floors below as I ran past, making sure a lift-car would take ages to get up to the twentieth. They might choose to take my route, but by then I'd be lost in the concrete labyrinth of the Barbican. I was pretty confident that, on home turf like this, I was fairly impossible to outwit.

As I passed the lift, the doors opened with a chime. A tall man stepped out: sleek suit, long but neat hair tied back, keen grey eyes. This had to be the third brother. I sensed the warning in my gut: a shark had swum out of the weeds among the shoals of little fishes. I fixed a vague smile on my face, thanking my lucky stars that he didn't know what I looked like.

'Want me to hold the car for you?' he asked politely, putting his hand in the gap where the doors slid back.

'No thanks,' I said breezily. 'Just going to my friend's.' I gestured down the hall.

He moved away, letting the doors slide to, slipping his key into his back pocket. I wondered for a brief mad second if I dared freeze him, but as I didn't know his strength, I couldn't risk it. I let him go. I walked purposefully on, eyeing the entrance to the stairwell as I passed. Vick entered the apartment and shut the door.

Now or never. I ran back and pushed the metal bar to open the fire door, bounding through so quickly that the alarm had barely started ringing when the heavy door crashed closed. The stairwell was an ugly grey space smelling of concrete car parks, very different from the carpeted luxury of the corridor. One floor below, I broke through to the next floor and punched the call button for going down. I could hear the hum as the car Vick had used began to move. I then summoned all the other lifts. Down two more floors and I repeated the delaying tactic. That was all I had time for. The Benedicts wouldn't waste seconds waiting for lifts when they knew I had left by the stairs; I had only a brief space before they sorted out their plan to recapture me.

Twenty floors is a heck of a long way. By about eleven I was unable to focus on the treads—they had become almost like an abstract painting of lines—and nearly lost my footing. My concentration wasn't helped by the sound of pursuit. The Benedicts were not shouting or making a fuss, rather they were relentlessly thudding down the stairs like an army squad on fitness training. Of course, it helps if your buddies also speak telepathically.

Phee, stop this madness!

So Yves had decided to try and reach me then. I'd half expected him to have attempted it earlier but I guess he and his brothers were too busy planning how to cut me off. I was banking on them not considering that I knew about the underground car park below level one. While Vick or whoever waited to catch me in the lobby after succeeding in summoning one of the lifts, I was going to be slipping past them a floor below.

Ground floor. Basement. I pushed the bar and stumbled over the sill into the dark warren of the car park. Turning sharply left I raced towards the Barbican Centre, knowing I'd be much harder to spot in a crowd than on one of the empty pavements along the traffic-choked roads. The walkways to the arts complex were filling up with people coming to dine at the restaurants before the evening performances began. Flat rectangular ponds reflected the buildings crowding the skyline, water barely ruffled by some optimistic ducks gliding on the surface. I wove in front of one large party of German tourists and slowed to a walk. Running would only draw attention to me. Breath coming in painful gasps, I tried to act normally. I caught a red-dressed lady looking at me curiously as she strolled by arm-in-arm with her husband.

I gave her a sheepish smile, flapping my hand to cool my cheeks. 'Have you got the time? I'm worried I'm really late.'

My rush accounted for, she glanced at her watch. 'Five-thirty.'

'Thanks. Yeah, I'm late.' I gave her a parting smile and began to speed walk past the square concrete planters brimming with summer blooms.

Yves had given me fire-flowers. No one had ever thought to do that for me.

Phee, tell us where you are, please! We're not angry with you— we just want to help you.

I wasn't going to answer in case he sensed my direction from a stray thought.

Phee, please! Don't try this!

The Barbican Centre lived up to its name, appearing like a modern fortress of brown-grey concrete, so completely miserable that I couldn't understand how an architect could get away with designing it. Cities were dispiriting enough without the buildings slumping into a deep, untreatable depression. The interior was better: wide foyers for mingling with the marks, discreet corners to check what you'd lifted out of a handbag— it was very well organized for those in my profession. I'd overheard the visitors remarking that the theatres and concert halls were excellent but that wasn't the kind of place people like me got to see. For us, all the drama happened offstage.

Phee, don't give up on us before we've even had a chance! Yves's pleas were becoming more desperate.

I followed a sign down a flight of stairs to the Ladies and ducked inside. A cheap retreat perhaps, but I doubted they would break in unless they were sure where I was. Standing at the sink I gazed at my reflection. A wild-eyed frump stared back. I needed a serious make-over if I wasn't going to turn heads for the wrong reasons. I'd abandoned my bag at the Benedicts' flat so had to do my best with soap, handtowels, and my fingers. I smoothed my hair down and splashed my face. I then remembered I had a stub of eyeliner and a tube of lip gloss—one of the advantages of frumpy clothes is capacious, line-destroying pockets. With a dab of make-up, I began to look more myself. Then, retreating into one of the cubicles, I unzipped my skirt and wriggled out, to reveal my shorts underneath. I unbuttoned my white shirt and reknotted it under my breasts. I felt like one of those circus 'quick change' acts—ta-dah, no more Wimpy Wendy, now we have Slinky Phee rising from the ashes. I rolled the skirt up and tucked it under my arm, planning to swipe the first plastic bag I saw to put it in.

Checking my appearance for a final time in the mirror, I was pleased with my transformation. A couple of elderly ladies came in and frowned disapprovingly at my display of midriff. Yep, I'd got it right.

Phee, we know you're in the Barbican Centre.

How did they know? Or were they just guessing and hoping to catch me out? These questions mingled with my doubts as my brain went into spin cycle. Was I doing the right thing running like this? Did I have another choice? Leaving my soulfinder, even if it was for his benefit in the long term, felt like sawing off my own arm.

Look, cut messing us around and meet us. I'm standing by the shop on the ground floor.

Yeah, yeah, and his brothers were staking out the other exits. I wasn't born yesterday.

Do you want me to beg? He was getting angry with me—I couldn't blame him. I had hit him where he was vulnerable, striking at his confidence dealing with girls, and I was sorry for it. He was perfect as he was and didn't need to be shy. But he couldn't be mine. *Can't you just give me one little chance?*

Sorry, no can do. Not in my world. His only chance was to keep away from me so my life did not infect his.

I took a final look at myself in the mirror. I could do this. Leaving the Ladies to head straight for the exit on the lower ground floor, I sent a final wish.

Be happy, Yves.

Big mistake. I stopped in my tracks. Yves was standing with his arms folded, his brothers either side, directly opposite the Ladies. He had tricked me into thinking him upstairs.

Nice. Like the new look. He didn't sound as if he liked it one tiny bit. He sounded fit to be tied down and given a dose of sedatives.

How did you find me?

Unique energy signature, remember?

I took a quick survey of my options. Back up and wait them out—but no they'd just come in after me. Go with them, and let the Seer hurt Tony tonight and then them when he came for me. Use my power on them—too many people and they would know to resist. A fourth option—make a fuss. They couldn't haul a girl from a public place if I kicked up enough noise. Though I hated drawing attention to myself it sounded a pretty good moment to learn.

Don't even think about it or Vick will have to do his thing on you, warned Yves, who must have read my intentions from my furtive glances around the foyer.

Then a fifth option arrived, one none of us had anticipated. Unicorn and Dragon walked swiftly up from behind the Benedicts and passed them before they knew it.

'Phee, great to see you!' Unicorn said with false friendliness. 'I thought we'd be late for the concert. Come along.' He hooked my arm on one side, Dragon on the other.

Now it had come, I wasn't sure I wanted this rescue.

'Who the hell are you?' Yves made to intervene, but Vick held him back with a speaking look. A brawl in the Barbican was not a good outcome for any of us.

'We're her brothers.' Unicorn squeezed my arm painfully. 'You won't see her again. Sorry if her light-fingered ways bothered you. She'll be punished for it.' So Unicorn thought this was about a steal that had gone wrong. That made sense: why else would the three Americans be chasing me through the Barbican. He whipped the skirt from under my arm and shook it out. 'She's not got the stuff on her so I suggest you check the Ladies. She's probably stashed it there.'

Dragon wrenched my arm behind my back. 'Say goodbye to your friends, Phee. Sadly she can't stay to play.'

I said nothing.

'Go on, say it!'

'Bye.' God, I was so tired of bullying men.

The gold bracelet around Dragon's wrist began to glow with heat. 'What the—!' He let go of my arm and shook the band off. It melted into a flat disc on the tile.

Yves gave him a challenging look. 'No one hurts Phee.'

Wrong. They did all the time. But Yves had made a mistake and revealed that he was a Savant, which propelled this confrontation into a new dimension. Dragon sent an arrow of a look at the metal and glass sculpture hanging overhead a little way behind the Benedicts. With a rattle of bolts coming loose, it fell diagonally towards them as he pulled it with his power.

'Yves!' I screamed.

The three Benedicts threw themselves out of its path as it smashed to the floor, losing shape like a beached jellyfish, a mess of splinters and wire. The resulting commotion of screams and officials running to the site of the incident allowed us to slip away. Unicorn and Dragon shot out of the entrance onto the underground street before the Benedicts had time to recover their feet. At Unicorn's hail, a taxi peeled from the rank and stopped to let us get in. I felt the urge to laugh crazily—my second ride in the back of a cab, so fast on the heels of my first. Boy, was I living it up.

Yves, are you OK? I had to know.

Yes, just a few cuts. He sounded relieved that I cared. *But, Phee, are you OK? Who are those men?*

My brothers, maybe. I hunched in a corner, head against the window as the taxi pulled away. *Goodbye, Yves. It would've been nice to know you. I'm sorry it didn't work out.*

Chapter 8

There was no need to be told that I was in dire trouble. Dragon and Unicorn chose not to mention it before the taxi driver but they were seething. Some of their reaction might have been down to post-battle adrenalin, but I knew that I had added insult to injury when I had warned the Benedicts, spoiling Dragon's attack. The Community were supposed to stick by each other; I'd made my split loyalties all too clear. I could only hope they would not make too much of the fact that Yves had known my name and stepped forward to defend me. I dreaded to think what they would do with the knowledge that I had discovered my soulfinder.

The electronic clock on the taxi dashboard showed that it was still only six when we got out a street away from our temporary home. So early? I'd lived through so much today that I felt it had to be at least midnight. I shivered, horribly cold in my shorts. Unicorn had managed to drop my skirt during the scuffle—no loss to fashion but I'd had a few things in the pockets I would've liked to keep. Then again, the missing skirt was the smallest of my problems at the moment.

A sheet of newspaper tumbled-turned down the alley and

wrapped itself around my legs. I kicked it away. 'Do I go back to my room?' I asked, not really expecting a reprieve.

'You're joking?' mocked Unicorn. These were the first words we'd exchanged since getting in the taxi.

'Oh, Phee, Phee,' Dragon took hold of my arm again, 'why did you do it?'

I wondered what exactly he meant. Get caught? Shout my warning? Fail in my mission?

'After talking to you last night, the Seer knew something strange was going on. He sent us to keep watch on you and it was as well we did.' Anger made the tendons on his neck bulge as he clenched his jaw. 'You spent five hours in our enemies' company.'

In what way were they enemies? To me, Yves had started out as just another mark.

'Makes us wonder what you told them.' He used his power to open the fire-door, not waiting for Tony to answer a knock.

'I told them nothing! I escaped as soon as I could. There were three of them, Dragon, in case you didn't notice!'

Heads quickly withdrew from doorways as we passed. No one wanted to be picked out for being too curious.

'Three people who know all about us now. Three Savants. Three problems. And maybe more if they tell others.'

'But there's nothing to tell!' I could feel that my protests were falling like cries in deep space—in the emptiness of Dragon's heart, there was nothing to carry the sound. Unicorn was worse: his soul was stuffed with evil and cruelty. Being on the wrong side of him was to be a mouse in the paws of a vindictive alley cat.

'Yeah, yeah, explain that to the Seer.' Dragon shoved me up the stairs.

We reached the fifth floor. I was cursing my decision under my breath. I should've taken my chance with Yves; coming back hadn't saved Tony but only made everything much, much worse.

Phee, I can feel you are upset. Speak to me. It was Yves, trying to find me again. His telepathic message was faint as he didn't quite know where to direct it. I couldn't reply. Some telepaths can eavesdrop on the conversations of others and block them if they try. One of the Seer's companions, a woman called Kasia, had these gifts and she was never very far from him. The last thing I wanted was Yves and his brothers to storm into a fight they could not possibly win.

Unicorn went on ahead into the Seer's rooms while I stood with Dragon on the balcony. This must be what it felt like to wait for an execution. I was consumed by a strange kind of panic, searching for options while knowing that there was no escape. Yves's voice whispered pleas but I had to ignore him.

Unicorn came back too quickly and nodded to signal that we could enter. I was alarmed to see most of the Seer's hangers-on were leaving, only his core team of a couple of henchmen and Kasia remaining behind. I studied her quickly, hoping for an ally. I had had several OK conversations with her in the past months. A bleached blonde thirty-something with the prematurely aged skin of a heavy smoker, she wasn't unkind, just very much under the sway of the Seer. I often wondered if he used his gift to plant the seed of adoration in his female companions, knowing that a normal woman would be repulsed by being close to him.

No one spoke as we approached the Seer's throne. My knees were shaking—something I was sure everyone had noticed as I could barely stand.

Sprawled on the sofa, the Seer turned to me, his small, dark eyes as malevolent as the button features of a voodoo doll's face and about as human.

Still no questions.

Unable to stand the tension, I gave a little whimper of distress, quickly swallowed.

He raised a finger. I was lifted into the air and let fall back to the floor, landing on my back, all the wind knocked from my lungs by Dragon's mental punch to my stomach.

'You betrayed us.'

I curled up, hands over my head. 'No, no, I didn't.'

Dragon's next attack sent me spinning over the floor to crash into the wall like a squash ball. Pain slammed through my body.

'You told the Benedicts about us and now the Savant Net will be aware of our cell.'

'Please, I said nothing. I escaped as soon as I could, but I was tired and weak—I had to rest before I tried to break out.'

My excuses disappeared like raindrops falling on cracked, dry earth. I was never listened to, never heard in the Community; just a tool to be used. The Seer turned to Unicorn. 'Did she have anything on her?'

Unicorn folded his arms. 'Nothing. She was trying to evade them in the Barbican Centre when we caught up with her. If she managed to steal any items she must have dumped them.'

The Seer flicked his gaze back to me. 'Did you?'

'No, I tried.' He glowered. 'I really did, but they had a fail-safe mechanism, a kind of self-destruct. There was an iPhone and an iPad but both were destroyed.'

'That is unfortunate,' the Seer tapped his fingers on his stomach, 'for you.'

I curled up even tighter.

'So what do we do now, sir?' Dragon asked, perhaps to distract him from thoughts of inflicting immediate punishment. Some flicker of brotherly sympathy might still glow in the depths of his heart like the light of a dying star. 'And what's going on? Unicorn and I, we were wondering why you wanted her to hit these men in particular.'

The Seer played with a gold ring squashed on his puffy finger. 'I suppose there is no harm in you knowing. The Savant Net has recently come to my attention—and they have crossed some other Savants, business contacts.'

'What is the Net?' Unicorn frowned at me as I made to crawl out of the Seer's eyeline. I lay still.

The Seer debated for a second if he was prepared to share information; he usually kept all knowledge to himself, aware it gave him extra power over us. This time he made an exception. 'It's an international organization, very loose-knit, a group of fools misusing Savant gifts for what they term "good" causes.'

Unicorn smirked; Dragon laughed; but for me the news was welcome. So there were good Savants? Gifts did not have to be used in the shadows like we did with ours? That was encouraging to know even if it was unlikely to help me.

'They try to crack down on the activities of those of us who wish to be free to exercise our powers in whatever way we see fit. If they give the authorities too much of an insight into our methods, we will find our hunting grounds much reduced, and some of us may even be put out of business.' The Seer flicked a hand at me. 'Phoenix was sent to acquire the possessions of the one in charge of communications but she has disappointed me. I'd counted on her gift to get the information our colleagues require to eliminate the threat to our operations.'

'What kind of information?' asked Unicorn.

'Names, addresses, all kinds of valuable intelligence about those involved in the Savant Net were stored on that Savant's computer and now she tells us they have gone up in smoke. That data was our bargaining chip and now we don't have it.'

Savant Net? I could make a guess what he was talking about—an online group of those of us with gifts—but why did he want to know about it now? I could understand that he saw it as a threat but the Seer was usually only interested in the gains of petty theft and quick money; taking on the Savant Net was in another league. Normally he would move on if he thought the authorities had got wind of us. Had his horizons expanded to selling information in some form of Savant espionage? Or had he already been involved and I had just never known? It had not escaped me that the fact that they were talking so freely in front of me was not a good sign. No indication of trust, it was more likely they knew I'd be unable to share what I was learning.

Dragon folded his arms, standing over me like a prison warden, ready to kick me if I dared move. 'There were three of them chasing her. Are there more?'

The Seer nodded. 'Many more. That particular branch destroyed the Kelly business empire in Las Vegas last year. As far as we can make out, they are at the centre of the US operations of the Savant Net.'

'Forgive me, sir,' Unicorn said smoothly, 'but you have said "we" a number of times. I'm not quite sure who you mean.'

The Seer glared at him, his head sinking deeper into his triple chins. 'I'll tell you when I'm ready to tell you and not a moment earlier.'

Unicorn backed down immediately. 'Of course, sir.'

The Seer took a cigar from a box at a sidetable and lit the tip. 'I see you clearly, Unicorn. Like the creature I named you after, you have only one point and you'll skewer anything on that horn of a brain of yours to get your way. You want to rule and you secretly look down on me.'

'No, no, sir.' Unicorn went quite pale. 'I'm just curious.'

The Seer gave a poisonous bubble of laughter, a belch of cigar smoke. 'I do not mind your ruthless drive for power, my son, as long as you do not act on your thoughts to dispose of me.' He leaned forward, the sofa creaking as he moved. 'Let me tell you now, you won't be able to. I have planted enough seeds of loyalty in all your brains to make any step against me the same as suicide.'

Of course he had. We all knew that trying to escape him was impossible.

'If—when—one of you takes over, it will be by my invitation. But you should know that there is a world of other Savants outside my organization, one that I will very soon introduce you to, but on my terms and on my say-so. Understood?'

Cowed, Unicorn nodded. 'Completely, sir.'

'Now, Phoenix.' He sucked on the cigar.

Oh God, he was turning his attention back to me.

'I fear you have not told us everything.' His power was pushing at my mind but I was too terrified to have any thoughts but fear; he wasn't learning anything that way.

'She spent all afternoon with them,' Unicorn said hurriedly, trying to prove his suspect loyalty by tattling on me.

The Seer blew out a stream of smoke. 'And you wish us to believe that you told them nothing about us?'

Dragon hauled me from the floor on to my knees. 'Answer the Seer.'

I grappled for safe things to tell them. 'They gave me something to eat and sorted out a burn I got when the gear went up in flames.' I held out the reddened palm. 'One of them is a healer.'

'A healer!' snorted the Seer. 'Not much of a threat then. And what else happened?'

'He . . . they let me sleep. Then I escaped.'

Unicorn strode towards me, hand outstretched. 'She's wasting our time. Let me use my power on her to loosen her tongue.'

'No!' The Seer stopped Unicorn in his tracks. 'Phoenix has

other uses. Her youth is part of her value to me. I don't want her made to talk that way.'

I breathed a subtle sigh of relief—too soon.

'Fetch Tony. I've noticed that there seems to be some attachment between the two of them. Perhaps she will talk to save her friend.'

'Please, there *is* nothing more to tell you!'

But Unicorn had already left.

The Seer ignored my frantic pleas, turning to the television as if nothing out of the ordinary was happening. I crouched against the wall, hands covering my head to drown out the hateful sound of him crunching his way through a handful of peanuts. A talent show burbled away on the screen with its manufactured tension and false emotion, leather-faced judges passing judgement on those who were foolish enough to put themselves through the torture. The Seer was a bloated version of them, manipulating the futures of others with his least word, his punishment for failure not expulsion, but pain or death.

Tony shuffled into the room, his worried dark eyes flitting from me to the Seer. 'You sent for me, sir?'

The Seer switched off the screen with a blink midway through some dance group. 'Yes, Tony. I need your help.'

Tony was understandably surprised by this statement. He smiled wanly. 'Of course. Anything. You know I am loyal to you.'

'Phoenix here is having difficulty telling us everything we need to know. We want you to persuade her otherwise.'

Tony had no idea he was being toyed with. He turned a shaky, cajoling smile on me. 'Come on, Phee, you know the Seer can't be disobeyed. You have to tell him all you know.'

I dug my nails into my knees. 'I have, Tony, only he doesn't believe me.'

Tony rubbed his mangled hand with his good one. 'I see, I see. Not sure what we can do then.'

Then, in a fraction of a second, the mood in the room shot into the red spectrum. The Seer sent Unicorn an unspoken order. The younger man grabbed Tony by the scruff of the neck.

'How old are you, Tony?' the Seer asked as my friend quivered in Unicorn's grip.

'Fifty-eight I think, sir.' Tony turned desperate eyes on me.

'Please, don't!' I whispered.

'You would give your life for me?' the Seer continued.

'Of . . . of course,' agreed Tony.

'Good. I want ten years now.'

Smiling hungrily, Unicorn closed his eyes and spread his gift over Tony. I could see the dark grey pall falling over his victim; Tony's hair was drained of colour, turning pure white, skin more lined, body stooped as bones bent arthritically. Oh God, oh God.

'Phee!' gasped Tony in shock. 'Help me!'

I scrambled up to my feet, intending to break the connection by force, but Dragon threw me back down with a flick of a finger.

'Tell us what we want to know,' droned the Seer.

My mind howling with rage, I felt as if I was being ripped in two. Unicorn was killing Tony—I had no choice.

'All right, all right, please stop!' I screamed. 'There's one more thing I can tell you. But, please, I beg you, please stop hurting him!'

Unicorn lifted his hand. Tony slumped to the ground, chest heaving.

I swallowed. 'The reason why the Benedicts took me in—it's because I'm Yves's soulfinder.'

Silence met this claim. What had I done?

'You have a soulfinder?' Dragon said incredulously. Like me, he probably had doubted they even existed.

I nodded. My whole body was shaking as though I had been shut in an industrial freezer, unable to get any warmth to my core. I had betrayed my other half.

The Seer rocked slightly on the sofa making the frame groan. 'Interesting. This has . . . possibilities.'

Forgotten until this moment, Kasia laid delicate fingers, nails painted scarlet, on his shoulder. 'It's true. I can sense him trying to find her. I ignored it until now, not sure of what I was hearing, but there is a search underway.'

The Seer glanced back at me. 'And has she replied?'

Kasia gave me a pitying look. 'No. She's blocking him.'

The Seer tapped his fat lips with the tips of his fingers. 'Curious. That seems to support her claim that she's loyal to us. Perhaps I've judged her too harshly.' He then noticed Tony lying at his feet. 'Take the man away and make sure he's looked after. He did well.'

Tony's eyes fluttered open as he was lifted up by two of the Seer's guard.

'I'm sorry,' I whispered.

His tired eyes closed, giving me no absolution.

'So, tell us, Phoenix, what is it like to have a soulfinder?' The Seer seemed genuinely interested. He patted the sofa cushion next to him. 'Come and tell your daddy all about it.'

I wished he would go back to torturing me. Choices long since given up, I moved to the seat he indicated. 'It feels . . . ' Frightening? Awful? Wonderful? 'Special.'

'And would you do anything to keep your soulfinder safe?'

This question was much more dangerous. 'I . . . I suppose. I hardly know. I only met him this morning.'

He stroked his lips thoughtfully. 'And does he like you?'

I gave a choked laugh. 'Like me? How could he? I've tried

to steal from him—I ran away from him. I imagine he is pretty fed up with me right now.'

He leaned over and patted my cheek. 'You underestimate yourself, Phoenix. You have your mother's looks and an interesting gift: he won't have given up on you yet.'

I wished he would. I did not like the direction this conversation was taking.

'You may have failed to get the intelligence this time, but how much will he give to keep you, I wonder? Would he sacrifice the Savant Net if he knew that was the only way to save his soulfinder? A fascinating dilemma.' The Seer licked his lips, calculating the fallout of human misery from his little experiment using me as bait.

I doubted very much that Yves would put his family and friends at risk for me. Now we'd met, he had to know I wasn't worth it, even with the soulfinder link between us. The legend was that your soulfinder was supposed to give a Savant completeness, contentment and new strengths to their gift, but Yves could hardly hope for that when I was such a disaster area. The presence of the Seer in my life was like being raised in the shadow of the faulty Chernobyl nuclear reactor; I was going to be living with the effects of the radiation for years.

The Seer offered me the peanuts but, as the bowl had been lodged on his lap, I would rather have eaten scorpions. 'I think I will take you with me this evening,' he mused. 'Get dressed for a night out, my dear. You and I have some friends to meet. They will be eager to hear about our interesting situation.'

'Going out?' I'd never heard of the Seer venturing from his squalid penthouse, but then I had not dared track his movements.

'Yes. The Waldorf Hotel. Kasia, make sure she is suitably kitted out to impress. You may use the jewellery.' He tossed her a key from his top pocket. Kasia snatched it from the air.

'I'll need you along to ensure no security leaks.'

'May I wear something from the box too?' she asked hopefully, caressing the key in her fingers.

The Seer sighed, hating the idea of any of his riches leaving his vaults. 'I suppose you must. But my daughter gets the diamonds. Nothing above pearls for you.'

Kasia flashed him a radiant smile. 'Thank you. Come with me, Phoenix.' She frowned at my scratched knees and faded shorts. 'I can see I have my work cut out.'

Chapter 9

For the first time in my life, I was all dressed up with somewhere to go. If I hadn't felt so depressed about Yves and Tony,
I might have even enjoyed the experience. Kasia and I had had
plenty of outfits to choose from as the Seer's apartment had
rooms stuffed with designer clothes, shoes, and jewels, none of
which could have possibly been used, as his companions were
usually to be seen in cheap imitations of the real thing. I was
even more perplexed by his mentality of surrounding himself
by tat when he easily could afford so much more. I could only
guess that there was a strong miserly streak to the Seer, con-
tent to possess without enjoying, a character bent towards the
gutter rather than aspiring to the swanky parts of town, like
the West End, where we were now heading.

A white stretch limousine had been hired for the evening.
What the chauffeur made of picking up the little party of
the Seer, Kasia, Dragon, Unicorn, and me outside a rundown
estate, he was too wise to share with us. The Seer wore his
usual white suit; Dragon and Unicorn were in black dinner
jackets. Kasia had found a white beaded cocktail dress with
matching bolero, the better to display her pearls. She had gone

overboard with her cosmetics and hair products, ending up a bit too much like Marge Simpson by the time she'd finished. I'd been ordered to wear a violet silk gown, cut to flatter my slight build. Long enough to cover my scratched knees, it kept shoulders bare, the better to display the long trail of diamonds around my neck. With a disapproving cluck of her tongue, Kasia had earlier repaired my poor haircut with a pair of deft scissors, then set it in an upswept style so the droplet earrings fashioned to match the necklace could be seen. She had taken out my extra earrings, replacing them with discreet studs, making me look less 'street' and more classy. With a pair of delicate silver sandals, I felt worthy of my seat in the back of the car.

The narrow streets of the East End gave way to the tower blocks of the City, great canyons filled with traffic fumes, late-working bankers and stockbrokers.

'Who are we going to meet tonight, sir?' Unicorn asked, careful not to push too hard with his questions after his earlier slap-on-the-wrist.

'Some allies: those of us with the gift that stand against the Savant Net.' The Seer sprawled on the rear seat with only room for Kasia beside him. He studied my appearance as I sat facing him. 'You look very elegant, Phoenix. I am pleased.'

Kasia preened under the implied praise of her skills. 'I did my best with her.'

'Thank you,' I choked out.

'You will come into the meeting but I do not want you to say anything unless asked a direct question.' He gave a wheezing cough. 'Understood?'

'Yes, sir.' I rubbed my fingers against the smooth fabric of my gown, marvelling at the softness. I'd never felt anything like it before.

The Seer smiled. 'I see you are fond of life's little luxuries.

If you do as I say, I can promise you much more like that in the future.'

He had got the wrong girl. I might like pretty things but I wasn't to be so easily bribed. I'd wear sackcloth and ashes if that meant I could escape him. 'Thank you, sir.'

The Seer tapped his stomach with his slug fingers. 'Perhaps you should call me "Daddy" tonight. It will make the right impression.'

I'd prefer to get in a bath of live snakes.

Unicorn and Dragon couldn't help exchanging an alarmed look at this concession.

'Only Phoenix,' the Seer warned. 'A daughter may take such liberties; my sons will carry on treating me with fear and respect. I will not lose face with these men.'

Who could we be meeting that even the Seer felt in awe of them? I'd never seen him doubt his image before, but then I'd never seen him step outside the confines of the Community. Perhaps this, for him, was like a reunion of petty despots in the margins of the United Nations General Assembly, all lining up to measure who was the biggest human rights abuser.

The car swung into the Waldorf and a uniformed porter rushed to open the door. Dragon got out first to check the lie of the land before helping the Seer on to the pavement. I was the last to follow. Smoothing down my dress to enter the smart entrance hall, I couldn't tear my eyes away from the hotel: it was beautiful. I loved the row upon row of lit windows in a stately sweep of a building, about seven storeys high; the alert staff seeing to the guests' every need before they even thought of it; the quiet elegance of the place, the opposite of where we had begun our journey. The porter kept his expression blank as he stood back to let the enormous bulk of the Seer inside, though I did see a glimmer of interest as his eyes lighted on my necklace. The diamonds were superb. I had to hope the original owner was not dining in the West End tonight.

'May I help you, sir?' asked the doorman on duty in the foyer.

'I have a reservation in the restaurant. Name of London,' the Seer said crisply.

'Of course, sir. The rest of your party has already arrived.' The doorman led the way to the restaurant, handing us over to the head waiter. 'Mr London.'

The waiter conducted us smoothly to a table in a private dining room at the rear of the restaurant. We had to weave our way through the diners sitting at the white-clothed tables; candles, flowers, and silver and glassware all adding to the atmosphere of privilege. I saw a couple in one corner holding hands, the man brushing the woman's fingers tenderly with his thumb. Something that felt suspiciously like sorrow brought tears to my eyes.

Yves.

Phee, where are you?

I'd reached out to him even though I hadn't meant to. Kasia sent me a startled look. I shook my head slightly and blocked the connection I'd made. She nodded, acknowledging that I had repaired my mistake.

Entering the dining room, we found six men sitting around the table, their bodyguards standing against the wall behind them. They stood politely to shake the Seer's hand.

'Gentlemen, I hope I am not late?' The Seer gasped a little after walking from the car, a marathon to one who spent all day on a sofa.

The ginger-haired man at the head of the table shook his head. 'No, Mr London, we had only just got around to ordering drinks. I'm New York.'

The Seer smiled a little queasily. He was not comfortable to hear that they had all had a chance to discuss him before he arrived. 'Good to meet you at last.'

The others muttered their names as he went round to greet them: Moscow, Beijing, Kuala Lumpur, Sydney, Mexico City. No real names, only locations.

The Seer waved Kasia, Dragon, and Unicorn off to stand with the bodyguards before bringing me forward. 'My daughter, Phoenix.'

Mr New York took my hand. 'Charming.' I could feel his gift brush over me like a cool breeze as he tried to guess my strength. I kept my thoughts blank, not sure how his worked. To be in charge of other Savants required some control of minds so I guessed that all the men in the room had skills in that direction. Baffled but not disappointed, Mr New York let go and clicked his fingers for the waiter. 'Another place for Miss London. Perhaps here between her father and me.'

So Mr New York had appointed himself as the ringleader, had he? I glanced around at the other faces of the men gathered; none protested, but neither did they look entirely pleased by the arrangement.

Mr New York decided to make a joke of it. 'I apologize, gentlemen, for monopolizing the fairest dinner companion. My only excuse is a delight in beautiful women.'

Two waiters hurried forward with place settings and an extra chair. When I took my seat, everyone else sat down, a weird, old-fashioned gallantry that did not fool me that they cared in the least for my presence among them. They were merely aware they were on show before strangers and were going through the motions of polite behaviour.

Mr New York signalled to the staff to begin taking our orders. I stared at the long list of choices on the menu, unable to understand the curly writing. Here my patchy education let me down. My experience of restaurants was limited to fast food.

'Phoenix, that's a pretty name.' Mr New York snapped his menu closed, having made his decision.

'Thank you, sir.'

'Call me Jim.' He winked, his gaze lingering on the diamonds. 'So, you are the apple of your daddy's eye, are you? Bet you got him twisted round your little finger.'

I shivered, aware that the Seer was listening. 'No, sir. Mr London keeps us all under strict control.'

'Ah, that rare thing: an obedient daughter. Maybe you could come and give my girls lessons, at least get them to keep a lid on their account at Bloomingdales?' He chuckled at his own joke. The waiter bent at his shoulder. 'The quail's eggs followed by the shoulder of lamb.'

'Excellent choice, sir,' murmured the waiter obsequiously. 'Miss?'

The words danced before my eyes, so many unfamiliar terms. 'Is there a vegetarian option?' I whispered.

The waiter's eyes softened a little. He gestured to the curly 'V' entered by the vegetarian dishes. I am so dumb sometimes.

'Vegetarian? What are you doing, London, allowing your daughter to starve herself of protein?' scoffed Mr New York. 'I invest in prime beef herds in Argentina; I find it difficult not to take non-meat eaters as a personal slight.'

The Seer frowned. 'My daughter will have the foie gras and the Angus steak.'

The waiter hovered at my side, bravely giving me time to correct the order. 'Miss?'

'I'll . . . I'll have what he said.' My nails curled into my palms, leaving little half-moon pressure marks.

'And how would you like the beef done?' His voice was gentle.

'She'll have it medium-rare,' interrupted Mr New York. 'If we are to make a convert of her, she should eat it at its best—not dried out like a hunk of old boot leather.'

The serving staff withdrew, leaving the dining room devoid of outsiders to our little meeting.

'So, Mr London, did you get the information you promised us?' asked a man further down the table; Mr Sydney if I remembered correctly.

The Seer sipped sparkling water from a wide-bellied glass. 'No. They had it rigged. The electronics went up in smoke when my operative stole them.'

A ripple of disappointment went round the table.

'I see. I suppose I would've been disappointed had our enemies been so easily compromised.' Mr New York exchanged a glance with Moscow and Beijing. I could tell they had little respect for their host. 'But tell us, London, why exactly are you here, then? I thought it was understood that this data was the price of your entry to our organization?'

The Seer leaned back, the chair creaking under his bulk. 'Because I have something better to put on the table.'

Before anyone could comment, the waiters were back with the first course. A plate of pale pink-brown paté was put in front of me. Two lacy cheese wafers sprouted from it like wings. I didn't bother to pick up a knife and fork as it was clearly animal in origin.

'Amazing dish, foie gras,' Mr New York said conversationally, while the waiters circulated, filling wine glasses for the men. 'They force feed geese to get that velvety texture from the liver.' He enjoyed watching me turn a shade of green as I pushed the plate away.

The waiter pounced. 'Miss is not enjoying her hors d'oeuvre? Can I bring you the asparagus soup instead?'

'Nonsense,' mumbled the Seer. 'She loves it, don't you, Phoenix?'

I picked at the side salad before he forced me to eat a mouthful, like one of the geese that had died to provide the dish.

Defeated, the waiter retired from the fray, taking the rest of the staff with him. They had to be under orders to leave the gentlemen alone between the necessary duties of fetching, carrying, and pouring. The hulk of a bodyguard closest to the door stood in front of it to prevent anyone else entering.

'Mr London, we would be most interested to hear what you think is better than information.' Mr Beijing, a tall Chinese man with a narrow face and pebble-hard eyes, invited the Seer to continue.

'Fate has handed us a gift, a way to bring down the Savant Net from the inside.' The Seer stabbed a scallop from his plate, smearing butter on the white rim as he mopped up the sauce.

'Go on.' Mr New York swirled a straw-coloured wine thoughtfully.

'I have identified the soulfinder of the sixth Benedict son.'

'A soulfinder? A rare treat. That indeed would be useful. Where is she?' The American's eyes flicked in my direction.

The Seer said nothing but merely looked at me, confirming his guess.

'Her? Your own daughter?' Mr New York began to chuckle. 'Well, if that don't take the prize!'

'The irony is delicious.' Mr Sydney raised his glass to me.

'As I said, I would bring something better to the table, and here she is.' The Seer enjoyed his moment of triumph, receiving the congratulations of his new allies. I had been his ticket into their company.

Mr Moscow cleared his throat, ending the little round of praise for the Seer. 'The question is, how will we use her?' He studied me, pale green eyes in his square, pasty face suspicious. 'Is she loyal?'

'All my people are loyal,' corrected the Seer. 'They have to be or they die.'

His statement met with general approval.

'What had you planned to do with her?' Mr New York asked, for the first time treating the Seer as an equal.

'I will seek a meeting with the boy—in secret. Find out how much information he will give in return for her safety.'

Mr New York smiled sceptically and patted the back of my wrist. 'But he won't believe you will hurt your own flesh and blood.'

'Really?' The Seer's expression was glacial. 'Do you doubt me capable of that—and more—to ensure our businesses can function without their interference? Dragon.'

My steak knife leapt into the air then arrowed down to dig the tip into the back of my bare forearm, making a shallow cut. Moving slowly up to my elbow, it drew a line of fiery pain. I knew better than to move—it could be my throat next—but I couldn't stop the tears springing to my eyes.

Mr New York batted the knife away. It flew into the corner and lay still. 'Enough, you've made your point!'

I pressed a napkin over the cut, staining the white linen with blood. Pushing my chair back, I got up. 'Excuse me.'

The Seer waved me away. Napkin concealing my cut, I dashed out in search of a refuge.

'Are you all right, miss?' My waiter caught me at the door.

'Yes, yes, just a little accident.' My heart was pounding and I knew I must look wild-eyed. 'Where are the . . . ?'

He caught my meaning. 'Through those doors, miss.'

I took cover in the plush toilets. Thick handtowels in a wicker basket on the marble top, automatic taps that worked with a wave of a hand, a beautiful flower arrangement, a collection of top-of-the-range toiletries: all so perfect that I had a mad urge never to leave and return to my grubby world outside. I seemed to be spending a lot of time hiding out like this. Approaching the basin, I ran my cut under the spray of water, rubbing in some soap to clean the wound. It was only superficial but it stung. All the pleasure I'd taken earlier in the evening swirled down the plughole with the red-stained water. I may be all prettied up for one night but I was still only a tool to the Seer, now being fashioned into the means of Yves's destruction. I couldn't bear the thought that I'd be used to hurt him.

Kasia came in and stood beside me, arms folded. She frowned at the water spots I'd splashed on my dress. 'I was sent to see if you're OK.'

'I'm fine,' I lied. I didn't meet her eyes in the mirror.

'There was no need for Dragon to do that to you.' Kasia picked up my wrist and studied the cut. 'It spoils the look. Do you think it is going to start bleeding again?'

I wondered if she was worried for me or for her white gown. 'I don't think so.'

'Probably best to leave it then. A bandage would be very obvious.'

'And spoil the look,' I echoed.

She squeezed my fingers briefly. 'It's important to please the Seer and not let him down in front of his business contacts.'

He should have thought of that before he ordered Dragon to start carving me up in front of them.

'Why are you with him, Kasia?' I found myself asking. She seemed at heart a nice enough woman; what on earth was she doing in this set?

She smiled at me in the mirror, her eyes fever-bright. 'The Seer is the most wonderful man. You'll understand in time.'

I understood he had planted the belief in her mind. She was to be pitied as she really didn't know that she was a prisoner, as I was for different reasons. Of the two, I'd pick my kind of servitude. Patting my arm dry, I wondered if my mother had also held this false confidence in the Seer; I couldn't remember her well enough to know what she had really thought, but I had no memories of her ever saying a bad word against him. Indeed, she had impressed on me just before she died that I was to try and stay in the Community, making it sound as though it was the only home open to me. And I had trusted her to know. Another false belief planted, this time unwittingly by someone I was sure had loved me. Throwing the soiled towel in the waste bin, I reflected that she was the only one who had. Even Yves was never going to feel real love for me as the situation had been forced on him by fate or genetics, whatever. I acknowledged that I could fall for him, for his gentleness, intelligence and (here I admit to being shallow) to his all too handsome appearance, but what would he find in me to love?

Kasia waved her hand in front of my face, waking me from a daze. 'Hello. Earth to Phee.'

'I'm coming.' I took a final look at the elegant girl in the mirror, the one marred by the scratch on her arm. It didn't feel like me. Then again, I didn't know what 'me' felt like.

Chapter 10

In the car on the way home I held myself apart from the post-match analysis of the meeting indulged in by the Seer and his two sons. They were pleased with how the business had been conducted, congratulating our leader on his wrong-footing of the others by producing me as a surprise star player on his team. Tuning them out, I reflected instead on the waste of food on my plate. I'd not eaten anything but side salad, vegetables and bread rolls—the waiter had kept me well supplied with those so I wasn't feeling hungry. The men had decided to skip dessert and go straight to brandy and coffee. If I hadn't already known they were crooks, their aversion to the best part of any meal would have condemned them. I'd managed to swipe a couple of handmade chocolates with my latte but, really, what was the point of dining for the first time in my life at a five-star restaurant and coming away with so little to appreciate from the experience?

I knew I was making myself think such inconsequential thoughts to avoid dealing with the key point of the evening. The Seer had promised to use me as bait for Yves and I was in no hurry to find out what form this would take.

Back at our 'home bitter home', I followed the Seer up to the fifth floor, hoping this would be the end of the evening, but I was not to be so lucky.

'Phoenix, a word,' the Seer gasped at the top of the stairs. He mopped his sweating brow with a red silk handkerchief.

His court was waiting for him in his lounge, the women all cooing over his smart appearance.

'Ladies, give us a moment,' he announced, gesturing for them to leave.

Watching them file out without a protest at their dismissal, I realized he had created a bunch of robotic women to serve his every need, like, what do you call them? Yeah, Stepford Wives. It was obscene. The Seer lowered himself onto his favourite spot on the sofa. 'I am sure you understood what we want of you.'

I shrugged, wrapping my arms around my waist. 'I . . . I think so.'

'You are to arrange to meet your soulfinder tomorrow. Tell him to come without alerting his brothers. He has to be alone or it will be the worse for you, understood?'

Threats, threats, and more threats. 'Yes, I understand. Where should I meet him?'

The Seer rubbed his cheek. I hoped it was a sign of the onset of really painful toothache. 'The Millennium Bridge. That way we'll see if he really has come alone.'

A suspended footbridge over the Thames between the Tate Modern art gallery and St Paul's cathedral, it was a good choice for a clandestine meeting.

'And then what?'

'Take him into the Tate. We'll meet in the Turbine hall.'

'You . . . you are going to be there?' I was unable to hide my shudder.

'Of course. I have business to conduct with your young

man. You're not bringing him back here.' He shifted, letting out a belch. 'That reminds me. He'll pressure you to tell him what this is all about. You must say nothing of what you heard tonight. As far as he is concerned your meeting is only about being his soulfinder. He'll believe that soon enough if the legend of the soulfinder is true.'

I nodded, appearing to agree as I did not know what else to do while my mind was so confused.

He beckoned me closer and gripped my scratched arm. *You will tell him nothing of what you heard tonight.*

I closed my eyes briefly, feeling sick as his power smeared my mind, destroying my free will in this matter.

He let go. 'Good girl. Now go get some sleep. Contact your soulfinder first thing in the morning and don't give him long to make the meeting. We wouldn't want him to have a chance to make counter-plans.'

No, we wouldn't want that, would we?

'I'll have Kasia monitoring what you say, so do not think to double-cross me in this.'

'I wouldn't dare,' I muttered truthfully.

'Goodnight, Phoenix. Oh, and leave the diamonds with Kasia, won't you?'

Relieved to be dismissed, I slapped the necklace and earrings in Kasia's hand and backed out hurriedly before anyone else could try and get something from me. I hadn't forgotten Unicorn's attempt to steal a march on the Seer by making me promise yesterday to show him first what I'd stolen. That had proved to be a big zero, but I did not believe Unicorn for one moment had abandoned making other plans for his own benefit if he could think of a way to do so without crossing one of the Seer's lines of loyalty. Fortunately, the Seer ordered Dragon and Unicorn to stay behind to discuss what to do tomorrow if Yves agreed to meet me. Not invited into this inner circle, my only choice was to return to my room and work out how exactly I was going to keep Yves out of this sordid mess.

Slipping out of my finery, I hung the dress up on a hook behind the door and put on my pyjamas. I lay down for an hour but sleep eluded me. I got up and paced my room like a mouse running a maze in a scientist's laboratory until three, when exhaustion made me curl up under the duvet. Among my worries was Tony, but I felt too scared to go and see him—any contact I had with my friend only made things worse for him and I guessed he would not thank me for bringing more attention to him. Was I really the cause of him ageing ten years, or had I stopped it before so much was taken from him? Unicorn's power could not be reversed. No one had yet worked out how to keep someone young or the Seer would have been bottling it and selling it years ago; Unicorn could only speed up nature and make his targets age.

And what was I going to do about Yves? I was going to have to arrange to meet him—if I didn't do it willingly, the Seer would force me—but perhaps I could warn him somehow when we met as to what was truly going on? I'd be blamed, of course, when he didn't come to the meeting at the Tate, but that was better than letting the Seer anywhere near him.

I must have drifted off eventually because morning had already arrived when I woke up, the few birds that braved our part of town doing a brisk job of greeting the dawn. Taking a quick shower in cold water—my flat didn't run to the luxury of hot—I dressed, making each piece of clothing like a bit of mental armour to defend myself against the day. Shirt—I had to protect Yves. Jeans—I had somehow to live through whatever punishment my failure to please the Seer entailed. Shoes—I must allow no more harm to come to Tony. Eventually feeling ready to make the first move, I sat cross-legged on the floor and reached out for Yves. Seven thirty. If I arranged to meet him in an hour, we would have the crowds of commuters using the bridge camouflaging us. That might make Dragon and Unicorn's job of keeping track of our movements more difficult, something the Seer had not thought about when he proposed the meeting place.

Yves. Hi, it's me.

Phee? Where the hell are you? He'd answered on the first hint of a message from me; he had to have been listening all this time.

Good morning to you too. I smiled, sensing his huff of annoyance mixed with relief that I'd contacted him.

Nothing good about it until I see you.

Excellent—he had given me my cue. *OK then. Meet me on the Millennium Bridge at eight thirty. You know where that is?*

No, but I'll find out. Just tell me, are you OK?

Good question. *Just meet me. We'll talk then.*

Phee!

And come alone. Don't get your brothers involved in this or you won't see me.

I cut the connection. He might have a pretty good idea of my direction now I'd reached out to him but I doubted he had the telepathic skill to pinpoint my location.

Dragon, I've done as I was asked. I didn't like using this method of communication with people in the Community—it gave them too much access to your mind—but I decided talking to Dragon this way was the lesser evil. I could get out without seeing them that morning.

When? His thoughts in my brain were like the stamp of heavy machinery compared to Yves's butterfly touch.

Eight thirty. I told him to come alone.

Jeez, Phee, you didn't leave us much time to get there ahead of you.

The Seer told me not to give him much warning.

He didn't mean it to apply to us too! And the Tate won't even be open—did you think of that?

No. But, hey, tough cookies. Not that I said that to him, of course. *Sorry, I didn't think.*

Yeah, yeah, you never think. Still, it's done. We'll be in position. The Seer can arrive at the Tate as it opens at ten—that gives him more time.

I'm heading out now. Don't want to be late.

How's the arm? I could feel a smirk behind the question.

Been better.

Remember, won't you? You may think you're daddy's little girl, but that counts for nothing.

He had no need to be jealous; I had no illusions about my importance. *Don't worry, Dragon, the diamonds wouldn't have suited you in any case.*

I cut off, pleased to get in the last word for once. Dragon could hurt me, true, but somehow he no longer scared me, not like his brother and the Seer.

Vanity saw me dipping quickly back into the bathroom to put on a whisper of lip gloss and mascara. Though tired, I definitely looked better than my Wendy disguise. Perhaps Yves wouldn't be ashamed to be seen with me in public this time? It would be nice to think so. Hurrying out, I jumped on a bus heading through the City to St Paul's. It wasn't far but I still went upstairs to occupy the front seat, the one above the driver which gave you the illusion that you were in charge of the bus. I had to share it with a school kid who was listening to music on his phone so loud I swear I could hear the lyrics. The absurdity of the not-silent-headphones made me laugh and I hummed along until he started giving me dirty looks. His problem—if he didn't want me to share his tracks then he really should invest in a better pair of earbuds. He was lucky I hadn't nicked his mobile—normally I would've done so just to see if I could get away with it, leaving him mid-song, wondering what the hell had just happened.

I admit it was strange to be in such a good mood when everything in my life was so dire. I could only explain it as a response to the awareness that I was going to see Yves again in a few minutes, my soulfinder. I didn't need to steal other people's stuff to give me a mood-lift because I could steal myself a little happiness just imagining that things were different.

I got off the bus in the shadow of the great cathedral. White walls rose from the narrow streets like cliffs of grubby sugar candy. This close you can't see the dome well, but I knew it was above me, sitting on the cathedral like one of the serving dishes the waiters used at the Waldorf to cover the plates as they brought them to the table. I could imagine a heavenly hand coming out of the sky and lifting it off with a flourish, revealing the tourists and tombs inside.

Sun was shining on the Thames as I walked down Peter's Hill. The sounds of traffic mingled with the shouts of the boys in the grounds of a school right by the footbridge. I was swimming against the tide as commuters battled up the hill towards the City from the rail terminuses south of the river. It was exciting to be among so many people, to feel briefly part of the vibrant life of London. I could almost imagine I had a proper reason for being here, a job perhaps in one of the cafés on the South Bank, a normal life with friends and a flat somewhere cheap in the suburbs. Some people might think that a boring life choice, but to me the independence sounded like heaven.

I didn't have my own watch so I stopped a harassed-looking woman hurrying north, one of the few not occupied with talking on her phone. Without breaking step, she crisply informed me that it was eight-fifteen. Perfect—I had plenty of time to get in position. I thought the centre of the bridge would be the best spot, giving me a chance to watch out for trouble from either direction. I had been serious about ducking out of the meeting if Yves brought his brothers with him. Stepping onto the bridge, I admired the catapult-shaped supports, musing that, if my heavenly hand had finished serving the cathedral, it could pick up one of these and fire a pellet at Kent.

Shaking my head at my absurd imaginings, I wondered if anyone else saw things like I did. Would Yves understand the way my mind worked?

'Phee?'

I almost jumped out of my skin at the light touch on the shoulder. I spun round—Yves, of course. He'd got here before me and had lain in ambush by the entrance to the bridge. For all my plotting, I'd forgotten that he too would have made his own plans in the short time I'd allowed him.

'Yves, you came.' I pressed my palm to my pounding chest.

'You didn't leave me much choice.' He glanced behind me. The sunlight kissed his skin, turning his tan golden. He made me feel like some mortal visited by a demi-god in one of those Greek tales—and none of them had ended well for the human if I recall. 'Are you on your own?'

I nodded. I was—sort of. 'Are you?'

His face could not hide the brief spasm of his annoyance that I'd doubted him. 'You asked me to come alone so I did. You need to learn to trust me.'

I started walking, leading him to the centre of the bridge, away from the dangers that lurked near the busy entrance. Anyone could hide there. 'And you need to be more suspicious. Not everyone can afford to be so trusting.'

He let that pass without comment but instead caught up with me.

'So, to what do I owe the pleasure of my summons this morning?'

I could forgive him his sarcasm: our encounters up to this point had not been promising.

'I don't want to steal anything from you today, if that's what you're asking.' I dug my hands in my pockets.

'Can I hope that this is you finally realizing that soulfinders have to stay together?'

We reached the middle of the bridge. I leaned on the balustrade and gazed down into the muddy-green waters of the Thames. An orange plastic bag tugged against the plinth of the bridge support, rippling like a poisonous type of seaweed. Yves stood next to me but his eyes were on my face, not on the river. 'Phee?'

I didn't want to answer his question. I just wanted to stand for a few stolen minutes with my soulfinder, enjoying the sunshine and the feeling of quiet happiness that being with him gave me despite everything in our way. 'You know, Yves, you are a really lovely person.'

'Why does it always sound as if you are saying goodbye?'

Because I was. 'You have a great family too from what I've seen. You'll be OK.'

He folded his arms. 'What are you trying to tell me?'

'I think if you stayed with me, I'd be very bad for you.'

He shrugged that away. 'Soulfinders can't be bad for each other—they *are* each other. We aren't complete apart.'

'You see, Yves,' I picked at the paintwork, 'the thing is I've been brought up in a . . . a bad crowd and I can't get out of it.'

'I'll get you out.' The firm line of his mouth told me he would not settle for less.

'My leader controls us.' I could feel a nervous shiver running down my spine but so far I hadn't broken any rules set down by the Seer; I was only forbidden to say what I had *heard* yesterday. 'I tried to tell you what it was like, about the things that happen where I come from. My friend was . . . hurt in my place because I'd been seen with you.'

All stiffness went from his stance. He closed the gap between us and put an arm round my shoulders. 'I'm sorry, Phee. Is he OK?'

'I don't know.' My voice sounded thin even to me. 'And then yesterday I met some new . . . well I suppose you'd call them "allies" of my leader. I can't tell you what was said, but it isn't good—for you, I mean.' A pain like a drill in my skull warned me not to say any more. I took a deep breath. 'That's all I can say.'

'Phee?' His tone was gentle.

I looked up at him, wishing I could lose myself in his warm brown eyes.

He stroked my cheek with a finger. 'You don't have to look after all of us, you know? You worry for your friend, for me; when are you going to let someone care about you?'

I swallowed, tears close. No one had ever put me first. I didn't expect it.

'And I don't think you really understand about soulfinders.' His fingers were trailing fire over my too-sensitive skin, tracing the line of my jaw, the hypersensitive place by my ear. 'Sure, you know the theory but you've not seen it in practice. My parents are soulfinders—and I've had months to watch my brother Zed and his soulfinder, Sky, together. Forgive me, but I think I know more than you do on this subject.'

'You do?' Why was my voice so husky?

'Hmm-hmm.' He bent a little closer. I could feel him shaking a little, as if he wasn't sure if I was going to push him away again. He didn't realize that I was caught up in the magnetic attraction too. 'I can see you are not going to believe me unless I show you.' He gave me a shy smile.

'I'm not?'

'No.' Sliding his arm down to the small of my back, he tugged me towards him until our bodies were touching, his boldness growing as I made no sign to discourage him. 'You know, I quite liked Wendy, despite her old-lady clothes and funny attitude to Geoscience, but I really like Phee: she's beautiful, determined and protective. I was so wrong yesterday to say I was disappointed to be matched with a thief—I gave you no credit for doing what you had to do to survive and I want you to know that you could never, ever disappoint me.' I could feel his breath on my cheek; my eyelids fluttered closed of their own accord as he closed the gap. His lips began a gentle exploration of my mouth, peppering soft kisses at each corner. 'Relax—I won't bite,' he whispered, caressing the side of my face to get me to soften my jaw.

I unclenched my teeth and began kissing him back. His tongue tickled my lips then eased in to caress my mouth. I could feel my knees beginning to turn to water; all that was stopping me from crumpling was his hand at my back holding me tight against him. I could feel the heat of his palm against my spine, fingers carefully flexing against my taut muscles as he coaxed me to let myself trust him. I'd never felt so precious to anyone before in my life—so respected. And I had thought he wasn't sure of his moves around girls; boy, was he proving me wrong! This guy aced this test as he did all others.

He was the one to break the kiss. I came out of my lovely dream with his forehead pressed against mine. An elderly passer-by gave us an indulgent smile, reminding me that we were in the middle of a crowd. 'Young love,' the man muttered to his companion, patting her arm. 'Remember what that was like?' They strolled on, heads bowed together affectionately. Yves grinned after them, then turned back to me with a very male smile of satisfaction.

'Understand now?' he asked.

I wasn't sure. I'd been set on fire and could not put out the flames. My body seemed to spark with new energy as if, after months with batteries running down, I'd just been connected to the mains. I ran my fingers over my mouth. 'And I thought you didn't know much about girls.'

He frowned. 'Why? Did I do it wrong?'

I gave a shaky laugh. 'No. But your brother said—'

'Oh, you heard that, did you?' Yves laughed and brushed a strand of hair off my cheek. 'I won't claim his broad expertise but I've kissed my share of girlfriends.'

Annoyed at the idea of other girls being on the receiving end of those kissing fireworks, I made to pull away, which seemed only to amuse him.

'Don't. That was before I knew you. With you, I'm completely different. I need you like I need oxygen. No kiss has ever affected me like that one. You know, socks blown off.' He grinned and I couldn't help but smile too. 'The first kiss of many, I hope. Look, Phee, we don't have a choice about being together; we just have to work out how to clear away the obstacles.' He muttered a curse. 'That came out wrong. I meant to say that I want to be with you—it's not just the soulfinder thing speaking. I know you're thinking I'll be fine without you; that might have been true last week, before I met you, but not today. If you care even a tiny bit for me, you have to give me a chance to prove I can help you.'

'No one can help me.' But I began to hope, to pray, that I was wrong.

'That's not true. At least let me try.'

Chapter 11

We stayed like that for a few minutes, his arms wrapped round me, holding me close, his fingers shifting through my hair, massaging the back of my neck. All the tension wound inside me began to ease. I couldn't deny what he was saying, as I felt it too. With him I was no longer desperate and alone. Too often, I experienced life like a heart patient who has undergone surgery and been left with an aching hole in the centre of my chest; in Yves's arms, that gap was filled, leaving me cared for and complete. How could I think of giving this up if there was even a slither of a chance that we could have a future together?

'Feeling better now?' he asked, reading the signs my body was broadcasting, no longer held at the point of taking flight.

'Yes. Much.'

'Tell me why we are here.'

I traced the pattern on the front of his T-shirt with my fingertip. 'I was sent to get you. I'm bait.'

He didn't pull away. 'Go on.'

The Seer's mind virus stopped me saying that I knew about the Savant Net or the threat to me. 'My leader wants to talk to you. He's going to be in the Tate.' I pointed to the factory-like building at the southern end of the bridge. 'He won't be alone.'

'What does he want to see me about?'

'I can't say.'

'Can't or won't?'

He was shrewd. 'Can't.'

'What would happen if you did say?'

Could I tell him that? The Seer had not ordered me to keep quiet about his skills; he hadn't even imagined I'd want to confide that to Yves. 'It would hurt me. A lot.'

Yves dropped a kiss on the top of my head. 'OK, I get it. We've met guys like him before—the ones who can do sick, twisted stuff to brains like some sort of computer bug. I don't want you hurt. How long have we got?'

'About an hour. The gallery opens at ten.'

'Have you had breakfast?'

We had a meeting with the Seer in prospect and he was thinking of breakfast? 'Er . . . no. But shouldn't we, like, make a plan or something?'

'We can plan while we eat.' He took a step back but kept hold of my hand, tugging me towards the southern end of the bridge. 'Come on.'

'What?' I stumbled after him, not sure if I should laugh or cry.

'I have my soulfinder to myself for an hour; I'm intending to make the most of it.'

We found a little kiosk café on the Embankment and sat down at one of the metal tables. Red and white parasols flapped in the light breeze, rippling like fête bunting. A seagull balanced on the top of a lamp post, lord of all that he surveyed with his pebble-black eye.

'What do you want?' Yves cracked open the laminated menu. 'Coffee, coffee, more coffee, tea, tea, another kind of tea. Buns. Oh, you've got to have buns—that sounds so

English.' He had the delighted expression of someone making a gold strike.

I smiled, trying to reign in my errant thoughts at all this talk of buns. 'OK, I'll have tea and a hot-cross bun.'

He winked. 'So will I. I'm now living out one of my dreams.' He slapped the menu back on the table, weighting it down with the sugar bowl.

'You dream about hot-cross buns?' I teased.

He took my hand and kissed my knuckles. 'No, I dream about having my soulfinder to myself, somewhere in the sunshine. I didn't know it was going to be London, but I'll settle for that.'

'All right, love, what'll it be?' With ninja skills, the motherly waitress pounced, making us both start.

Dropping my hand, Yves quickly placed the order.

'You want jam with that?' She tapped her pad. 'Or are you sweet enough?'

Yves gave her a sheepish smile and said that, yes, we would like jam. I found it cute how the adoration of women of all ages embarrassed him so easily.

'I do like Americans,' she declared to me. 'Always so polite.'

As she bustled off, I touched Yves's cheek. 'You're blushing. What is it about you and older women? They all flirt with you.'

He trapped my hand against his skin. 'Do they? I didn't notice. I'm only interested in one girl flirting with me.'

I grinned. 'Good recovery.'

'Glad I've not lost my skills.' Yves checked his watch. 'OK, Phee, you've got an hour to tell me everything about yourself.'

I pulled my hand back, ashamed of my shabby life. 'What kind of things?'

'I know there's a lot you can't tell me but there's so much I don't know about you, surely you can share some of it? You're vegetarian. Why? You like reading. Do you have a favourite author? What makes you laugh? Cry? Do you prefer the old *Star Wars* films to the ones they made later? What kind of music do you listen to?'

I held up my hand, relieved none of these questions went to the heart of my situation. 'OK, OK, I get the message. Right, um . . . I don't like killing animals so I won't eat them. That makes me cry too.'

He nodded. 'Fair enough.'

'I like all sorts of writers. I never had anyone tell me what to read so I guess my list is a bit odd. I kinda grab things off the library shelf.'

'Tell me who you've grabbed then.'

'Isaac Asimov and Jane Austen—see, in libraries you start at the As.'

He tapped his chin with a forefinger, eyes sparkling. 'Inter-esting—*Pride and Prejudice* in space—has possibilities.'

We stopped talking as the waitress returned with our or-der. When she left I continued. 'Willa Cather, Agatha Christie, George Eliot. So many that I would take the whole hour just listing them.'

'That's fine by me.' He sliced open the bun and slathered on the strawberry jam from the dinky pot the waitress had given us. 'Bite.'

Obediently, I took a chunk out of the half he held for me.

'You know, I'm going to get a lot of pleasure from feeding you up. Xav thinks you are undernourished.' He took a bite from the same place I had eaten from, keeping his eyes on mine the whole time. I found it so sweet that he was flirting with me—no one had bothered before.

I changed the subject, not liking the reminder of where I had come from. 'Not seen them.'

'Not following.'

'*Star Wars*. Not been on at a cinema when I had a chance to sneak in.'

He rolled his eyes in mock-horror. 'We'll have to fix that immediately. Lots of popcorn and a DVD fest.' He suddenly got embarrassed. 'Not that I'm a *Star Wars* fan or anything.'

I giggled. 'I don't believe you. I bet you go to those conventions all dressed up.'

'I'd better hide my light sabre before you come to my house, then, or my credibility will be ruined.'

'Too late: you're rumbled. What was your last question?'

'Music.'

'Oh yes. I don't know. I haven't got anything to listen to music on.'

He put down his mug of tea. 'You haven't . . . er . . . acquired an MP3 player, or an iPod?'

'I don't keep the stuff I steal, except a few clothes from time to time. It isn't allowed.'

Yves brushed the back of my wrist, a gesture to say he understood, but he didn't really. Would Mr Strait-laced-and-Respectable really understand that I'd liked being a very good thief?

'I hear stuff in shops though; I'm not completely out of touch. So,' I said with false brightness, 'what about you?'

He stirred his tea. 'This very unnerdy person's view on *Star Wars* is that the new ones are best—I go for lavish special effects and the acting doesn't bother me. Could never get past the Princess Leia hairstyle and the teddy-bear creatures to like the first three, though I have to admit that Harrison Ford is uber-cool.' He started counting his replies off with a wave of the teaspoon. 'I eat meat but would be happy to try the vegetarian way for you and it would be better for the environment so maybe I should do it anyway. I read but mostly non-fiction. My favourite novel is *My Name is Asher Lev* by Chaim Potok.'

'Whoa, sounds learned.' I was glad I hadn't admitted to my soft spot for popular romantic literature.

He laughed. 'It's a great story—very deep. But I like a good murder-mystery too, and sci-fi. As for music, I like classical but I also go for lots of other styles.'

'Like what?'

'R&B for a start. You know, songs like 'Billionaire'—great lyrics, very funny.' He sang the first few lines in a rasping tone.

I smiled. 'You, a billionaire?'

'Don't take it literally. But, hey, don't you think I'd make a great lead singer?'

'Sorry to break it to you, babe: you might have the looks, but you don't exactly have the voice.' I patted his hand consolingly.

'Bang goes my dream of stardom. I'll have to settle for being an environmental scientist instead.'

I giggled. 'The world of geo-whatsit will be much the richer for it.'

'And everyone else very relieved?'

'You said it.'

We laughed together. I couldn't believe this: we had an hour out of ordinary life and he had managed to make it a golden time. I hardly remembered all the things hanging over us, caught up in just enjoying his company with no yesterdays or tomorrows to spoil the moment.

'What about your family?' I sipped my tea.

'You'll meet them soon, I hope.' He grimaced as he tasted his own drink. I have to admit it was a bit strong even for me.

'You should've ordered coffee.'

'But when in London . . .'

'Londoners drink coffee too these days. We're not all "cor blimey, mate, have a cup of Rosie Lee".'

He gave a bark of laughter. '*What* are you talking about?'

'You know, cockneys, EastEnders. Rhyming slang.'

He cupped my cheek and brushed a thumb across my nose. 'I don't know—we don't have "Rosie Lee" in Colorado—but I look forward to you teaching me all about it.'

I blushed, afraid I was making a twit of myself.

'No, you aren't. You're cute.'

I frowned at him. 'Stop picking thoughts out of my head.'

'No need. It was written all over your face.' He demolished the last piece of bun and set about buttering the second. 'My family. I have six brothers as I told you. You've met numbers two and five.'

'Do you like being called by your numbers?'

He looked up, interested that I had picked him up on this. 'No. In fact, we hate it but it makes it easier to explain. I think all of us just want to be ourselves, not defined against each other. That's natural in big families like mine.'

'I see. You could never be anything but Yves to me—not number six.'

'Good to know. I knew there was a reason I liked you.' We shared a smile. 'Eldest is Trace. He is a cop in Denver and has a gift for sensing the background to objects when he touches them. He's one hell of a tracker and never, ever cheats, unlike other brothers I could mention. Uriel is most like me, I guess, in that he is academic. Quiet and thoughtful compared to the rest. He's doing post-grad in forensic science at college and can connect to the past, something like having glimpses of the future but in reverse.'

I couldn't stop a sceptical snort. 'I get the past thing, but like anyone can *really* tell the future. The ones I've met who said they can have been fakes, even in the Savant world, not much above a palm-reading gypsy in a caravan at the fair.'

Yves offered me another bite. 'Then you haven't met my mom and my youngest brother, Zed. They both see flashes of what's to come. They also have an uncanny gift for knowing what you are thinking.' He winked.

'So do you.'

'Minor. Not like them. I'm better with energy.' He snapped his fingers and a flame appeared on his palm.

I clapped my hand over it to snuff it out before anyone noticed. Yves folded his fingers over mine, keeping me close.

'Will is tuned to sense danger, like my dad. He's really laid back but great to have at your side if it comes to a fight.'

I could hear great affection in his tone and guessed he had a soft spot for this particular big brother. 'You're lucky to have so many to love.'

'Yes, I am.' He stroked my hand absent-mindedly. 'I love them all, though Zed and Xav can get really annoying.'

I sensed he didn't mean it. He was clearly devoted to them.

'They seem to think I'm not macho enough, just because I prefer science to sports and talk to girls about books and ideas. And I think they are idiot jocks, so we get on fine.'

'But you'd do anything for each other.'

'Goes without saying.' Yves signalled for the bill.

'Not where I come from. Families don't work like that.'

'You've not had a family, Phee, not for a long time. From what I've heard, you've had no one.' His expression took on a determined cast. 'But that changed yesterday. You now have a whole family of annoying brothers to look out for you—and a sister in Sky, my brother's soulfinder. And just you wait until my mom realizes you don't have your own mother. She's always wanted a daughter and I think you'll fit that description perfectly. She'll be taking you shopping and doing all that girl stuff before you know it.'

I smiled sadly. 'Sounds lovely.'

'It will be, you'll see.' Yves passed the waitress the bill folder with a ten-pound note tucked inside, once again not waiting for change. This time I didn't protest. 'Let's talk about our plan.'

We got up from the table and I linked my arm through his. We began to walk slowly down the wide pavement of the Embankment on the Thames, moving aside to let a skateboarder weave past.

'Do you have strong shields?' I asked, feeling a bit sick now we were heading towards the Tate.

'Sure. If you live in a family of Savants who can read your mind, you develop them double-quick.'

'Don't let our leader get inside your head. He does this thing where he plays with the switches in the mind. I'm not even sure what he's planted in my brain but I guess he's protected himself against any of us turning against him.'

'OK. I'll make sure he can't get at me. I can help you with yours too if you let me.'

He sounded too sure of himself for my liking. I wondered if he realized that his intellectual skills, which took him to the top of the class in most of the places he hung out, were useless when it came to my world. I watched a water taxi beetling its way towards Greenwich, churning the water to leave a white wake. The roar of the city drowned out most other noise; I could barely hear the boat's engines. 'How can you do that?'

'I can grab energy from the environment and feed it to you so you can reinforce your shield.'

'Really? That sounds brilliant. But my defences have always crumbled really quickly when I face him.'

'They won't this time. Ever since I was a kid, I've had to learn to control my own gift to stop me blowing up stuff that annoys me so I'm pretty good at keeping a grip under pressure.'

'Except around me.'

'Yes, well, I'm working on that. Give me a break—it's only been a day.'

I sighed. 'He won't like me resisting him. Perhaps you'd best not try anything today as he'll find a way of punishing me if I put up a struggle in public.' I touched the scratch on my arm, recalling yesterday's demonstration of power.

My movement brought Yves's attention to the cut. 'He did this?'

I shrugged. 'Indirectly. I wasn't lying when I said he had no problem hurting us to make us obey.'

Yves struggled with his outrage before clamping down on it by taking a deep breath. 'OK. Let's just take this slowly. When the rest of my family arrive we'll have reinforcements to help you resist. Today we'll just find out what he has to say.'

'You won't like it.'

He swung me round so my back was to the embankment wall and rested his chin on the top of my head. 'No, I don't suppose I will.'

'So we go in. You hear what he has to say and then you leave.' I spoke to his chest, not wanting to come up for air.

'Yes, except there's one little correction: *we* leave.'

'He won't allow that.'

'We'll see.'

I was scared for him, my sweet, intellectual soulfinder. He didn't know what he was facing and I had to protect him from underestimating his enemies. I felt I was leading my beautiful leopard right into the range of the hunters' guns. 'Look, if it's a choice between you leaving without me or a fight, please just go. I'll be fine.'

He looked hurt that I didn't think he could stand up to them alone. 'Phee, don't try to put yourself between me and danger; I won't allow it.'

'So what are you going to do? Beat your chest and go all

caveman, swinging your club at anyone who threatens me? I'm not a little woman you need to defend.'

His face hardened. 'That's exactly what you are: you're *my* little woman and I'm not having you sacrifice yourself for me.'

'Back at you, mate, though I'd have to substitute "big man" for the "little woman" dig.' We were being ridiculous and, deep down, I suspected we both knew it. I took a moment to calm myself. 'OK, OK, I get where you are coming from because it is the same place for me. Let's just agree not to risk each other, share the burden.'

'I've got bigger shoulders than you.'

'And a bigger head by the sounds of it. Stop the "me heap big man" act and be rational. We can only go in there if we are united on the best way forward.'

Yves tapped my nose in reprimand. 'My dad's Native American, did you know that? I could have you arrested for perpetuating racial stereotypes with your "heap big man" crack.'

Oops. 'No offence intended.'

'None taken. But in return, you have to let me run this show. If we both try to call the shots we'll end up stumbling over each other into the crossfire.'

I didn't like it but I could see some sense in his suggestion. My fear often paralysed me when it came to dealings with the Seer; I could allow that he would be more objective on this occasion. 'OK, I'll let you lead this once, but only if you say you won't do something stupid and put yourself in danger. We go in, hear the deal, and then try to leave together.'

He gave me a hug for my grudging concession. 'Yes, that's the plan. I won't push the last point too far and get us hurt, but I want you to know I'll be aiming for taking you with me. Stand back and let me make the running—I'll know what I'm willing to concede to get you out safe.'

I closed my eyes briefly. 'I've got a bad feeling about this.'

He placed a gentle kiss on each eyelid. 'Trust me, Phee. We'll be fine.'

'You don't have your brothers somewhere nearby, do you? As, like, back-up?'

He shook his head. 'I promised I'd come alone this morning. I haven't even told them where I've gone.'

Shame. Part of me wished he hadn't been so honourable. 'OK, let's do this. I'm supposed to make sure you come alone so maybe it's just as well that they don't know what we're up to.'

'The only ones who might know are Mom and Zed, but they are in the air heading for London.' He gave a crooked smile. 'If they do get a future news flash, I'm going to be in deep trouble when they land.'

I squeezed him back. 'Don't worry: I'll protect you from them.'

'Now that I can allow.'

Chapter 12

First through the doors as the Tate opened, we entered an empty Turbine Hall. This exhibition space was cavernous, like an ugly back alley in a giant's castle. The current display added to the uncanny atmosphere: huge metal spiders crouched splay-legged on the concrete, invaders from space in a 1950s 'B' movie poster. Several hung suspended as if about to descend on our heads; tiny ones scuttled up the walls to exploit any cracks in human defences.

'Nice,' Yves commented ironically.

We wandered among the metal forest of arachnid limbs, killing time.

'What makes an artist spend their life making these?' I asked with a slightly hysterical laugh.

'Exorcizing nightmares maybe?'

'And giving them to us?'

'Phee?'

We turned warily on hearing Dragon call my name. He was alone, standing framed by the pincers of the largest of the metal spiders.

'Um . . . hi. Dragon, this is Yves.'

The two glared at each other.

'We met yesterday,' Yves said curtly. 'Let's hope modern art has a better day.' He cast a significant look at the suspended spiders, reminding us all of the fate of the mobile at the Barbican.

Dragon gave a gloating smile. 'Don't go putting ideas in my head, mate.'

'I doubt you need my suggestions to cause pointless destruction, *dude*.'

Enough sabre-rattling. 'Dragon, I've brought him here as asked. What happens now?'

With the arm looped casually around me, Yves squeezed my waist, reminding me who was supposed to be in charge of this little confrontation. But if he insisted on picking a fight with Dragon before we'd even got off the ground with the negotiation, then of course I was going to intervene!

'The Seer is here.' Dragon folded his arms and nodded up at the wall separating the main body of the art gallery from the Turbine Hall. A couple of floors up, there was a window, a perfect vantage point from where our leader could look down on us, much like he did at home. Naturally, he wasn't going to put himself anywhere near an enemy; he was too much of a coward, and he always sought to make us feel subordinate.

Yves curled his lip in a sneer at the white-suited hulk of a man surveying us. 'Is that him?'

I felt humiliated letting him glimpse even this much of my background. 'Yes.' I could see Unicorn beside him. Kasia was probably lurking to check we weren't using telepathy to anyone outside but I had forgotten to warn Yves of this possibility.

'How are we supposed to talk?' Yves asked. 'Megaphone?'

Tell him I will speak through you.

I gasped as the Seer forced his message into my head. 'Me. He's using me.'

Yves rubbed my back in sympathy. 'OK, then, let's make this as short as possible. We can do without him bouncing round inside your mind. Ask what he wants.'

The details of the members of the Savant Net.

'And what's he going to do with that, as if I couldn't guess?'

That's for me to decide. Your soulfinder only has to hand them over. Tell him.

I couldn't imagine Yves agreeing to any deal like that. This was hopeless.

Yves pondered the deal he was being offered. 'And then what? You're allowed to leave? He'll let you go?'

The Seer chuckled at Yves's audacity. *Phoenix stays with her daddy.* I couldn't bring myself to tell Yves that part so I didn't relay it to him and just shook my head. *Explain to your soulfinder that he has to remain within the Net and feed me all the information I require. He will spy for us.*

'And why would I do that?'

Because if you don't, Phoenix will suffer.

On his signal, Dragon forced a miniature spider from its wall bracket; it rocketed straight for me. With quick reflexes, Yves pulled me down so that it passed overhead to smash against the far wall, leaving a dent in the concrete.

'You forget: you're not the only ones with powers.' Yves stared up at the Seer and smoke began to curl from his suit pocket. As his wallet burst into flames, the Seer and Unicorn frantically tried to put out the blaze.

'Yves, stop it!' I whispered.

He reluctantly extinguished the blaze. 'I went for his heart and that was the nearest I could find to one,' Yves explained to me with a wicked smile.

We were so going to pay for that—but I had to admit the sight was one to savour for the rest of what was probably now going to be a very short life.

Tell that Yank of yours that he had better produce the goods or you'll be the one to burn! screeched the Seer in my mind, his voice like the grating of metal on metal.

'He's not happy,' I glossed for Yves.

'I bet he didn't put it quite like that.'

'No. Not exactly. I'm the hostage for your good behaviour, much as we expected.'

'And you've lived with *that* squatting on your life?' marvelled Yves, his disgust at the Seer all too apparent. He was sure to despise me if he ever discovered that the man could be my father. I hoped he never found out; I had more than enough points against me as it was.

Under his own set of orders, Dragon stepped forward and attempted to pull me away from Yves. 'Time to leave.'

Predictably, my soulfinder would not let go. Fury sparking in his eyes, Yves pushed me back and placed himself in Dragon's way. 'If you touch her, I'll singe every hair on your head.' And he would too—I could see determination in his expression. 'She's staying with me from now on.'

'Not happening. She belongs to the Community.'

'She belongs with her soulfinder.'

'Look, mate, I've played nice so far. There're three of us and one of you. How exactly do you think you are going to get out of here with her?'

Yves gave a ripple of a shrug. 'Tell your leader that if he wants that information, he has to let her go with me, or there's no deal. I don't trust you not to hurt her while she's with you and there's no point in this for me if she's not safe. What I do, I do for her.'

'How touching. I think I'm gonna throw up.' Dragon rolled his eyes at Yves's defiant talk.

I wanted to butt in and forbid Yves from promising anything that put his family and the Savant Net at risk but I remembered in time that I'd said I'd let him make the running. It terrified me that he was getting in over his head, but I'd given my word.

Yves stood firm. 'I'm sure it is not beyond the capabilities of your Seer to put in safeguards to keep her from spilling your secrets, but my interests are only protected when I can see her. That's a red line for me.'

Dragon must have been reporting what was said for the Seer came back quickly with his counter-offer.

Tell him he can have you for forty-eight hours and then he must bring you and the information to me.

'Where does he want to us come?'

To the London Eye.

The Seer's concession was more than I had expected. I passed the message on to Yves. 'Are you OK with that?' It would give us time at least to untangle this mess.

'We'll take it.' He checked his watch. 'We have until ten thirty, Friday.'

But Phoenix, you must come up here first. I have a message just for you.

That would be the safeguard. 'I have to go up there. He won't let me leave otherwise.'

'I'll come with you.'

'No,' Dragon interrupted. 'We're staying right here.' He then changed tactics; rather than push at Yves, he used his power to tug me free. Yves had to let go or risk hurting me. I staggered but caught myself on a spider leg before I fell. 'Up you go, Phee. I'll babysit your soulfinder for you.'

I hated the idea of the two of them being alone together for any length of time. I worried that Yves would lose his temper and set fire to something—Dragon probably. 'I'll be quick.'

Call if you need me. Yves didn't look happy to let me out of his sight.

I didn't reply, fearful of eavesdroppers, but nodded. Sooner this was done, the better. I ran up the escalators to the floor where the Seer waited. He had commandeered the entire window niche for himself, Unicorn deterring any tourists who wanted to share the privileged view down on the exhibits. His spotless suit was marred, the jacket now sporting a blackened circle on the pocket. I hid the gleeful smile that threatened to give away my pleasure at the small humiliation Yves had managed to hand him. I couldn't remember anyone ever getting one over on our leader.

The Seer had his back to me, still looking down on Yves and Dragon who were circling each other like two wild cats about to rip at each other with their claws.

'So that is your soulfinder. Interesting. He is foolish and bold to come here for you. The bond must be as strong as legend says for him to risk himself. And for what? A girl he met only a day ago.'

There wasn't much I could say to that.

'As for my safeguards, I know how to ensure he keeps his word. Come here.' The Seer beckoned me closer. In this public place, he didn't demand I kneel; instead he took my hand and covered it with his other. Anyone looking at us would think he was a caring father offering me an affectionate pat on the back of my wrist as we enjoyed the gallery together.

If he reneges on his deal to bring us information, if he betrays us to anyone in the Savant Net, you will punish him by hurting someone he loves. And you will come back to us after forty-eight hours—nothing will stop you even if you have to fight to the death to return.

He dropped my hand and patted my shocked face. 'Don't look so horrified, Phoenix. If you were loyal to us, you would be happy to agree to do these things without compulsion. Are you faithful to us or should I think again about letting you go with him?'

Please no. 'You can rely on me.'

'Good girl. I expect a full report when you get back. Learn as much as you can about the Savant Net. Now run along before your soulfinder and Dragon draw attention to themselves. I can already see the security guards gathering in anticipation of trouble.'

With a nod to Unicorn, I hurried back to the escalators. I reached Yves just in time. He must have just insulted Dragon because the latter was about to take a swing at him.

'OK, ready now!' I announced chirpily, bouncing into the middle of the fray. I caught Dragon's arm by darting under his guard and giving him a mock-friendly hug, propelling him back and away from Yves. 'Glad to see you are getting on so well but we must go.' On tiptoes, I put my mouth near Dragon's ear. 'The Seer says "behave". He doesn't want trouble.'

The gaggle of worried guards gathered by the main doors visibly relaxed on my arrival to defuse the fight. One spoke into his walkie-talkie, cancelling his request for more staff.

Dragon gave me a crushing bear hug in retaliation. 'Tell your pretty boy that this isn't over between us.'

'See you later.' I held out a hand to Yves. 'Let's get out of here.'

Yves didn't need asking twice. He sent Dragon a last challenging look as he took my offered palm. I immediately felt a hundred times better, his warmth replacing the shivery feeling left over from my encounter upstairs.

'How bad?' he murmured as we escaped up the slope and out into the sunshine by the side exit.

'Bad,' I admitted.

'Can you tell me?'

'Yes. I think he wants you to know. If you go back on the deal, I hurt someone you love. If you don't return me, I fight to the death to make the meeting.'

He swore.

Remembering how studiously polite he had been to me only the day before under the provocation of my repeated attempts to mug him, I wondered what I was doing to my soulfinder to lure him into using vocabulary outside his normal comfort zone. 'I'm a really bad influence, aren't I?'

Yves looped an arm over my shoulder, the now familiar weight feeling just right in that place. 'I don't know exactly what you are, Phee, but I certainly saw red in there a couple of times. All of the people you grew up around act like monsters.'

'OK. I was raised by wolves, I admit it. But remember that, won't you? You can't expect me to behave better than them when the chips are down.'

He shook his head. 'No, you're nothing like them.'

I was everything like them, probably even sharing the same tainted genetic inheritance. 'Kind of you to think so, but consider yourself warned. I'm a crappy bet for a soulfinder.'

'I'll take the gamble.' He rubbed my upper arm. 'You come first with me now. No monsters are going to drive us apart.'

We arrived back at Yves's flat without settling the major issues hanging over us. I wasn't going to let him betray family and friends for me; he refused to talk about what he was planning to do. I could understand that: if he'd said immediately that he had no intention of going through with the deal, then I'd have to hurt someone—not the best introduction to his parents. Still, he insisted that I came first in his decisions and he wouldn't let me down.

'Trust me, Phee. It'll work out,' he said as we took the ride up in the lift.

I shook my head slightly, keeping my eyes fixed on the changing floor number.

142

'Easier than the stairs, huh?'

I winced. 'Yes. Sorry about that. I thought I had to go home.'

'So we saw.'

'I think it was a bad decision.'

He smiled at that. 'Yeah, I think so too.'

'I should've disappeared—just gone away. Then you wouldn't be in this fix.'

Yves frowned. 'Now that would have been a *really* bad decision.'

Getting out at the twentieth floor, we walked up to the entrance to the flat. Fitting his key in the lock, he pushed the heavy door open to let me enter first. The sight that greeted us was a pile of luggage in the hallway.

'Uh-oh.' Yves gave me a pained smile.

'They've arrived?'

'Yeah. That's amazingly quick. They must have hopped on the first flight.'

'We've only just got here.' A tall man in late middle age came out of the nearest doorway, arms stretched out. I thought he was heading for his son, but he came at me instead. I almost cringed back but Yves's firm hand on my shoulders prevented me from doing so. I was folded in a hug that had the strength of the Rocky Mountains behind it—stone, forest, and river. He smelt of trees too—a pine-scented aftershave. Yves had already told me that his father, Saul Benedict, had been born and bred in Colorado. He had the thick, black, grey-streaked hair of his forefathers and a burnished skin from spending most of the year outside. I could see where his sons got their stature from: he had to top six feet easily. 'You've found her.'

Yves cleared his throat, overcome with emotion at seeing his father's unquestioning joy for him.

'Yeah, Dad, I did.'

'Great news, Yves.'

No sooner had Saul let me go than a small woman bustled into our midst. A fraction shorter than me, she squeezed me to her chest and kissed the top of my bent head. 'Clever Yves!' she exclaimed in her throaty voice.

'I was lucky, Mom.'

'Karla, let the poor girl breathe!' chuckled Saul.

Karla pushed me gently away and then thumped her son in the stomach. 'But where have you been, you bad, bad boy? Your brothers have been frantic—they didn't know what to do until we turned up! Zed told them that you would be OK and that was the only thing that stopped them calling in the police!'

'Love you too, Mom,' said Yves, replying with an apologetic squeeze of a hug. 'So you knew we were coming?'

She waved that point away as if of no importance. 'Yes, yes, he saw you turning up here with Phoenix, none the worse for whatever you have been doing to fetch her.'

All this family stuff was both heart-warming and excruciating. I wanted to crawl deep inside to protect myself from the unaccustomed swirl of emotions.

A third Benedict stepped into the hallway; it had to be the youngest one, Zed, as he held hands with a shy-looking blonde girl and I already knew he was the only brother with a soulfinder. 'Hey, Einstein, I see you've found your magic formula at long last.'

Xav bounded out behind him. 'Yeah, Phee equals You-She squared. I've been working on that one: like it?'

The blonde girl groaned. 'That really sucked, Xav. Not even worth a place in a cracker.'

'Aww, Sky, you are so cruel! I don't know how Zed puts up with you.' Xav tweaked her long plait.

'Hands off my girl,' growled Zed, mock-wrestling his brother away from his giggling soulfinder.

Yves laughed at the battle while I marvelled at the impressive, tousle-haired Zed in front of me. Someone had overdone the share of good looks when it came to this family: there wasn't a runt among them.

Ending their tussle as abruptly as it had started, Zed flicked his gaze to me as if I had spoken. He laughed, slapping Xav on the back. 'She just wondered if I was the runt of the litter!'

'Truth will out.' Xav grinned.

I blushed. 'Did not!' I whispered, clapping my hands to my cheeks. How could Yves live in a family where several of them could pick thoughts out of your head?

Sky elbowed him in the ribs. 'Shh, Zed, you're making her feel uncomfortable. Her colours have gone all pink and purple.'

'Sorry, Phoenix.' Zed gave me a charming grin.

I revised my opinion that the girl was timid. She appeared to have her giant well under control and a disturbing ability to know what I was feeling.

Yves pulled me further into the flat, dropping my hand to embrace first Sky, then Zed, murmuring thanks for them coming so quickly. I laced my hands together nervously, out of my depth.

'Come through to the kitchen, Phoenix,' said Karla brightly. 'We were just having breakfast—or is it lunch? My body-clock is all out of sync!'

Victor waited for me by the kitchen counter. I realized I hadn't actually properly met him—you couldn't call our confrontation in the Barbican an introduction. He held out a hand to me.

'Phoenix, I'm Victor, Yves's big brother. How're you doing?'

'Fine.' My voice had disappeared along with my confidence. Where was Yves? This trial by family was too much for me.

A warm palm splayed on the back of my shoulders, calming me before the seeds of panic could bloom. 'Hi, Vick. Sorry I didn't tell you where I was going. I couldn't.' Yves met his elder brother's penetrating gaze.

Victor read the message then nodded. 'OK. I understand. Just, in future, an "I'm-not-going-to-get-myself-killed" note would be appreciated. And, Yves, you got to remember you have a tendency to take on more than you can deal with. Next time, use back-up.'

Xav slapped Yves lightly over the top of his head. 'Dog breath.'

That appeared to put an end to their complaints about being left worrying what had happened to him. I wasn't sure I could've been so forgiving if it had been me.

'So you got Phoenix back,' declared Karla, clapping her hands in delight. 'That's lovely.'

'I'm more on loan,' I muttered.

'Yeah, my little library book.' Yves guided me to a barstool at the kitchen island. He helped me up then stood behind me as the rest of his family took seats. We'd interrupted their breakfast: half-drunk mugs of coffee waited by plates of buttered toast.

I thought I should make an effort to be friendly, filling the expectant gap in conversation with a polite question. 'Um . . . how was your flight?'

'Very pleasant. Victor has so many useful friends.' Karla smiled at her brooding son, the only female in creation who was not bothered by his air of danger. 'We had lovely first-class seats. I slept like a baby.'

Saul rolled his eyes. 'Only after I persuaded you to take a sleeping pill. She's been worrying about you, Yves.'

Smart woman.

'I can imagine.' Yves poured us both a coffee from the filter jug.

'So, Phoenix, tell us how you met?' Karla looked at me

146

with her bright brown eyes. With her long, dark hair loose, she managed to look far too young to have seven grown-up sons.

I choked on my drink.

Yves stepped in. 'Mom, Phee has a difficult background. It's not easy for her to talk about it.'

She frowned. When I checked her mental patterns, I could see that she was searching me for something, like a sniffer dog after drugs.

'Karla.' Sky tapped her mug with her knife to draw attention from me, her English accent standing out against all the Americans. 'You're doing your thing.'

Karla shook herself, her misty expression clearing. 'I was? Sorry, I must be more tired than I thought. Don't mind me.'

'I found it spooky when you first did it to me; maybe you should give Phoenix a bit of space?'

This Sky was an astute reader of character. Or perhaps she just knew what it was like to be dropped into this family with no preparation? She caught my eye and nodded reassurance, letting me know without a word that I had one ally at least at this table.

'I think that is a very good idea, Sky,' Saul rumbled, giving his son's soulfinder an affectionate look. 'We came here to help Yves and Phoenix; not scare the living daylights out of her.' He brushed his fingertips over his wife's arm in a tender gesture. 'And I can sense that the threat has not gone away. Am I right?'

Yves nodded.

I closed my eyes, hoping that if I did not see him betray the Seer, my orders would not be triggered. *Hold me back if I attack one of them*, I begged Yves.

I'm not going to renege on my deal, he promised.

Saul's eyes narrowed. 'And I sense something from you, Yves. You're registering as a threat to us. Like to explain that?'

Really not, I thought.

'How can I be a threat?' Yves asked innocently.

Saul corrected himself. 'More a risk.'

Yves shrugged but the silence felt awkward for all of us.

'So what's going on?' Zed bumped Sky from her chair, sat down, then pulled her onto his knee.

'We can't tell you. Neither of us can do anything to help you find out.'

Yves's statement wasn't met with outrage as I had expected, but another silence. Then the family appeared to come to a collective decision to postpone the reckoning.

'O-K,' Xav drawled after a painful few seconds. 'Pass the OJ, then.'

Zed shoved the carton of orange juice to his brother with a wave of his hand. 'So, Sky, are you gonna show me your old haunts in London?'

The Benedicts just accepted Yves's statement and changed the subject. They were amazing. If it had been me, I would have demanded answers.

They trust me—well, mostly, Yves whispered. *I just wish you would too.*

I rubbed my hands on my jeans. *I'm working on it*, I admitted. But I couldn't see how he could square his loyalty to them with his promises to me.

Good. The rest of the occupants of the kitchen were fully aware we were talking telepathically but politely pretended not to notice. Yves smiled affectionately at them all. 'Now, we should let these guys get some sleep.'

Karla reached over and patted my arm. 'Take the rest of the day off from worrying, Phoenix. You're with family now.'

Not worrying was easier said than done.

Chapter 13

The arrival of so many of Yves's family caused a reorganization
of sleeping arrangements. Mr and Mrs Benedict took over Victor's room; Sky and I were given Yves's double, and the boys
were to share Xav's queen bed and the sofas in the living room.
At Yves's suggestion, I followed Sky to have a rest for a few
hours. The stress of the last two days had taken its toll on me
and, besides, it was less traumatic than staying in the kitchen
to make conversation. If Yves was going to tell his brothers
the truth, I didn't want to hear it. I was hoping that ignorance
would protect me from carrying out the Seer's order.

Sky kicked off her shoes and lay down on the right side of
the bed. 'Bliss. I didn't sleep much on the flight. We were all
too stirred up about Yves's news.'

I hovered by the other edge wondering if she would mind
if I shared the double with her or if I should sleep on the floor.
'What exactly has he told you?'

Sky patted the mattress. 'There's plenty of room. Why
don't you lie down?' Gingerly, I unlaced my shoes, took them
off, and stretched out. She smiled. 'Yves didn't say much. We
know he met you at the conference but you're in some kind

of trouble, mixed up with a bad crowd of Savants. He said he needed help getting you out of the country. Saul and Victor are going to work on sorting a passport for you. And he thought that I might be able to understand more about where you're coming from, being British too.'

I doubted that. How many people come from a seedy background like mine?

Sky wasn't deterred by my silence. 'How old are you, Phee? You must be nearly eighteen if you're Yves's soulfinder.'

'I am?'

'His birthday is first of July. You don't know?'

I stared at the white ceiling. No cracks, unlike my room at home. 'Birthdays don't figure much where I come from. I think I remember my mum making a fuss of me each year in the summer but she's long gone and I don't recall details, like the day or anything.'

'I didn't know my birthday either. My parents and I had chosen the day of my adoption so it was a bit of a shock to find I was probably younger than I thought.'

Her strange comment pricked my interest. 'How did that happen?'

'Zed's birthday is fifth of August; because of the link between soulfinders, that makes mine around then too.' She turned on her side to look across at me. 'But I've kept first of March as my birthday as I like to tease Zed about dating an older woman. And my parents wouldn't understand if I told them about the soulfinder bond and tried to change it.'

'They don't know?'

'Well, I think they've picked up that there's something special between Zed and me but I'm not sure how I'd even start to explain to non-Savants. I wasn't exactly overjoyed when Zed filled me in about it all the first time.' Her smile broadened and I sensed there was a story behind that statement.

'What did you do?'

'Thumped him with a shopping bag and told him he was a jerk.'

'Ouch.'

'So how was it for you and Yves? Love at first sight?'

'Hardly. I nicked his stuff and he made it explode.'

Her fair eyebrows winged up. 'Oh my gosh! That sounds exciting. And then?'

I sensed I could confide in her without scaring her off. Watching her mind-kaleidoscope for a moment, I saw that her powers gave her similar insight into people, though she saw moods rather than thoughts. She was watching my colours, seeing my face ringed by pale pink and grey like the first flush of a sunrise on the horizon. 'What's a lie?'

She caught on quickly. 'You can see what I'm doing?'

I nodded.

'I can't help it these days. Spending so much time with Savants switches on my antenna for emotion. Do you mind?'

I shrugged. 'I see thought-patterns so I suppose I should be the last one to object.'

She brushed a strand of her long wavy hair off her face. 'Yellow.'

'Sorry?'

'A lie. Can you tell one too?'

I thought about it for a moment. 'Not sure. I can see how people are thinking so if they are conscious of the lie then they might give it away by having conflicting images passing through their heads. Your approach is much more straight-forward.'

'Is that the extent of your gift—as far as you know, I mean?'

'No, I . . . um . . . can freeze your thoughts—it feels like time is suspended for a few moments.'

She considered this. 'Cool. You might find you can do even

more with Yves. That stuff about soulfinders completing each other really is true. I'm finding new strengths when I work with Zed. My telekinesis is getting very good—I sometimes beat him, which he hates, naturally.'

'I've never tried. You think I might be able to do other things? At the Community . . .' I paused, worried that I was betraying too much information about myself.

Sky met my eyes soberly. 'Go on. Think of me as a friend.' She sighed when I looked blank. 'That means I won't tell anyone, not even Yves, what you say to me.'

I'd never had a proper friend; it would be nice—not that I was ready to accept her offer just on a few minutes' conversation; I was too streetwise for that. 'Where I come from, we concentrate on developing our main skill. Even telepathy isn't used much. The Seer—'

'Who's the Seer?' She twirled a lock of fair hair around her finger.

'Our leader. He uses it most—to give us our instructions. I wouldn't want anyone else in my head. I think we all feel the same.'

'Doesn't sound as if you want him in your mind either.'

'Yeah, true.' I tried to even out my breathing. Just talking about him made me feel close to panicking.

She let the lock fall back in place. 'You know he's abusing you, don't you? You have every right to your own privacy. Shoving his voice into your head is just as bad as keeping someone imprisoned against their will or beating them up.'

I gave a gulp of laughter. 'There's plenty of that too.'

She reached out and touched the back of my hand. 'I do know what it is like, you know.'

'How can you?' I whispered. She was so perfect—a tiny fairylike creature, all sweet and pretty, floating on a bubble of love above the taint of everyday life; I felt like the ugly gnome next to her, living a life grubbing in the lowest muddy dregs of humanity.

'I'm not what you think, you know. I was abandoned as a child at a service station after years of abuse—broken bones, bruises, the full works. I couldn't speak for many years and even forgot my name.'

'What . . . ? How?'

'It's true. My parents saved me first, then Zed finished the job, with his family's help. I thought I had it rough but now I see that I had more luck than you. How long have you been alone?'

Her understanding triggered a welling of emotion. Disobeying my mind's order not to be weak, tears crept down my cheeks, heading for the pillow. 'It seems like for ever. Mum tried, but she was under the Seer's control, much like I am. I don't know any other kind of life, Sky. I'm really worried I'm all wrong for Yves—I'm gonna mess him up. I'm toxic.'

She shook my shoulder, a gentle reproof. 'Rubbish. There's nothing wrong with you. It's a miracle you still care as much about others as you do.'

'But Yves . . .'

'Don't worry about him. He's a strong person, quite capable of looking after himself despite what his brothers say about him. Don't let that studious outside fool you; he's got fire within.'

I thought of the confrontation at the Tate. 'I think I've seen it.'

'Trust him. He deserves this chance to make things right. And you can rely on the rest of the family too.'

Wanting to believe her even if I wasn't convinced, I smiled and snuggled down into the pillow. 'He's gorgeous, isn't he?'

Sky laughed. 'They all are—Zed most, of course.' I didn't

agree—I'd take my sleek leopard any day over the tiger she was with. 'It's quite exhausting if you're the jealous type.'

I bit my lip, wondering how I could want to smile so soon after crying. My emotions were yo-yo-ing all over the place. 'Yves attracts older women—they all flirt with him.'

Sky giggled. 'Oh my, I never knew that. I can't tell Zed—he'd tease him unmercifully. How does he handle it?'

'Gets all embarrassed. It's so cute.'

'Yes, all my friends think he's . . . well, you probably don't want too hear that. But they've told me—the lucky ones that have dated him—that he's the perfect gentleman.'

I wasn't sure that was how he behaved with me; I seemed to press too many buttons to allow him to keep his cool. 'So does Zed attract the cougar-women too—the older ones?'

She let out a snort of laughter. 'No, they all cross the road when they see him coming. He can project this quite scary aura when he's not thinking. Funny really, as his powers are nowhere near as lethal as Yves's.'

'It's the quiet ones you have to watch.'

'Yes, so it seems.' She yawned. 'Ready to have a sleep?'

I nodded, more at peace than I had been for days. 'OK.'

'Wake me at four if you get up before me. I promised to ring my parents and let them know we arrived safely.'

I envied her the network of people who cared what happened to her.

'Don't,' she said softly, astutely guessing, or maybe reading, my emotions. 'We care. You aren't on your own now.'

That was what Karla had told me. The problem was I had a hard time overcoming the training of my upbringing. The first lesson of this new life would be to accept that there might be some truth in their claim to care for me.

I woke a few hours later to find Sky still asleep, her breathing a soft whisper, eyelashes curling on her pale skin. She looked like a fairytale princess waiting for her prince to wake her with a kiss. Checking the time on the bedside clock, I saw that she still had a few hours before her phone call so I slipped off the bed and padded on my bare feet out of the bedroom.

Glancing in through the open door to Xav's room, I saw Zed stretched out on the queen mattress, his arm hugging a pillow as if he felt Sky's absence at his side. I guessed he had left the door ajar so he could hear if there were any problems in our room. I was reassured by this more normal level of suspicion where a stranger was concerned. He wasn't to know that I wouldn't turn on his soulfinder and I approved his precautions. I tiptoed on into the kitchen, discovering Yves, Victor, and Xav all at work on laptops.

'Hi.' I paused in the doorway, wondering if I was welcome.

'Phee.' Yves looked genuinely pleased to see me. 'Hungry?' He uncovered a plate of sandwiches which he had kept ready for me. 'They're all veggie.'

'Thanks.' I took the barstool next to him, studiously keeping my gaze off their screens. The less I knew about anything, the better.

Victor closed his with a snap and opened a pad. 'While you're eating, Phoenix, would you mind telling me what you know about your parents?'

The sandwich went to sawdust in my mouth. 'Why?'

'I want to track down your birth certificate so we can get you a passport. Without that, it's going to be really hard getting you out of the country.'

Yves nudged me. 'Something wrong with the sandwich? I can make you another. I think we even have some disgusting stuff called "Marmite" in stock on Sky's insistence.'

I swallowed. 'No, the sandwich is fine.' Of course they'd need papers for me, but when had I been asked if I wanted to leave the country? 'And don't diss Marmite—it's the food of the gods.'

'Strange British gods with cockney accents who drink Rosie Lee?'

'Yeah.' I took a crisp from a bowl in the centre of the counter.

'I stand corrected.'

'Phoenix?' Victor repeated patiently, sensing my evasion.

'Call me "Phee", please. OK, here's what I know. I was born in Newcastle. My mother was called Sadie Corrigan. I don't know about a father.' By which I meant I really, really didn't want to know. What if the birth certificate listed the Seer? But then, I didn't know his true name so maybe no one else did? And he would hardly want an official record of his name anywhere. 'She always said my father was someone she met on holiday in Greece. A friend among the people I live with remembered me being born. I'm not sure if it happened in a hospital. I didn't ask him.'

Victor gave me an encouraging nod. 'That's fine. If there's a record, I'll be able to find it from that information. We'll start by guessing you were born in the month around Yves's birthday. If that draws a blank, I'll go a bit further either side. Lucky you have such an unusual name.'

'Hmm,' I said in a non-committal tone.

Yves rubbed the back of my neck. 'You've not asked what the plan is.'

I shrugged. 'Isn't it best if I don't know?'

Xav grabbed an orange from the fruit bowl and flipped it into the air, making it hover and then orbit the table before catching it. 'You are part of this now, Phee. We keep everyone in the loop.'

'But it's dangerous. Hasn't Yves explained?'

'Dangerous smangerous,' scoffed Xav. 'We eat evil Savants for breakfast in our family.'

Victor clipped him over the head. 'Stop fooling, Xav. She won't think we take this seriously if you clown around.'

'Lighten up, bro. Phee knows I'm a sensible soul at heart.'

'I do?'

He began peeling the orange. 'Don't sound so sceptical. You'll dent my confidence.'

'I doubt even being run over by a rubbish truck would dent your confidence.'

Yves gave me a hug. 'I'm so pleased you're such a quick judge of character. You've got him tagged.'

'Yep, toe-tagged, in the freezer, then buried six feet under.' Xav clutched his chest, toppling off his stool. 'I'll never recover from such character assassination.'

Mr Benedict appeared in the doorway behind his son. 'Xav, are you misbehaving? I hope you're not teasing Phoenix.'

Xav sprang up off the floor, trying to look the injured party. He failed. 'Would I ever?'

His brothers snorted.

'OK, OK, maybe sometimes. But you should've heard what she said to me.'

Mr Benedict shook his head with a smile. 'Nothing you didn't deserve.' He came forward to take the coffee Victor had poured for him. 'How are you, Phoenix? Feeling better after your rest?'

'Yes, thanks,' I replied shyly. It was so strange seeing a father with grown-up sons. The relationship was a difficult one for me to understand: he was clearly still an authority for all of them but it was tempered by affection and respect. If you could describe someone as being the exact opposite to the Seer in the way he handled people, you might come up with someone like Mr Benedict.

'Yves, why don't you and Phoenix go out for a few hours while we get to work on her papers? Go and enjoy yourself. Get to know each other.' Mr Benedict gave us a merry smile. 'I'll tell the conference people not to expect you again. Family emergency.'

Yves bounded up at that suggestion. 'That's a great idea. Thanks for handling it, Dad.'

I slowly grasped that Yves meant to leave the rest of his family when we had so much undecided, so many threats to sort through. 'But . . .'

'No buts, Phee.' Yves pulled me off my stool. 'I want you to relax and enjoy yourself for once.'

Victor dug in his pocket and pulled out a white envelope. 'Here, take these.'

Yves raised an eyebrow.

'Front-row seats for *Wicked*—supposed to be a great musical. I got them for myself and my . . . um . . . colleague from Scotland Yard, but looks now like I won't have time to use them.'

'Was that the willowy brunette detective by any chance?' murmured Xav.

Victor shrugged. '*C'est la vie.*'

'Little brother is playing havoc with our love lives while he sorts out his own,' complained Xav with a good-natured chuckle. 'Glad I'm not the only one suffering.'

Mr Benedict took my vacated stool. 'When you both meet your soulfinders, we'll jump through hoops for you too.'

Xav stretched. 'Great. Like to see Yves doing the hoops for me. Pay back big time.'

Mr Benedict blinked, as if hearing something none of us could. 'I'd get going, Yves, if I were you. Your mother is about to get up and I doubt she'd let you escape without another inquisition.'

Yves laced his fingers through mine. 'Message received. See you later. Don't wait up.'

'Of course we will,' called Mr Benedict to our retreating backs.

Chapter 14

In the foyer of the Shakespeare Tower, Yves paused to check for directions on his London A–Z. I tapped my foot, irritated that the Benedicts had decided my future then organized my afternoon without asking me. I was going to have to do something about that.

'You don't need a map.' I pushed it away. 'Just tell me where you want to go.'

He smiled and tucked it back in an inside pocket. 'I forgot; I'm with a local.'

'Yeah, sort of.' I zipped up a maroon hoodie I'd borrowed from Sky. It matched Yves's T-shirt from that first day: Wrickenridge White Water Rafting on the back. I couldn't claim I belonged in London like he so clearly did in his little town, but I knew my way around. At least here I would be in the driving seat.

He scanned the tickets. 'OK. Let's find out how good you are: the Apollo Theatre?'

I'd picked pockets around Victoria Station on many a night when the theatres were turning out. I wonder if he'd given any thought to how I obtained my local knowledge. 'We should go to Victoria.'

He opened the door for me to go first and playfully bowed me through. 'I thought we'd have something to eat first in Piccadilly but I'm in your hands.' Somehow he made the comment very flirtatious.

'Really?' I paused and wiggled my fingers. 'Do you trust them?'

He took my wrists and pressed my fingers to his lips, laughing as he jostled me around a corner and out of sight of the lifts. 'Oh yes.' His mouth gently brushed each one, sending shivers down my arms, linking to my spine and from there to every nerve in my body.

'Yves . . .' He was only touching my fingertips and I was melting into a breathless heap.

'Hmm?' He didn't break off his gentle assault, his hum resonating against my sensitized skin. Turning one hand over, he nuzzled the palm.

'Should you be . . . doing this?'

'Definitely.' He progressed from my hand, up my arm to lay a kiss on my jaw. 'Can't kiss you with all my brothers around, so it has to be here. I've been dying to touch you for hours now—it was killing me.'

'Touch me?' My voice was an unimpressive squeak.

'Uh-huh. You go round with this little frown mark between your brows, did you know that?' His thumb brushed the spot. 'Sure sign you're worrying about something. I've been wanting to kiss it away.'

I choked. 'Like I haven't got stuff to worry about!'

'But not now. Not here.' He moved to meet my lips. 'You have a day off from worrying.'

With his mouth pressed to mine, I couldn't think of anything but the sensation of being held and caressed by my soulfinder. This gentle boy with fire in his heart had stormed my defences and made me fall for him so hard I knew the landing would likely kill me. But, oh the descent was wonderful. I didn't want to think about what would happen when we met reality.

Hands cruised from my shoulder blades to my waist.

I pulled away to rest my head on his chest. 'This is amazing.'

'My kissing that good, huh?'

'No.'

'What?'

Oops, again I'd scratched his confidence—and he'd been doing so well too. I'd been thinking about being held, something that hadn't been part of my life for years. 'Of course, your kissing is amazing.'

He huffed in my hair. 'Tell me I'm the best kisser you know and my bruised vanity may recover.'

I rubbed his back consolingly. 'You are. You're the only boy I've kissed.'

'Is that so? Are English boys blind?' He pulled me closer.

'I don't think so. I just haven't met any nice ones and kept away from the bad ones. The Seer doesn't let boys get near me—not ones he doesn't approve.'

'So I could be terrible at kissing and you'd never know the difference?'

'Believe me, I think I would. If any kiss made me feel this way, then it would be outlawed.'

'You're right. Let's break the rules then.' He tilted my chin to explore the possibilities.

Finally, we broke apart, arms loose around each other.

'So are we gonna stand here all day?' I asked his sternum.

'Yep.' His fingers wandered through my hair, messing it up so that the feathered ends went every which way. 'Fine by me. Who wants to see a boring old award-winning show, anyway?'

Put it like that . . .

'Um . . . me?' I'd never been inside a theatre. I couldn't

help a thrill of anticipation at the idea of actually seeing a live performance.

He groaned. 'Me too. Come on then. But take a rain check on that kissing thing.'

'Rain check?' I smoothed my hair back into some semblance of order.

'American speak for a delay, not a cancellation.'

I grinned. 'OK. I'll go with that.'

Caught up in the swirl of city life once on the tube, we got off at Piccadilly and joined the crowds surging up the escalators and out on to the circus, with its iconic statue of Cupid surrounded by buildings decked with flashing advertisements. Yves insisted we stop and pay our respects to the arrow-shooting god, walking around the plinth until we stood directly in the line of fire. With a wink at me, Yves mimicked being struck in the heart.

'Go on: your turn.' He waited for me to copy him.

I looked nervously over my shoulder, not so happy to be caught in sentimental fooling around. 'Is this, like, a tradition or something?'

His eyes twinkled. 'Is now.'

Quickly, I clapped my hand to my chest. 'Satisfied?' I felt stupid.

He folded his arms. 'Nope.'

We were attracting the attention of the tourists on the steps. A Korean couple had taken snaps of Yves staggering dramatically with a pretend arrow wound. They looked very disappointed by my feeble performance.

'Can we go now?'

'Not until you do the Cupid-arrow thing properly.' He leaned closer. 'One of his arrows is nothing to the power of being a soulfinder.'

Realizing that I had to do the full clown routine to get away from here, I went for over-acting, taking the bolt, spinning, staggering and collapsing into Yves's arms. The tourists applauded.

'And now?'

He put his arm around my shoulder. 'Awesome. Better than mine.' He paused. 'Shall I do it again?'

I tugged him away. 'No, you nitwit. Let's get something to eat before the show.'

'What's a nitwit?'

'Look in the dictionary and there's a picture of you.'

'Ouch.'

I smirked, but privately I wondered if he had meant anything by his fooling with Cupid's arrow. I knew I had fallen for him but I had no expectations that he should feel anything so profound for me. How could he? I understood that the soul-finder bond might make the physical part of our relationship more intense than a normal date, but such pre-programmed instincts did not equal love. My worst fear was that he was just acting that he liked me because he knew we were stuck with each other and was too polite to hurt me. I couldn't bear it if he was faking what he felt.

My self-torture lasted through dinner and up to the very door of the theatre. I was pleased to see that, though some people had dressed up for the evening, Yves and I were unremarkable in our casual clothes, even in the most expensive seats. The usher waved us through, and then another member of staff conned Yves into forking out a fiver for a programme full of adverts.

'They should be paying you to read that,' I whispered as we settled into our seats.

He refrained from commenting again on my Scrooge-like observations, restricting himself to a roll of his eyes.

'But you can buy a lot for a fiver.' I crossed my arms defensively, feeling cheap. I had an image of myself as one of those prizes kids get at hook-a-duck stalls at fairs that break in five minutes, compared to the exclusive handcrafted items around me, sold in Hamleys' toy department. A girl two seats along had stripped off a leather coat to reveal a snug red sheath dress and gorgeous Nicole Farhi shoes with ice-pick heels. She was eyeing Yves, flicking her hair in that 'come hither' gesture that I'd never even attempted and knew I would not pull off if I did. I gave her a hard stare, only slightly reassured to see that Yves hadn't noticed, his attention on the cast list. It was rather insulting to know she thought me so unimpressive as not to have considered me any contest.

'I've read the book, but can't imagine how they're going to adapt it for a musical,' Yves said to me, flicking through the programme.

'What?' I dragged my eyes away from the competition. Definitely a diamond-encrusted Barbie type.

'*Wicked*. It's a retelling of *The Wizard of* Oz from the point of view of the Wicked Witch of the West, a kind of prequel.' And of course my genius would have read it—as well as every other important book on the planet, no doubt.

'Oh.' Even with my dysfunctional childhood I'd seen that one—Dorothy, yellow brick road, and red shoes. I'd even read the original stories by L. Frank Baum, thanks to my library-haunting habits. 'Is there another side to tell?'

He put his arm on the back of my chair and let it slide to rest on my shoulders. I twitched an eyebrow which made him throw back his head and laugh. 'Smooth move, hey?'

'I wouldn't call it exactly *smooth*. Try obvious.' I tweaked his thumb.

This made him laugh even louder. I could see Diamond Doll fretting, probably wondering why such a nice guy was hanging out with such a sharp-tongued girl.

Yves ruffled my hair. 'Sassy—I like that about you.'

My next vinegar remark was cut short by the dimming of the lights. Yves squeezed my upper arm gently and leaned over to whisper:

'Just enjoy yourself. Everything from now on is going to be just fine.'

The performance finished at ten, turning us out on to the street as darkness swallowed up the sky and unlit back alleys. Out on the main thoroughfares, the neon lights kept night at bay, bathing us all in the cold sunlight of the commercial twenty-four-hour day. I could hardly believe how quickly time had passed. The rainbow colours of scenery and costumes, music from a live orchestra, actors just a few metres away from me: everything had been breath-taking. I'd been on the edge of my seat the whole time, drinking in every nuance of the performance. I'd wanted to weep at the injustice dealt out to the Wicked Witch; she'd never really had a chance in a world where being pink skinned and blonde was the standard of beauty. Us skanks didn't stand a chance against diamanté Barbies.

Needing to walk off my temper, I strode down Victoria Street towards the illuminated tower of Big Ben; I was still buzzing with the emotion, wanting to protest at the injustice of life as the witch had tried to do. Yves had to jog to catch up with me, as I'd marched ahead when he'd stopped to exchange a few friendly words with the usher.

'Phee, wait!' He grabbed the back of my jacket. 'What's wrong? I thought the show was great; didn't you?'

'Yeah, it was fabulous. But I'm really, really cross at how it turned out.'

He hugged me to his side. 'Life's not fair, even in fairytales.'

'I want to go and punch the Wizard.'

Yves bit his lip, humouring my anger on behalf of a fictional character. 'I know what you mean.'

'Being green and misunderstood is something I can relate to—not the green bit.' I could not—would not—bear it if Yves laughed at me, and part of me was well aware that I was being ridiculous. 'I meant being a misfit.'

He nodded, manfully not making fun of my snit. He hadn't caught on to the fact that what I'd seen on stage had entwined with my self-doubts and fears like ivy on a crumbling wall. If he pulled at it with any teasing, all might come down on him like the proverbial ton of bricks.

'She tried to do the right thing, but the right thing turned out to be wrong,' I continued, now thinking of my own situation where I'd tried to protect someone I loved and dragged a whole family of innocent strangers into danger.

Yves tugged me to a stop outside a coffee bar. 'Phee, you seem really stirred up for someone who is supposed to have had a fun night out at a musical. I don't think you're supposed to take it so seriously. How about something to calm you down? Hot chocolate? Sky says it never fails with her.'

I shook him off, suffocated by his fussing over me, telling me what to do. I did not want hot milk and to be tucked in when I could barely stop myself screaming and lobbing a brick through a window. Fortunately for Yves, there was no target in my view—no Seer or any of the Savants I'd met the night before, or I would've got us both arrested. 'No thanks. I don't want to be calmed down. I want . . .' My breath was coming in painful, shallow bursts. 'I want to be understood!'

Yves held up both hands and took a step back, a lion tamer retreating from the swipe of a fractious wild cat. 'OK, OK. Can I *understand* you somewhere less public?'

'I don't care what other people think.'

'Maybe not, but I'd really like to get off the street.'

We were attracting curious looks as night revellers caught

on to the argument in progress—a one-sided debate where I was throwing all the anger and emotion against his even-tempered acceptance like the sea attacking a harbour wall. That made me feel worse, of course. Yves just stood there letting me splash and spray my fury all over him.

I swore at him.

He flinched but stood his ground. 'Phee, please.'

I threw an arm out towards him. 'Why do you let me do that? I just swore at you and instead of giving it back like a normal person and telling me to stop being such a jerk, you stand there like . . . like Nelson Mandela.'

He ran a hand through his hair, confused. 'You...you want me to argue with you? I thought you wanted me to understand you.'

Just at the moment he couldn't do anything right. 'That's not understanding me. That's tolerating me. Pitying me. I hate it.'

'O-K. Um . . . look, let's go and talk about this.'

I squeezed my hands into fists, tempted to hit out but knowing I really wanted to punish myself.

Yves's phone rang. Giving me space, he took it out and answered. 'Yeah, it's over. It was . . . it was good. Thanks for the tickets.' He glanced over at me. 'I think she liked it, maybe. Uh-huh. He did? OK. Yeah, I've got the message. See you.' He slipped the mobile back into his jacket pocket.

I folded my arms, trying to tear myself out of my mood like someone detaching their feet from a puddle of sticky tar. 'One of your brothers checking up on us?' I asked coolly.

'Er, yeah.' He glanced over his shoulder at the coffee bar. 'I need a drink. Come with me if you like.'

He entered and joined the queue at the till, posture spiky and stressed. His new tactic worked and I felt obliged to follow him. Where else could I go?

'What'll you have?' he asked.

'Decaf something.' I was wired enough as it was without

adding a shot of caffeine to the bloodstream.

He ordered two decaf lattes and suggested I go find a booth. I slid into one near the back of the shop, a dark corner where I could mope. God, I was horrible. He'd tried to give me a nice evening and I was messing it up going on a chaotic emotional stampede, flattening him in passing.

The bench squeaked as he sat. He pushed the tall glass over to me, a peace offering.

'Thanks.' I ran my fingers up and down the warm surface.

'I should warn you, Zed saw you running off. Vick phoned to tell me not to be a jackass.'

'It wasn't you.' I couldn't meet his eyes. 'I'm sorry. I flew off the handle.'

'The show's not real, you know.'

Whosh! My temper flared again at that spark. 'Of course I know that! I'm not stupid!'

'I wish we'd seen *Phantom* instead,' he said plaintively.

Turn it down, Phee, turn it down. 'But even though it's a fantasy, *Wicked* is true to experience—mine at least. Best intentions get screwed up.' Then I leapt feet first into what was really bothering me. 'You have to tell me, are you going to betray your family—the Savant Net? I can't stand not knowing.'

His hands flexed around his drink, fingertips going white. 'You have to trust me.'

He was still ducking a straight answer. 'I can't believe that you will—and so I'm wondering what's going to happen the day after tomorrow. I won't hurt them. You can't take me back to that flat.' I crumpled up a sachet of sugar spilling the brown sugar over the table. 'You can't do that to them—or to me.'

'If you can't trust me, at least trust my family to do what they do best.'

I kicked the granules around with my index finger. 'And what's that?'

'Look after each other—and us.'

He still didn't get it. 'But that's their soft spot. They don't realize you've brought a snake into the nest. I don't want to turn and bite them but that's what's gonna happen and you know it. You told the Seer you would keep your bargain but you can't—you just can't. I won't let you betray them.'

He took a gulp of his drink, controlling his knee-jerk response to my cutting and slashing at him. 'You don't really know, Phee, what I can do—what my family can do.'

I took a deep breath, realizing that I had just been putting off the moment that I would have to leave him. If I truly loved him—and I now knew I did—I had to make the choice for him. 'No, I don't. But I know what these men can do if they get their hooks into you. You think you have a safety net—a loving family, your home in the States—but they are everywhere, your enemies. They will take everything away from you—strip each petal off the flower. You are walking into a trap.'

'With my eyes open.'

'Open—shut—it doesn't matter.' I slid to the end of the bench. 'Look, I know you think you've got some clever way out of this, but you really haven't. I'm primed to hurt your family and then go back—I'm the weapon the bad guys are using against you. You've had a go at deciding my future—without asking me, by the way, don't think I didn't notice.' He looked a little shame-faced as he realized I had a point, which gave me space to make the rest of my speech. 'I've been trying to ignore the obvious. Make all the plans you like but I can't stay with you. Look at me—I'm a thief, Yves. I even like being one.' I can see that this shocked him. He'd been persuading himself I was more a victim than a criminal.

'But you never kept the stuff—you did it because you had to.'

'Yeah, yeah, you go on telling yourself that, sweetcheeks. I'm not a good person. I like it because it's the only damn thing I'm good at. In the bad column is everything else, including relationships.' I felt something crack inside me. 'Oh, what's the point? It's been . . . it's been lovely meeting you. I'd better get going.'

I was out of the door by the time he caught up with me.

'Running again? I thought we'd been there, done that.' His tone was clipped. Hurt.

'Yeah, well, maybe my first reaction was the right one.' I kept walking, heading up Whitehall towards Trafalgar Square. He was still following. Dodging through the crowds mingling by the fountains, I crossed the road by the National Gallery and turned into the Strand. I could hear him keeping step with my feet but he didn't try to stop me.

'Lady, want to see the menu?' A waiter paid to hustle tourists into his restaurant got in my path.

I hunched over. 'No, thanks.' And steamed on past. Yves continued to follow.

When I reached the Strand, I tried to shake him by taking a random bus just as the doors began to close. He shoved his shoulders in the gap and got on behind.

'Need a ticket, love?' asked the driver, tapping his machine.

'Yes, please.' I hadn't the foggiest idea where the bus was heading. 'What's your next stop?'

He gave me a funny look. 'Embankment.'

'Yeah, that'll do.' I dug in my pocket for some spare change.

'No need. She has a travel card.' Yves flashed the Underground tickets we'd bought earlier that included bus trips above ground.

The driver decided not to ask why I was looking daggers at my helpful companion. He shook his head and pulled away from the kerb.

I slumped down on a seat near the rear door. Yves sat in the row behind me.

'This is stupid,' I muttered to no one in particular.

'Yeah, it is. Glad you realize that.' Yves stroked my shoulder but I got up, putting myself out of reach. The bus swung round onto the Embankment and I rang the bell. The doors hissed open and I jumped out, Yves only a step behind. Nearly shouting with frustration, I took a suicidal dash across the busy road to reach the wall overlooking the Thames. The granite pillar of Cleopatra's Needle beside me, Waterloo Station opposite, this was a busy stretch of the river, restaurant boats churning the dark waters, glass cabins holding dinners like transparent-skinned crocodiles swimming past with their last meal inside, revellers oblivious to the fact they'd been swallowed whole.

I went to the very edge and hopped up onto the parapet.

'Phee, what are you doing?' Yves was alarmed. Finally, he had twigged I was serious.

'I'm making a choice. If you don't back off, I'm going over.' I glanced over the edge: I had no intention of killing myself but I'd not enjoy a dip in the muddy water below. The point was to get him to leave me alone.

'Get down from there!'

'When you go.'

Swearing softly, Yves looked away from me, then threw his hands up in the air. 'OK, you win. I'll go. Have a nice life.' With that he spun on his heels and stalked away towards the tube station, disappearing inside.

My sudden victory shocked me. That was it? He was giving up so easily? It was what I wanted—of course it was—but he hadn't tried very hard to persuade me to stay with him.

Feeling stupid on the parapet, I jumped down and sat on the steps to the Needle, knees huddled against my chest.

Why did winning feel so much like a defeat?

Chapter 15

Thunder rumbled over Tower Bridge. Storm clouds moved in and it began to rain. Not a gentle ladylike weeping but a great howl of tears from the sky, crying with no thought to what you look like, nose running, mouth open in an 'O' of misery. I knew how that felt. I was soaked in a matter of minutes, hoodie dripping at the sleeves, wringing wet at the shoulders, water working its way through to my T-shirt. I got up, squelching in my shoes. Wrapping my arms around myself, I shivered, eyes closed, brain too frozen to think what I should do next.

Arms caught me and hugged me to a hot, wet chest. 'How can you even think that I would walk away?' he said bitterly.

'Yves.' The emptiness suddenly filled; protest became a shout of happiness.

'I saw you sitting there—you really thought I'd gone. You didn't even trust me enough to look twice, did you?' He had got up a good head of steam, temper finally escaping. 'And standing on the edge like that, threatening to throw yourself in—I can't believe you said that to me!'

'I'm . . .'

'I don't want to hear it. Every time you open that mouth of yours you say something dumb that gets me angry, so I'm gonna stop you the only way I know how.' His lips swooped down on mine in a hot, forceful kiss, spiced with fury and frustration. Firecrackers exploded behind my closed eyes, sparkles in the pit of my stomach. I could feel the muscles of his chest bunching as he shifted to move me to a better angle, his fingers slipping under the damp material of my T-shirt to brush my waist. Responding to this new side to him, I shoved my hand under the tight belt around his jeans to touch the small of his back, palm resting against the strong notch at the base of his spine. His skin was so warm, so perfect.

He raised his head to take a breath. 'Don't you dare say we don't belong together,' he warned. 'We have this—and so much more. I'm not letting you throw it away.'

Please don't let me, my mind echoed. I pressed my ear to his chest, seeking out the comforting rhythm of his heartbeat.

'I promised I'd handle this and you've got to let me keep my word. For once in your life, reach out and rely on someone,' he whispered fiercely into my hair. 'I've got the information the Seer wants already on a memory stick. We are going to that meeting the day after tomorrow together. Even if you run away now, we both have to be there, remember?'

I nodded.

'No one will get hurt if you just keep to my plan. That's another promise.'

'But they'll take the information and use it to unravel your network of good guys.'

'You're thinking that the Savant Net doesn't have its own defences. We're not novices at this game, Phee. We've been up against these guys for a while now.'

'But the Seer's trying to make you into his sort. He'll get you to unpick those protections.'

He shrugged. 'One of us walking on the dark side is not going to bring the Net down. It's bigger than that.'

'But you are the one I care about.'

He shivered then rubbed his palm up and down the bare skin of my back, trying to distract me from the fact that he wasn't going to give me a straight answer. 'You're soaked.'

'So are you.'

'Let's go home.'

I didn't move. 'No one will get hurt? How can you square that circle?'

He tipped my face up to meet his eyes and wiped the rain from my cheeks. 'Your soulfinder is a genius, didn't Sky tell you? I can square circles in my sleep.'

I sighed. He wasn't going to reveal the plan to me—probably couldn't—how he was going to reconcile betraying his family with what I knew about his character. He had a trick up his sleeve; I had to have faith that it would be clever enough to get us both out of this bind. Yet I couldn't forget what his own dad had said: Yves's decision to stick with me had turned him into a threat. Even geniuses could get things wrong—look at Einstein's unfortunate choice of hairdresser. But what could I do? I was strapped in this car for the ride now. 'OK.'

He quirked an eyebrow. 'OK what?'

'Let's go home.' I pulled back to sneeze. 'Quickly. I'm freezing.'

He looked up the street into the stream of oncoming traffic then raised his arm.

'Not another taxi!' I groaned as one drew up at the kerb. 'We've got tube tickets.'

Yves held out the now sodden bits of cardboard. 'We had tickets. And if you think I'm going on the Underground with you in wet clothes so all the drunks can leer at you, then you've another thing coming.'

Oh. I crossed my arms. 'Good point. Taxi's a great idea.'

Cold, shivering, but somehow purged by the stormy encounter on the Embankment, I huddled on the back seat, Yves's arms looped around me so I could rest against his chest. I was finally beginning to believe that he would never let me go, even if that meant we both stumbled into darkness.

The next morning, Karla and Sky insisted on taking me shopping for some clothes. My wet jeans needed a spin in the machine and neither of them had trousers that would fit me, both being a couple of inches shorter. I made do with a pair of trackies borrowed from Sky—not my finest fashion hour as they ended well above my ankles. On my suggestion, we set off for the new mall near St Paul's, boys not allowed, to indulge in some serious retail therapy. Yves had given me a hundred pounds to spend, saying I could pay him back eventually but only through legal means. He hadn't forgotten my admission that I enjoyed my craft and was evidently still set on reforming me. I fingered the pouch containing the crisp new notes in my shoulder bag, marvelling that I was holding so much and could spend it on myself.

Diving into the shopping centre, we soon found a boutique we all liked. I scanned the cheaper racks of jeans, hoping to find something to fit. I would never have thought to ask but as soon as Yves's mother saw I favoured a certain pair, she demanded to see more sizes in the 'pants' I'd picked out. This made Sky and me giggle—childish I know, but Sky knew exactly where I was coming from, having suffered in the States for her British English. The right size found in the stock room, Sky grabbed a blouse from a rack to keep me company in the changing room.

I wriggled into the grey jeans then stepped out to look in the big mirror in the corridor. 'What do you think?'

Sky was admiring her blouse. 'This was an impulse, but I think I might get it.'

It suited her—a bright turquoise that made her eyes shine. 'Go for it.'

She surveyed my selection. 'They look great. You're really slim and they show your legs off.'

I twisted round and read the tag. 'You know, I've never bought a pair before.'

Sky began unbuttoning the top. 'Never had grey jeans? They are so useful—go with almost anything. I've some back home.'

'No, I mean, never bought anything from a shop.'

That stopped her in her tracks. 'What, never?'

'When you don't have any of your own money and can freeze the staff so they don't notice you walking out, what else can you do?' I disappeared back into my cubicle and unbuttoned the jeans to tug them off. Through the gap in the curtain I could see Sky's shocked expression in the mirror. 'I could hardly go round naked.'

'But . . .' Sky shook her head.

'Yeah, I know it isn't fair on all the other customers. Shoplifters like me are the dregs. Logically, I know that it's selfish, that everyone else pays, but it never feels like that. The rush is too addictive.' I was truly shocking her now. Perhaps there was a thing as too much truthfulness when you are trying to make a friend.

'I hope you never have to steal again. I'm sorry, Phee, but it sucks as a way of life.'

'Yeah, but it's all I have.'

'*Had*, you mean.' Sky smiled. 'I don't think you'll need to worry about money after this.'

I stepped back into my borrowed trackies and came out with the jeans draped over my arm. 'Of course I'll worry about money. I've got nothing and I don't intend to live off the Benedicts.'

She looked at me through her eyelashes as she bent over to lace her trainers. 'You don't know then?'

'Obviously not.' I ran my hands through my hair, trying to get it to look halfway decent.

'Yves is obscenely rich.'

'You mean the Benedicts are?'

She shook her head. 'No, just Yves.'

'How come?'

Sky re-hung the blouse. 'You've twigged that he's clever?'

'Yeah. Hard to miss.'

'He invented this security app for the iPhone—came out of the work he was doing for the Net. The Apple people bought it—it's quirky and makes protecting information fun—so now he's got a big nest egg for college and he's become this kind of informal consultant for them. He wanted to share the money with the rest of the family, but they all told him to get lost. So it's his. He hates it. I tease him that he spends money like a dog shaking off water after a dip in a pond.' She mimed a shudder. 'Brr, there goes another hundred bucks!'

'Nice problem to have.'

She smiled. 'I know. I expect he's relieved to have someone to share it with. Prepare to be showered in dollars. Hope it makes you feel less guilty about buying a pair of jeans on his tab.'

I clipped the trousers back on to the hanger. 'I'm going to pay him back. I'm not a . . . you know . . . gold digger or whatever the term is.'

'We never thought you were.'

At that point, Karla burst into the changing room with a heap of clothes folded over her arm.

'Darlings, I have something for you. I couldn't resist!'

To my surprise, Sky paled. 'Oh no,' she mouthed at me.

'My Yves will buy you the jeans, but I will treat you each to a pretty dress.' She clasped her hands to her chest. 'I have never had daughters—you are my girls.'

'Um . . . thanks,' I muttered, feeling embarrassed at her enthusiasm to sweep us to her maternal bosom.

She patted my cheek. 'After seven boys, you are doing me the favour. Put them on—put them on!'

I now focused on the clothes she had hauled in with her. Ah.

Sky smiled sweetly at Karla. 'Why don't you wait outside while we change so we can surprise you with the full effect?'

Karla looked doubtful.

'And perhaps you could find something for yourself?' Sky continued.

Karla's face brightened. 'You're right! I shall see if they have one in green.' She whirled out with a whisk of curtain, taking her dauntless energy back to the shop floor.

'Oh my word,' groaned Sky, 'what's she chosen this time?' She fell on the clothing and held up a pink ruffled dress. 'Yours or mine, do you think?' She gave a hysterical gulp of laughter.

'Who . . . what?' I scratched my head, wondering how Karla had managed to find something quite so ghastly. It looked like the cross between a bridesmaid's outfit and the kind of thing you would wear for a party. When you were five. 'Do you think it's meant to be ironic?'

Sky frowned. 'In this boutique? Yeah. Accessorized with Uggs it might work. But not on me. Kate Moss might get away with it but I'd look just sweet and about eight. Let me tell you, though, as far as Karla is concerned, there's nothing ironic about this. She wants every girl to dress like a Disney princess. I only usually go shopping with her when I have my mum along for protection. She's good at heading Karla off from her worst picks.'

I gingerly shook out the powder blue version of the same dress. 'So what do we do?'

Sky stepped back behind the curtain and began to change into the pink, knowing from my expression that I wouldn't even consider that shade. 'Well, we can either offend someone who only wants to please us, or we can suck it up and suffer.'

Resigned, I stripped off my top. 'I'm good at that.'

Lost in the skirt, Sky began to giggle. 'Actually, Phee, I've just had a fabulous idea. Let's keep these on and try them out on our boys—see how they react. It'll put them in a really tight spot—us in clothes selected by their mother. They are just gonna die trying not to offend anyone.'

'Are you sure?'

'Yeah, I'm sure.'

We had just done up each other's backs when Karla returned, her arms empty this time. She clapped her hands to her mouth.

'Oh my gosh, don't you both look pretty!'

We looked like rejects from the auditions for *The Sound of Music*.

'I will have to buy them—they are meant to be yours!' Karla waved her credit card around like a wand. 'What a shame they didn't have one in green for me. But then, it is a young girl's style. I would've looked foolish.'

And we didn't?

'Karla, Phee was just asking if we could keep them on, seeing how my trackies don't fit her anyway.' Sky elbowed me as I opened my mouth to protest.

'Of course! Just give me the tabs and the new pants and I will pay for everything. We'll have to get you shoes to match the dresses before we go home.'

She was gone before I could pass over the money Yves had given me.

Sky began folding up her old clothes. 'Thank goodness all my old friends live over in west London.'

'Isn't this a bit of an expensive joke?' I tugged the sweetheart neckline straight.

Sky smiled. 'No. We were not going to get out of here without some questionable dress or other; this way we can have fun with it. Besides,' she squinted at me, 'the Disney princess look really suits you.'

I threw the trackies at her head.

As we approached the flat, Sky held me back and closed her eyes. 'Just preparing the way,' she explained. 'I want to get Zed and Yves on their own.'

Karla sailed into the kitchen, bestowing kisses on the older Benedicts gathered there, regaling them with tales of our shopping adventures. Sky's telepathic message had sent Zed and Yves into the living room. I could see them in the reflection from the window opposite the door, both standing by the sofa wondering what we wanted.

Sky grinned at me and grabbed my wrist. 'Play it serious. That makes it harder for them,' she whispered.

Then we were in the room.

'Hi, darling. We've had such an awesome time shopping with your mother.' Sky dropped my hand and brushed a kiss on Zed's jaw. She held out her arms and spun. 'What do you think?'

I smiled shyly at Yves. 'Your mum insisted she bought them for us. It's my first dress.'

Good one. Sky's voice dipped lightly into my head—not an invasion but a welcome visitor. *Rub it in.*

I frowned and looked down at the shiny material. 'I wasn't sure, but I thought it kind of suited me. With the right shoes and everything.' I displayed the new blue pumps. 'I wanted to look, you know, pretty.'

Yves gaped. I felt a little bit sorry for him. 'Um . . . Phee, I don't know what to say.'

I let my bright expression dim. 'You . . . you think I look horrible in it?' My voice rose in a convincing squeak of distress.

He put his hands on my shoulders. 'No, you look great. You always look great, no matter what you're wearing.'

Zed laughed. 'Ouch. Wrong thing to say.'

'You mean that I don't look any different to normal in this?' I asked with a puzzled frown.

'Yes, I mean, no, this is lovely on you. Of course it is.' Yves glared at his brother who was cracking up at his attempts to be polite. I quickly scanned Yves's mental pattern seeing a frantic whirl of thoughts as he struggled to find the right thing to say. He thought the dress perfectly ugly.

Sky turned the attention back to her. 'So, Zed, isn't this a killer outfit?'

'Certainly a killer, baby,' he replied with mock seriousness.

'Good, because I've bought another five just like it.'

He picked her up and spun her round. 'You horrible, teasing fairy. If you really have more of those fashion disasters in your bags, I'm gonna hang you on top of the family Christmas tree in December.'

She wrinkled her nose, feet still suspended from the floor. 'You weren't fooled?'

He kissed her frown. 'Not for a second. I know my mother. I know you. Phee, I will give the benefit of the doubt.'

Yves looked flummoxed. 'What's going on?'

'The girls are pulling your leg, bro. Get used to it.'

'You mean, this is a joke?' He sighed with relief. 'Thank goodness for that.' He bent his head close to mine. 'You look like you should be on a biscuit tin with a parasol.'

I curtsied. 'Thank you, kind sir.'

Xav chose that moment to wander into the room. Seeing

Sky and me in his brothers' arms, his face was stricken for a second, then he smiled, recovering his usual good humour.

'You both look butt-ugly,' he said lightly, backing out. 'Sorry for interrupting.'

Sky pushed away from Zed. 'Xav, don't go because of us. We were just fooling around.'

'That's fine. Carry on fooling.' He went back into the kitchen and shut the door.

'Damn,' she muttered.

Zed stroked her arm. 'He'll be fine. Yves, how's the Savant locator coming along? We've five brothers still to pair up.'

'Working on it.' Yves released me. 'Almost got the programme written. Tell me you've got something else to wear?'

I nodded. 'Yeah. Be right back.'

'Narrow escape, brother mine, narrow escape,' I heard Zed mutter to Yves as I left.

Chapter 16

With a discreet knock on the door an hour later, Mr Benedict appeared at the threshold of my borrowed bedroom. After a decadent long, hot shower, I was busy painting my toenails with Sky's help. She insisted we did each one a different colour, just for the fun of it. We were surrounded by our purchases, which spilled haphazardly from the bags like presents at a toddler's party.

'Am I interrupting?' he asked politely. I sensed that this kind of behaviour was not really his department, having raised boys.

'Not at all. Almost dry.' I felt a little weird being caught with my rainbow toes elevated and he clearly felt uncomfortable interrupting girl-time.

He backed away. 'Come into the kitchen when you're ready.'

'Sounds serious.' Sky slotted the varnish bottles back in her make-up bag. 'I'd better come with you for moral support.'

Feeling comforted to have her at my side, I went into the kitchen. Yves, Mr Benedict, and Victor were gathered around a laptop.

'Hey, Phee, OK?' Yves asked. He'd had a shower too from the look of his wet, spiky hair.

'Hmm,' I replied, not committing myself to an answer until I found out what this was all about.

Victor looked up, took in the multicoloured nails, and cracked a smile. 'See Sky's influencing you already, huh?'

I wriggled my toes. 'Um . . . yes.'

'Don't look so scared, sweetheart.' With a warm smile, Mr Benedict beckoned me to come closer. His casual use of the endearment made me feel strangely emotional. He knew I'd made his son into a risk factor to the family happiness, yet still he welcomed me.

'Well, you all sound so serious, what do you expect her to think?' Sky slid round me to take a glance at the computer screen. 'Oh, I see.'

'What's up?' I tried to strike a careless pose leaning on the counter but I was anticipating being chucked out at any moment. Had they discovered who my father was? Maybe that was why they were acting so distant? Yves hadn't even looked at me properly.

'I think we've found you in the national records,' Victor explained. 'See for yourself.'

Oh God, I was right. I forced myself to cross the distance to the screen where Victor had the information displayed, a copy of a full birth certificate. My mother's name was clearly listed and the date and place of my birth—2 July in a hospital in Newcastle. In the father's slot, the registrar had written 'not known'.

Yves put his arm around me. 'I'm sorry. I wish we'd been able to find out more for you.'

Relief swept through me like a gale in an autumn wood, fears flying before the wind. I had a reprieve. They were worried I would be upset not to have a father when the opposite was true. My secret was still safe. 'Not important. It's OK.'

Victor gave me a penetrating look; I think he knew I was

hiding something. 'I wouldn't say it's unimportant. You should be able to trace your mother's family from this. We have her date of birth now. You might have grandparents, aunts and uncles—you never know.' He clicked print.

'Yes, true.' Not that I felt like following that up just at the moment. I was indulging in a private celebration that I was officially fatherless.

'On the positive side, it makes it easier to get you out of the country as there's no known family to interfere. I'll talk with my contacts in the Home Office, call in some favours, and see if we can get you a passport on the strength of this. You are almost of age so they shouldn't be too worried. I'll need a photograph.'

'Sure. I think there's a place in Liverpool Street where you can get those done.' I tried to strike a businesslike tone, pushing the messy kinship stuff behind me.

'Best take her now,' Victor told Yves, filing the copy in his computer case. 'When things get sorted out here, we'll not want to hang around in London for long.'

It would be nice to be asked if I was intending to go with them. Still, that reminded me. I paused in the door. 'By the way, the bad guys have Yves's passport details—I saw a copy of the page with the photo—that's how I was able to identify him the first day. I don't know how they got hold of it. No one said.'

'Really?' That caught Victor's interest. 'There must be one of theirs working in the system. I wonder if that means they know how many of us are here now? We were hoping they had not realized we'd sent for reinforcements.'

'It could've come from the States—the copy of the passport, I mean.' I pressed my fingers to my forehead, pain starting behind my left eye. 'I saw someone from New York who knew about you.' I tried to fool my brain that I wasn't breaking any rules, only reporting what I'd seen, not what I'd heard. 'There were others—Moscow, Beijing, Sydney.' The Seer's retaliation made my head hurt but I had to tell the Benedicts as much as I could. I couldn't bear for them to be unprepared. It wasn't just the Seer they had to worry about. 'They were together for a kind of summit meeting I think.'

'Phee, shut up.' Yves took a tissue and wiped my face. 'You're getting a nosebleed.'

Victor shot me a concerned look. 'I appreciate what you're telling us, Phee, but we already know there's a group of rogue Savants in London at the moment. That's why we are here.'

'I see.' That changed things. I had the sudden image of myself falling between a water taxi and the Thames wall, caught in the surge between two implacable forces. The Savants were well aware of the existence of the other group; I was the only one stupid enough not to realize that and was getting squeezed in the middle.

Yves steered me to a chair so I could put my head down. 'Don't tell her anything else, Vick. It's not doing either of us a favour.'

I wasn't so sure about that. Being in the dark would lead to me making mistakes, like putting myself through a migraine and nosebleed to tell them something they already knew.

Vick squeezed my shoulder as he passed. 'I think we can give the photos a miss for today. You should rest.'

The bleed had stopped as soon as I'd given up spilling the Seer's secrets. 'It's OK. I'll be fine in a moment.'

'I agree with Victor.' Mr Benedict spoke as if laying down the law, a kindly magistrate presiding over the family. 'We have only just found you, Phoenix, and, from what I understand from Xav, we need to look after you. The rest of the day on the sofa watching DVDs is what I recommend. I'm sure Yves will happily wait on you hand and foot.' From his words, I suspected they wanted me kept well out of harm's way. It can't have escaped their notice that every time I left I tried to make a run for it.

I sat up, head spinning, but decided to play along. 'Sounds fabulous. I don't think I've ever had a day off.'

'Then take it easy. I'll see you both later.' Mr Benedict paused to kiss Sky goodbye, a casual fatherly gesture. He hesitated then did the same for me. 'I'll send Zed back when Xav takes over from him.'

I leant against Yves. 'Where is everyone going?'

He shrugged. 'I think we'd best not ask.'

He was right. The Benedicts had split into teams, each dealing with the different jobs to be done, one of which was making me 'official'. I didn't want to guess what the others were doing. 'So, what shall we watch?'

Yves picked me up, ignoring my squeals and Sky's laughter, and deposited me on the settee in the living room. 'Not *The Wizard of Oz*, please. I can't revisit the trauma of arguing about the rights of green-skinned witches.'

I almost smiled, but I still felt too tender about last night to have the necessary distance to find my behaviour funny. I had been so emotionally overwrought I was embarrassed to remember.

Sky came in and dropped a DVD into my lap. 'There you go. *Ten Things I Hate About You*, a classic—and Yves?'

He retrieved the case, then crouched by the machine to put the disk in the slot. 'Yep?'

'You will not spoil our enjoyment by deconstructing this film with your clever comments on the history of cinematography . . .'

'Aw, Sky, would I?'

'Yes, you would. Neither will you tell us how the plot resembles *Taming of the Shrew* in every aspect, script, characterization etc.,

etc., capping it all with a review of all other films based on Shakespeare plays.'

'So you don't want to hear my analysis of *Hamlet* and *The Lion King*?'

Sky folded her arms. 'Nope.'

Yves gave a put-upon sigh. 'Yes, boss.'

'You will, however, make us microwave popcorn.'

Yves stood up and saluted. He then leaned over me to whisper: 'She's small but dangerous—just thought you should know if you're going to be friends.'

'We *are* friends,' Sky said firmly. 'And you are standing in the way of the screen.'

'Yes, ma'am.' Yves scooted off into the kitchen.

'You fit in well with them,' I commented, putting my feet up and pulling a rug over my legs.

Sky snorted. 'Not so well at first. Had them holding me off at gunpoint.'

I didn't believe her. 'Still, you're like family. Yves thinks of you as a sister.'

Her blue eyes took on a serious expression. 'They *are* my family, Phee. And now you are too. It'll take a while, but we'll all adjust.'

'Hmm.'

She tweaked the blanket over my toes. 'If there's one thing I learned, it is that blood families can sometimes be the pits; it's the one you make for yourself that really gives you a home and people to love.' Just before I could comment on that, she threw her head back and laughed at herself, stretching her arms up. 'Just listen to me: so wise, so young! I'll shut up. Press play and prepare to have fun.'

The day went so quickly after that. I cottoned on to the fact that Yves and Sky were babysitting me as other members of the family came and went. We saw Zed for a stretch late afternoon. He spent it playing cards with Yves, while Sky and I watched a weepy classic. They occupied half the game arguing, Yves claiming Zed was cheating by using his future sense, Zed claiming it was only fair when his brother had a 'fricking awesome' computer for a brain. It was unclear who won in the end—I think no one because they ended up wrestling on the floor with the cards flying everywhere. I was worried they were going to hurt each other, but Sky just laughed and told them to keep the noise down.

Yves came to me after the fight—hot and rumpled.

'Are you hurt?' I asked.

He squeezed himself between me and the arm of the sofa so I ended up half sitting on him. 'No. But Zed is—he's a wuss.'

Zed threw a cushion at him, which Yves killed off with a cool telekinetic counter move. It fell from the air like a shot pigeon.

'Now, now, boys, play nicely,' Sky mock-scolded. 'Phee, you look, well, shell-shocked.'

'Is this how families behave?' I asked her.

'Quite a lot of them,' she confirmed. 'Sorry.'

'No, no, I love it.'

'Love the fact that my big brother here just beat the hell out of me?' Zed limped to the armchair. 'He's a bully.'

This protest was highly suspect from a boy who looked as though he could bench-press the weight of a mini without breaking a sweat.

Yves made a shower of sparks sizzle over Zed's head, who batted them away like a cloud of annoying mosquitoes. 'Cut it out, Brains, or I'll tell Phee all about your other wives.'

'Er . . . what?' I laughed.

Yves groaned.

Zed grinned, knowing he'd found an excellent way to embarrass his brother. 'Oh yeah, Yves's been married at least three times, each one to really cute little girls.'

'In kindergarten,' growled Yves.

'Yep. He was irresistible. They had him divided up between them: Mary-Jo got to play bride on Mondays, Cheryl on Wednesdays, and Monica on Fridays.'

'You are so gonna burn for this,' muttered Yves.

'What happened on Tuesdays and Thursdays?'

'Mom kept him back at home. I mean she had to give our lover-boy here a rest, didn't she?'

Sky perched on the arm of Zed's chair. 'Ooh, I like this story. And what about you?'

Zed smirked. 'I wasn't allowed to play because I was too mean and rough. Yves has always been the gentleman in the family—perfect groom material for the under-sixes. Mom probably has photos somewhere that's she's saving for his real big day. Consider yourself warned, Phee.'

I gave him an uneasy smile. It was OK to joke but Zed was talking as if us getting hitched was a foregone conclusion—not something I could get my head around. 'He needn't worry. I can't take on a bigamist, can I?'

'Oh, he's a free man.' Zed hadn't caught the awkwardness between Yves and me produced by his comment. 'The divorces were brutal—tears, smashed toys—and that's just Yves. I think they are amicable now—wasn't Mary-Jo your Science partner this year?'

'Yeah, and she's going to Princeton. With her boyfriend.' Yves got up, signalling a change of subject. 'Something to eat, Phee?'

'Yes, please.'

'I'll do some pasta for all of us—how does that sound?'

'Great. I'll be cook's assistant.'

He took my hand and steered me into the kitchen. 'You can assist by sitting on a stool and keeping me company. I want you to promise me you'll never listen to another stupid story from my brother.' He wrinkled his forehead. 'Brothers,' he amended.

'Not sure I can promise that.'

'Not fair.' He pulled a heavy-based pan out of a cupboard and put it on the stove.

There was something incredibly sexy about watching Yves cook, the little frown of concentration as he planned his assault on our taste buds. Yves didn't just bung a lot of spaghetti in a pan as I would have done; he made a red sauce from scratch, slicing and dicing, crushing and stirring with as much attention as I guessed he would give to his science experiments. He cooked as though he was composing a new formula, testing the taste, asking me to judge the seasoning, all with an expert's eye to getting the perfect balance. I was allowed to grate the parmesan, but that was all the kitchen territory he was going to concede. And when it came to serving, he didn't ladle a splurge of pasta on the plates; no, he presented the food, each with curls of cheese and basil on the top.

'Dinner is ready,' he said with mock formality, tea towel over one arm like a waiter.

Zed and Sky joined us at the counter.

'Wow, I love it when Yves cooks!' enthused Sky.

I had to agree: it was the best homemade food I'd ever tasted.

'Traitor.' Zed poured us all iced water.

'Can you cook like him, then?' I asked.

'Yes.'

'No,' Yves and Sky said in unison.

'Real men don't cook. Real men grill.' Zed grinned, knowing his argument was indefensible. 'My brother is so metrosexual— all these city-boy skills. I worry about him.'

'Worry about yourself,' scoffed Sky. 'Our household is going to be strictly fifty-fifty when it comes to things like that and

I refuse to live on burnt pizza. I'm enrolling you on a course when we get home. No kissing until you cook me a decent meal.'

Yves chuckled. 'Revenge is mine.'

Zed looked anxious for a second, then smiled. 'You won't last.' He tugged Sky closer and planted a kiss on her lips. 'There. Told you.'

'The no-kiss rule starts when we're home and I've found you a class,' Sky said smugly. 'Read the small print.'

Zed folded his arms and pushed back his empty plate. 'She won't last.'

'We'll see.' With Sky's eyes promising retribution, they held each other's gaze for a scintillating few moments.

'Challenge accepted, my lady.' Zed gave her a flourishing bow.

Looking at them together, I had a feeling she might not be so strong-willed as she thought. On the other hand, she probably wouldn't mind losing.

Victor came home late, long after most of the family had gone to bed. I heard his voice echoing in the kitchen when I was in the bathroom and I wondered if he'd made any progress on getting me my passport or discovered what Yves was doing. From the sound of it, he must have found something to complain about because his tone was angry. Normally, I would run the other way when I heard raised voices but the other party to the argument was Yves. I clicked off the light and waited for the fan to stop churning. Once all was quiet, I crept into the corridor to eavesdrop. I made no apology for doing so—if Yves needed back-up I wanted to be there; if he didn't, it was best he didn't know I was spying on his brother. I had to risk it as ignorance hadn't served me well up until now. I didn't quite trust Victor. With his links to law enforcement, he had to despise me even if he had managed to hide it so far.

Victor stood with his back to the door, brandishing a sheaf of papers at his younger brother. 'Look, Yves, I'm running this operation. Your job was studying icebergs or whatever. I can't tell Scotland Yard my own family is going behind my back—I've worked to build up that relationship and, with their help, we're close to cracking this ring of Savants.'

'Yes, I know, but that changed when I met Phee.' Yves had to be riled because he was making a candle on the table melt super-fast, flame almost a foot long, as if he had to do something with his heated emotion. I was beginning to understand now that he had a choice with his gift: either keep his emotions cool and even, or find a channel to let them burn. If he didn't, I guess someone could get hurt.

Victor paced in frustration. 'She's just one small part of all this. I understand you want to rescue her—she has to be your priority—but there's more at stake and you know it. We have to run this operation by numbers. I can't have an amateur doing his own thing. That's the way to get one of us killed.'

'I'm not putting anyone in danger.'

'Bull. You're putting yourself on the line—and I won't have it. I let you get away with the closed-lip thing in front of the others, but I have to know what you're planning. Dad warned you—you could upset everything, ruin months of work by law-enforcement agencies across the globe. I can't run this gig if we're tripping over each other. Just tell me, damn it!'

I knew I should go back to my room; I might overhear something I really didn't want to be forced to tell the Seer tomorrow, but curiosity kept me chained in place.

The candle was now a lake of hot wax. Yves turned to spinning a sphere of fire on his palm. 'I can't.'

'Geez, don't you get it, Yves? This is not about your

soulfinder—it is about you and your arrogant assumption that you, a kid of seventeen, can out-think everyone else. Well, face it, bro, you can't.'

Yves stared mutinously into space.

'Aren't you listening to me or do I have to remind you of what happened to Zed and Sky last fall? You told us the security perimeter at home couldn't be breached—that your work was without equal, but a couple of Kelly's goons still got through and took potshots at them.'

'I thought you weren't going to remind me.' The ball of fire in his palm went out. 'And I've made improvements since then. No one can get through now.'

'Just listen to yourself—you're doing it again. You're clever, there's no doubt about that—but you forget that so are other people. They can out-smart you.'

Yves folded his arms. 'Our home is safe. Phee will be OK with me.'

'So you take her side rather than your family's?'

'It's not about sides—and she's family too, now.'

Victor slapped the countertop with the papers, annoyed with Yves and himself. 'Maybe.' Yves glared. 'OK, I know it, but she's pulling us apart.'

Yves pushed to his feet, his stance combative. 'She's not and I don't want to hear even a whisper from you that you blame her for this situation. My choices are my responsibility—mine alone. I can get the right result if you do your thing and let me do mine.'

'You're asking me to trust that your brain is street smart as well as intelligent?'

'I suppose I am.'

'Yves, you're killing me here. I look at you and I try to make myself believe you know what you're doing, but part of me thinks you're going to be just as stupid as the next guy when a girl comes into the picture.' He heaved a frustrated sigh. 'I don't want to argue with you. I want to help you. Of all my brothers, you are the one I least want thrown into this kind of business.'

'Why?'

'You're too nice. Don't see the bad in people, give them too much benefit of the doubt.'

Yves shook his head, not budging an inch. 'I hope you're not talking about Phee, because if you are I think you'll rapidly discover just how unpleasant I can be.'

Victor must have recognized that stubborn look and stopped pushing on a closed door. 'These are hers.' With an abrupt change of direction, Victor dropped the papers on the counter. 'You know she's not telling you everything, don't you?'

Yves shrugged and leafed through the documents.

'I could get her to give us full disclosure—use my gift.'

'No.' Yves's word was concise and final.

'No? You won't even consider it?'

'Too many people have messed around with her over the years, Vick. If we become just another group breaking trust with her for our own purposes, we'll never get her back. She's told us what she can. You saw her today—she gave herself a headache and nosebleed trying to warn us what we faced.'

Victor removed his jacket and tugged at his tie to loosen his collar. 'I don't doubt her good intentions in that, but my radar tells me she's hiding more—stuff that she could spill if she wanted. Things that disturb her so badly she's in denial.'

'So? Then it's personal and none of our business.'

'Is it?'

My spike of alarm must have given me away because Yves's eyes went to the dark doorway. Oh yeah, unique signature: I'd forgotten he was an energy bloodhound.

'Not asleep yet?' he asked coolly. Now he had another thing to be angry about: I had been eavesdropping.

Reluctantly, I came into the light. There was no point hiding the fact I was listening. 'I couldn't. I found your discussion too fascinating. I mean, I was the subject, right?'

'Yes, you were.' Victor took a seat, perhaps trying to make himself less threatening, as he had been looming over me, but I caught the 'I told you so' look he flashed Yves, underlining my untrustworthiness. 'I'm sorry you heard that, but I had to make my opinion known.'

'It's OK. I've been telling Yves that he shouldn't put any of you at risk for me. I'm not worth it.'

'I didn't say you're not as important as any of us, Phoenix,' Victor corrected. 'Just there's more to think about than what we do with you.'

I wasn't sure if that was any different; it was all a question of priorities and I wasn't number one for him. 'Of course, I get it—really I do.'

Yves now looked irritated by both of us: me for being so dismissive of my value and Victor for being so insistent on the worth of his operation. 'OK, Vick, we'll get out of your hair tomorrow. You go do what you have to do and we'll go sightseeing.' Yves pushed the papers over to me. 'Sign there, Phee.' He caught my distrustful expression and sighed. 'It's just a passport application, nothing more.'

We had the meeting with the Seer tomorrow. Wasn't he even going to tell his brother about that? 'But Yves—'

'Not now, Phee; I'm feeling angry right at the moment and don't want another argument. Just sign the damn papers.'

I wasn't protesting about the papers and he knew it. Biting my lip, I put my signature in the box. It was weird—the first time I'd ever signed anything. My name looked loopy and childish; I wished I'd thought to practise.

'Look, Phoenix, I don't want you to think I don't care about what happens to you.' Victor slipped the documents back in his leather bag. 'I just have a lot to balance right now. If you can persuade my brother to take me into his confidence it would be a whole lot easier.'

I nodded, knowing I'd get nowhere with Yves. 'Sure, I'll work on that. Um . . . good night.'

'Yeah, sweet dreams,' said Victor.

Doubtful. I anticipated a night of tossing and turning. I was now terrified as to what Yves was planning for tomorrow. As his brother said, he might be super-intelligent, but was he street smart? The two were not the same and Yves could well be led astray by thinking he was cleverer than the rest of us. I was going to have to come up with a plan of my own while Yves and Victor were busy on theirs.

Chapter 17

Our appointment at the London Eye came around too quickly. Despite the tensions, the previous forty-eight hours had been an oasis in my desert of a life, and I had no wish to get back on the Seer's caravan to nowhere, but what choice did I have? At breakfast, I could feel the order to make the meeting pushing away inside me like a cattle prod. Any time I tried to think of alternatives, my brain would short circuit and I would find myself at the door, heading out. Only Yves understood the reason for my bizarre behaviour; the other Benedicts were all too polite to make any comment but they must have thought I was the rudest house guest they'd ever entertained—and cruel to Yves as well.

'Give yourself a break, Phee,' he whispered as he let me rest my head against his chest, latest assault on the door foiled. 'It'll work out.'

I just did not believe him. Overnight, I'd come to the conclusion that the only plan that had any chance of succeeding would be for me to stop Yves handing over anything. I couldn't attack Dragon, Unicorn, or, God forbid, the Seer, but Yves wouldn't expect me to turn on him. I'd steal it off him as soon as I had a chance and make sure no one noticed.

So here we were, as I had always known we would have to be: ten fifteen on a breezy morning in the queue for the London Eye. White crests formed on the river where the wind went against the tide, seagulls struggling to hold their position as they glided overhead. I had to wait until we met up with the Seer before making my attempt; I didn't want Yves to abort the encounter if he realized too soon what I'd done. We had no idea exactly how the Seer would choose to make his rendezvous, so followed logic and bought tickets for the overgrown Ferris wheel with its views of Westminister, Big Ben, and the Houses of Parliament. We were just approaching the front of the queue when Dragon and Unicorn appeared beside us.

'Glad you made it.' Dragon's grin was all teeth. 'We have reserved a private capsule for our party.'

They pulled us out of the line and took us over to the VIP entrance. I shrank away from Unicorn.

Don't let him touch you, I warned Yves. *He's a life-stealer.*

It's OK, sweetheart. My shields are up.

Just make sure they are on full power, hotshot.

Hustling us past the security guards, we found the Seer already in occupation of the see-through car. The doors closed behind us and the capsule continued its slow revolution upwards.

'Excellent. I'm pleased to see you are on time. Then again, Phoenix would have made sure of that, wouldn't you, my dear?' The Seer's hateful voice crept over me like army ants that could cover and devour prey in minutes.

I muttered something and drew closer to Yves, running my hand over his jeans pocket in what I hoped he understood as an affectionate rather than exploratory movement. The journey time for the London Eye to fully revolve was thirty minutes— there would be no escape for us, no chance of help until we came back down. I could now see why the Seer had chosen such a public place to meet. He had to ensure that we were out of reach of the other Benedicts, and this was a flamboyant way of making sure all approaches were cut off, as we were as isolated as fish in an aquarium. Still, that was good for me; I could probably manage to freeze them all if I was careful, but where did Yves have the memory stick?

The Seer beckoned us to approach. Dragon and Unicorn remained at our side as we moved forward.

'We haven't met properly, have we, Mr Benedict?' The Seer tapped the place on his stomach that Yves had set on fire. His new white jacket today bore no scar but the impression had clearly lingered.

Yves brushed his fingers soothingly on my upper arm. 'No, I've not had that pleasure.'

'I know a lot about you. Quite the boy wonder from what I've been told.' The capsule edged out from the lower struts supporting the wheel, opening the view on all sides. We were leaving behind the things that anchored us to earth and sailing out with scant protection into a void. I already felt queasy, and normally I had a good head for heights. It had to be the company. 'My American colleagues have been watching you with particular interest since your inventive powers became public knowledge. And now I learn that you're my daughter's soulfinder. Fascinating.'

'No, don't say it!' my mind screamed but I held still, stapled to the spot by my own stupidity. It hadn't occurred to me that the Seer would want to claim the relationship. But why wouldn't he?

The only reaction Yves gave was to tighten his grip on my arm. 'Then you'll understand what she means to me,' he said calmly. 'And I expect you only want what's best for her, being her father, just as I do.'

When were you going to tell me? Yves asked me privately.

Never. I was too ashamed to meet his eyes. *And he's not. I refuse to believe it.*

The Seer smiled. 'But I imagine our views as to what is in her interests are different. You have to understand, Yves—I can call you Yves, can I not?'

Yves gave a cautious nod.

'Phoenix belongs to a very close-knit community. Her family. We can't have outsiders tearing the fabric apart just to please themselves. Even soulfinders.'

Like he really cared.

Yves dropped his hand to my waist, a possessive move claiming his girl. 'But the bond between soulfinders is unique— you must know that.'

The Seer gave a greasy smile. 'So the legends say. Let's see how much she's worth to you. Do you have the information?'

We were sprinting to the crisis; I had to act now. I'd never had the gall to try and freeze the Seer before and my audacity terrified me. Reaching out, I quickly grasped the mental patterns of Yves, Dragon, and Unicorn. Attention fixed on the confrontation, none of them were thinking about me so weren't prepared for my backdoor approach. Now for the Seer. Touching his mind was like plunging into sewage—thick, reeking, and repulsive. I couldn't grasp it; his mind slipped from my control like oil leaking through cupped palms.

The Seer chuckled with dark amusement. *Let them go, Phoenix. What exactly were you trying to achieve here?*

There was no defence he would find acceptable. I let go. The three started moving again, unaware I had frozen them.

I'll be considering my punishment, my dear. Enjoy the anticipation. He wasn't going to announce what I'd done.

And then I was too late. Hesitating slightly, Yves took out the memory stick on its keychain, letting it dangle enticingly from his index finger like a hypnotist's crystal. 'It's all here. What does it buy?'

He was talking a language the Seer could understand. 'Her health and happiness—for the moment.'

On this suicidal barrel-over-Niagara journey Yves had insisted we risk together, we were at the edge; if Yves handed the information over, there would be no going back. Blackmail never ends; surely Yves had to be smart enough to get that? It was not worth buying a few days of me being OK at the expense of his family's security. He had to see sense before it was too late.

'Yves, forget it.' I tried to snatch the stick from his fingers, intent on snapping it in half. He lifted it out of reach.

'Keep out of this, Phee.' He pushed me to arm's length.

Unicorn gave me a look that made me feel like a maggot. I was surprised to find I did have some residual loyalty to the Community, otherwise I wouldn't have minded what he thought of me. 'So she's not so loyal after all. I did wonder.'

Yves stepped between us. 'She's loyal to me. That's what soulfinders are. What she hasn't realized is that the game has changed. I've decided to defect.'

Pretending interest in the view of Big Ben, the Seer savoured the unusual word, not heard much these days. 'Defect?' His expression reminded me of a toad swallowing a particularly juicy bluebottle.

'Yeah. This isn't about Phee any longer, Mr Seer, though I admit she was the catalyst. After meeting her, I figured that you could offer me more than the Savant Net.' Yves's grin had turned brash, confident—the expression of a boy with more arrogance than sense. 'You know, someone with my brains can't make the kind of money they deserve playing for the good guys.' We all must have looked very sceptical for he made an attempt to explain. 'Look, it's probably not of much interest to you, but my family have been on my back for a while now, cramping my style, needling me about my mistakes. Meeting Phee has given me the kick up the ass to do something about it.' He twirled the memory stick. 'I want this to be the price of my admission. And you give me Phee.' He mentioned me as if I were an after-thought.

The Seer fixed his gaze on Yves, trying to breach his defences to sort out truth from lies. Yves had to be lying, didn't he? I scanned Yves's mental landscape and found only a resolution to strike a deal. He was keeping us out of any deeper probe and I doubted the Seer would see more than I could.

At length, the Seer threw back his head and laughed. 'Good try, Benedict. You almost had us believing you were sincere. But I cannot believe the Savant Net's good boy is so easily tempted to betray his family.'

'Try me.' Yves tossed the stick to Unicorn, catching him unawares. 'I take it you have a laptop?'

Unicorn nodded and drew a little computer out of a brief-case. Slotting the stick in the USB port, he waited for the information to come on screen. Distressed and confused by this sudden change of direction, I paced my end of the capsule, corralled by Yves and Dragon in case I tried to grab the stick again. Somehow I'd got myself in the position that they were all teaming up against me. Four against one—how had that happened?

'Looks good to me,' Unicorn confirmed. 'Savants listed by country and skills. I know a couple of the British names—they check out.'

Yves glanced over at the screen. 'Just don't copy that over from the memory stick.'

Unicorn snorted, showing he had no intention of obeying that restriction. 'Running a virus check right now.'

Yves shrugged. 'Your funeral.'

The Seer brushed his chin, rethinking his approach. 'So you are corruptible, I see, Yves. I thought you'd try to hand over false information, but if this holds for all the other names, then I have to admit I was wrong about you.'

'You credit me with far too pure motives, Mr Seer. It's simple really. I want to make my fortune and I want my girl: you can give me access to both. What else does a man need for happiness? I'm seventeen—almost eighteen—about time I shook off my babysitters, don't you think?'

'You'll understand if we don't believe you on the strength of this.' The Seer waved to the screen where Unicorn was now scrolling through the names. 'I'll have to consult my business partners and they will probably want to meet you. Can you do that without your family finding out? Your value to us is primarily as a source of inside information; we would not want them to question your loyalty.'

'That's fine. My family wouldn't believe me capable of this. Even if they see me talking to you this morning, they will still find an innocent reason for me doing so.'

Yves, no! I mentally beat against his barriers; he was keeping me out of his head just as I had done when we first met. I didn't understand what he thought he was doing.

The Seer nodded. 'Yes, you're quite convincing in your incorruptibility; I can see how they would fall for it. In that case, we'll take this information to my colleagues; check it out; and then send you a message where you should meet us.'

'OK. So what about Phee?' Yves wasn't looking at me, just tossed the remark out as if I were a dog he had to remember to kennel before he went on holiday.

The Seer shook his head. 'She has revealed that she's disloyal so I cannot let her out on loan to you again. There's a little matter that needs seeing to. She comes home with us.'

'Then I do too. This soulfinder business is weird; we're

programmed to want to stay together, even if your partner's a bit of a flake.' He winked at me as if that would make the insult better.

Dragon sniggered.

The Seer frowned, weighing up the risks. 'You can do this without alerting your people to what's going on?'

Yves shrugged. 'All I need say is that I've decided to go off with Phee for a bit of tourism. My parents really buy into the soulfinder thing and will expect me to want her to myself for a few days. They would rather I was out of their hair at the moment. That'll give us a day at the very least before they start looking for us. Is that enough?'

'It should be.'

We were coming down on the other side of the Eye. The Seer calculated that we only had a few minutes left to seal the deal and he was still unsure of exactly what he was getting.

'I need some surety if you come back with us. I prefer my activities to remain out of sight.'

'Of course you do. Only sensible.' Yves stretched as if completely at ease with the unfolding situation, waistband of his boxers flashing above low slung jeans, well defined muscles rippling.

From the glint in his eye, I guessed that the Seer did not appreciate the display of youthful body peacocking beside his own fat turkey of a form. 'Your shields are strong, Yves. I think a safeguard planted in your brain would not set—at least not to my satisfaction. I will use Phoenix again as it is clear, even as a . . . what did you call her? Oh, yes, a flake, unreliable. Flake or not, she is a large part of your motivation.'

Yves dismissed me with barely a glance. 'No, there's no need for that. I'll let you put the thing in my brain.'

The Seer tapped his lips with his arched fingers. 'No. I don't trust you—yet. I know Phoenix's mind and hers is very susceptible to my touch. It will take with her and this is too important to risk in an experiment with a Savant at full power, as I sense you are. Phoenix, come here.'

I clung to the rail at the far end of the capsule, shaking with anger. How could Yves denigrate me so? I couldn't believe it. 'You're all mad, all of you! Yves, stop this right now! I don't want you to come back with me, can't you understand that? Just leave!'

Dragon picked me up so my back was to his chest and hauled me over to the Seer. Yves did nothing to stop him, just stood with his arms folded.

'She gets hysterical like this from time to time.' My frigging soulfinder was apologizing for me! I kicked out, hoping to connect with his groin but my foot missed. 'Phee, calm down. No one's going to hurt you. It's just a precaution.' He turned to the Seer. 'What were you going to do?'

'I was going to suggest she kills you if you betray where we live to anyone outside the Community, but it looks as if she's going to do that anyway when Dragon turns her loose.'

They all laughed at me. It was only the hint that the Seer found my behaviour entertaining that cut off my protests. I went limp, head hanging. Dragon dropped me on my feet in front of the Seer.

'No one said a soulfinder relationship was plain sailing. I'll soon have her tamed,' Yves said smugly, patting the seat of my jeans.

I told him what he could do with himself—something anatomically impossible. The men laughed at my reaction, even Yves. This was so unlike my sensitive boy of the past few days, I couldn't understand what he meant by it. He had to be acting, but why? If he seriously wanted to treat me like a possession, he was going to find himself singing soprano.

'I'll leave the discipline to you, then,' smirked the Seer.

'I've been searching for a strong partner for her but it seems that fate has already selected you. I'm putting you in charge of keeping her in line, as well as fulfilling your end of the deal, understood?'

'Yeah, goes without saying.'

'And I take it something happening to her is worse than anything I could impose on you?'

Yves reluctantly nodded. 'Yeah, I guess.'

The Seer reached out and grasped my wrist. *Phoenix, if your soulfinder betrays me, the location, or any members of our Community, you will reject him.*

Happy now? I snarled at Yves.

He just shook his head, like a nursery teacher standing over a three year old's temper tantrum.

We completed the rest of the journey in hostile corners. Dragon and Unicorn stood guard on the computer; the Seer stayed at the front, studying the prospect as if he owned Westminster; Yves lounged against the railing in the middle of the capsule; and I, well, I'd retired back to the far end, hurt and puzzled by the course he was taking. He had said he wouldn't betray me, and so far he was keeping to his bargain with the Seer, but he'd also said he wouldn't hurt his family. How could handing over such sensitive information satisfy this pledge? And what was with all the disgusting macho behaviour? If he thought I would secretly swoon at being dominated by him, then he had better reconsider his options quickly or I'd do it for him.

The doors opened with a gentle hiss.

'Did you enjoy your flight?' the attendant asked, trying to hand me a customer questionnaire.

'Like a poke in the eye with a sharp stick.' I marched past her, ignoring the pamphlet.

Yves paused to smooth the woman's ruffled feathers. 'Vertigo,' he explained. 'My friend lost her head for a moment up there.'

No, I hadn't. He was the one who had done that, and now we were both in the Seer's trap, the very place I'd been trying to keep him out of since our paths first crossed.

Chapter 18

Finally left alone in my little flat while the information on the Savant Net was checked out, Yves and I stood awkwardly with the expanse of the room dividing us.

I folded my arms, trying to hold in my howl of fury. 'I can't believe you sold out.'

Yves dropped his eyes from mine and scanned the room. 'Nice.'

'I know it's not.'

He must have noted the lack of pictures or other decorations. All I had was a pillow, sleeping bag, towel and large holdall with the rest of my stuff. A spare pair of shoes was kicked under the bed. The floor was covered in worn brown lino, an old quilt cover stood in for curtains. At least my room smelt clean, unlike many of the other flats. I had made sure I scrubbed everything down before I unpacked.

'This makes me feel humble: you have less stuff in a place you've lived for a while than I have in a suitcase I brought for a week's stay.' Yves picked up my hairbrush and put it back down on the window ledge.

'Yves, please . . .' I couldn't stand small talk when he'd done such a terrible thing. He had to explain or I would go crazy.

He opened his arms wide, inviting me to walk in. I stayed on my side of the room. It would be easier, perhaps, to fall into the pattern of letting him steer me through this like some kid strapped in a chair on the backseat while he drove, but I couldn't live with myself if I did. It just wasn't in me.

He dropped his hands to his hips. 'OK. Look, I'm sorry about the way I treated you back there. I got the message that the Seer doesn't like to see people, especially women, expressing their own views. I thought if I gave the impression you'd transferred your loyalty to me, he'd be OK with that as long as I'm on his team.'

'So you *are* on his team?'

Yves shrugged. 'So it seems. For the moment. But really there's only one team that counts: you and me.'

'But what . . . how are you . . . ?' I ran my fingers through my hair and tugged in frustration. 'You've not really defected, have you?'

'Yeah, I have.' He sat down on the edge of my bed.

'No, you haven't.'

'I had no choice. I can't keep you safe otherwise.'

'That makes no sense. You no more want to walk on the dark side with this bunch than have a lobotomy!'

He had the gall to chuckle. 'Good image. Come and lie down with me. There's nothing either of us can do until we get our summons.'

'Can't you understand? I don't want to get more involved with you if you're like them.' It was the worst insult I could think of. 'And . . . and I don't believe it anyway. You're lying to me.'

He kicked off his shoes and stretched out. 'I promise you, I'm not lying.'

'But that's worse!'

'You keep forgetting the most essential point, Phee.'

'I do?'

'I've only asked one thing of you. Tell me what it is.'

'To . . . to trust you.'

'That's right. So get yourself over here and give me a hug. I need it even if you don't.'

Was he bad or good? I couldn't decide if he was lying or had made some disastrous choice, but whatever the truth, stretched out on my bed he was definitely tempting. He'd taken off his glasses, leaving his face somehow more open to attack. If I rejected him now I knew I'd be doing real damage.

'OK. One little hug.' I slipped off my shoes and joined him, nestling at his side. He eased his arm under my neck and pressed me close. I let my hand rest on his chest. 'You slapped my butt.'

He shifted to rub the offended part. 'Yeah, sorry about that, but I was making a point.'

'To me or to them?'

'Is "both" the wrong answer?'

I poked him in the stomach.

'Hey, don't blame me! I was acting like my brothers do at their most obnoxious. They're good teachers.'

'So it was an act?'

'Phee, come on: don't you know me even a little? Am I the kind of boy to go round treating my girl like a dumb babe?'

'I dunno. Are you?'

He tickled my ribs in retribution. 'Only when she says stupid stuff like that.'

I retaliated with a thump. 'No, I don't think you would normally do something like that but you're not acting normal. I'm getting confused.'

'I know, sweetheart.'

'You really think it's going to be OK?'

'Yeah, I really do.'

'Are you a hundred per cent certain?'

He grimaced. 'I wouldn't say that. If I'm honest, I'm thinking more like fifty per cent. Dad was right that I'm running a hell of a risk. I'm relying on a lot of people to do their part right and a lot could go wrong.'

That didn't sound good. 'Even me?'

'That's where the trust comes in.'

'I'm not going to follow you to the dark side, if that's where you've gone.'

'Honey, you're already there. This whole thing is about getting you out.'

That made him sound like the firefighter who went into the burning building to pull out a victim only to die in the blaze.

'So how are you going to do that?'

He smoothed a finger over my cheek. 'I've turned to crime, remember? I'm stealing you, of course.'

'You are?'

'Uh-huh. But first I'm going steal a kiss.' He went up on one elbow so our lips could meet in soft touch. He took his time, allowing us both to relax and enjoy the stolen moment of intimacy. There was something even more powerful about holding each other like this, lying down, legs entwined, his big frame brushing against me so I felt completely wrapped in his warmth. I'd been so starved of anyone touching me in a loving way that I was overwhelmed—dry earth soaking up a deluge.

He broke away and smiled at me. 'You really do stop time, don't you?'

'I wasn't using my power on you, I promise.' I had no intention of admitting to my failed attempt to freeze them all earlier.

'I know; I meant the effect you have on me. Kissing you has just become my favourite occupation.'

I returned his smile. 'Better than studying geo-whatsit?'

'Oh yeah, baby, you better believe it!'

We laughed together at his Austin Powers silly accent.

'I love you, Yves.' I said it before I could censor myself. Too late to call it back. 'I mean, I don't expect you to say it back or anything.' Idiot. 'Um . . . sorry.'

His eyes were glistening. 'Please, don't apologize. I'm only sorry you got to say it first. I've been waiting for the right moment to tell you.'

I tried to move away. He was just echoing me because he was incurably polite. 'Really, there's no need.'

He wouldn't let me budge. 'There's every need. You're good for me. I think our creator was very clever thinking up this soulfinder business, as he matches us not with what we want but what we require.'

I let pass the rather surprising admission that this science geek believed in God, not something I'd let myself do since I was little. Life had always seemed too much of a cruel joke to allow for a benevolent creator. 'And what did you want, then?'

He lay back down beside me. 'I thought I wanted someone like me—I was fairly shallow in my choices: a college girl, American prom queen material, someone who likes tennis and books.'

'I can do books, but tennis?' I snorted.

'But I play a mean game. I'll have to teach you.' His fingers brushed gently at the curve of my waist and hip. 'Though I should warn you: Zed sees it as another sign of my lack of machismo.'

'How?'

'Because the players wear whites, don't need a helmet and can't go dumping the other guy on the ground.'

'I see. Very suspect. So what did you discover you require in your soulfinder if it's not Miss Prom Queen?'

He went silent for a moment, making me wonder if he was

rethinking. I could almost see that perfect girl—she'd look like Jo-Grid; fragrant, with the air of the well-groomed women in perfume ads, wholesome as they bounded across flower-strewn meadows. If I came from an advert, it would be in a doorway in a Help the Homeless Christmas Appeal.

'Yves?' I tapped his chest: better to hear the answer, even if it was bad news, than be left wondering.

He smiled. 'Humility—that's what I need—someone who will challenge me about what it means to be intelligent. Someone who will test my control. I thought I wanted to go through life all calm and even-tempered; now I realize I need that fire or I'll never feel the sparks. I think—I hate to admit it—but I was in danger of turning bland. I'd be wearing cardigans before I was thirty if you hadn't come along.'

I smiled at the image. Perhaps cardigans weren't so bad if he wore nothing underneath and I had the honour of unbuttoning. 'But I'm not in your league, Yves. Never been to school.'

'You're clever in your own way.'

'There are huge gaps in what I know. I'm like Swiss cheese.'

'Even so, I've noticed you hold your own in an argument with me; I'm used to people folding because they think I know more than them.'

'You probably do.'

'Not really. Learning comes easy to me. I know facts and figures, but not real stuff. Unlike you.'

I felt a glow of pride in myself, possibly the first. He thought I knew more about life, did he?

'And you are all the things I said you were: protective, caring, determined to look after others before you give a thought to yourself. I'm awed by your selflessness, even more so now I've met the people you live with. You're a much better person than I am.'

'Rubbish.'

He covered my hand with his so both our palms rested against his heart. 'I'm serious.'

'I'm a thief. I liked it.'

'I would be too if I had been born into this life. Besides, I understand liking the rush of doing something well. For me, it's cracking a formula; for you, it's getting away with it. Why don't we find something else that gives you the same thrill without the illegal-you-might-end-up-in-jail bit?'

Kissing him would do that but I couldn't let him keep these illusions. All my sins bubbled out before I could think better of the confession. 'I got my friend hurt. Unicorn took ten years of his life because I wouldn't talk.'

He rubbed my neck in a comforting gesture. 'Not your fault. Blame the ones who did it. I'd like to meet your friend. What was his name again?'

'Tony.' I traced a circle on his chest with a finger. 'I'd like you to meet him but he's the only one. Keep away from the others.'

'OK. We'll go find him later if you think it's safe.'

'Nothing is safe here.'

'Less risky then.'

'Yeah, that's about it.'

'Just one thing, Phee.'

'Hmm?'

'I'm not going to trigger any of those switches the Seer put in your mind, so don't you do something that will produce the same result. If I'm going to sacrifice a pawn or two to keep you safe, I don't want you to go throwing my queen away.'

The way he was describing this, like a dangerous chess gambit, was not making me any happier, the stakes being so much higher than a handshake for the victor. 'You know what this feels like for me, Yves?' He shook his head. 'Like I'm blindfolded and walking along a rope bridge. I don't know if you've put a safety net there or if it's a river full of crocodiles.'

He kissed my forehead. 'I love the way you think. You have the most wonderful grasp of images, much more entertaining than my rather literal approach to life.'

He had skilfully avoided answering.

'So what is it? Net or crocs?'

'What do you think?'

'I think *you* think there's a net but you might not see the big holes in it. Didn't Victor and your dad both warn you?'

He rubbed my arm. 'See, I told you you were clever.'

'Basically, you are asking me to go into this blind—with the distinct possibility that my guide can't see the dangers either. I won't know until too late.'

He thought about this for a moment. 'That's about it. On the other hand, you might like to consider that the other guys might also be blindfolded—to some things at least.'

'I hope so.'

'I know so.'

Both rumpled and barefoot, sitting cross-legged on the bed, we'd just finished a picnic of my small store of biscuits and water when our summons came. It was by now late afternoon and I had been expecting one of my half-brothers, but it was Kasia at the door. She smiled at the pair of us.

'So this is your young man, Phoenix?' She gave him an approving once-over.

Yves looked to me to make the introduction.

'This is Kasia, Yves. She's the Seer's telepathy expert.' I hoped that was enough warning.

'Nice to meet you,' Yves said politely, standing up and holding out a hand.

Kasia brushed palms with him briefly. 'I've heard your voice for a few days now; nice to meet you in the flesh, Yves. You're

247

both wanted. Follow me.'

I slipped on my shoes and ran the brush through my hair. Yves tucked in his shirt and put on his glasses. We were as ready as we were ever going to be.

'Trust me,' he whispered as we left the haven of the flat.

As we walked towards the Seer's apartment, I could see Yves change. He stood up taller, his walk became more of a swagger, and he edged ahead a pace so I was left trailing behind him. He went first through the door.

'Yves, my dear boy, I'm sorry for my earlier suspicion.' The Seer did not rise but beckoned him to share a seat on the sofa next to him. Unicorn and Dragon scowled at my soulfinder from their corner by the big screen. 'Your information has checked out in all respects. My colleagues are very pleased with the details I was able to forward them.'

'You've sent it to them already?' Yves frowned. 'But I told you not to copy it off my memory stick.'

The Seer waved that away. 'Your data is not much use to us if we can't disseminate it, is it? Thanks to you, the Savant Net is going to be taken apart piece by piece. Slowly, of course. We wouldn't want them to suspect where we got the information from. And no one will hurt your people—that goes without saying.'

Because the Seer needed the Benedicts to carry on unwittingly feeding information through. I had no illusions that he was offering this concession for humanitarian reasons. More devastating was the realization that real information had been swapped for me; Yves had done exactly what he said he had: betrayed his family and friends. I felt the pain like a blow to the stomach. Somehow I'd been hoping for a miracle. I couldn't bear to think that his attachment to me had made Sky and his brothers into pawns he was prepared to sacrifice.

Yves clicked his fingers at me. 'Yo, Phee, get over here.'

'What?' I put my hands on my hips and glared at him. This was taking the role way too far.

'You're thinking too much. Mr Seer says I'm in, so come park your butt here where I can see you.' He leant to the Seer. 'She's still not with the programme—things are changing too quickly for her little brain. I want to keep a close watch on her.'

While I wanted to put a fist in his inflated ego, he'd also asked me to trust him. I was the only friend he still had if he'd cut his ties with everyone else for me.

With a flounce to broadcast my annoyance, I stalked over to the sofa and sat as far from him as the seat would allow. He was having none of this. Hooking an arm around my waist, he pulled me to sit on his knee, palm spread possessively on my midriff. The Seer missed none of this by-play, giving us his creepy smile of approval.

The Seer gestured to one of his companions to serve him a champagne cocktail. He offered a glass to Yves but not to me. I had no more role to play in this conversation than a sofa cushion. 'Now, son, the next step will be to meet with my colleagues this evening. They have a proposition for us.'

'What kind of proposition?' asked Yves, squeezing me in warning as I shuddered at the Seer's use of 'son'. No one said 'son' unless in a jokey 'all right my son' way—not unless they were making a heavy point to their audience.

'Business opportunities for us. Mr New York may argue for you to be absorbed into his organization as you'll be spending most time in the States, but I will press for you to remain on my books, what with you being my daughter's soulfinder. You're one of the family now.'

So they were going to squabble over the inside source, were they? Anything that drove a wedge between them was good news. Remembering 'Jim' New York, I was expecting him not to give up such a morsel without a struggle.

'And you'll want to come back and visit her frequently, won't you?' continued the Seer, sipping his drink. 'See how she's getting on here?'

Yves stretched his arms out on the back of the sofa, leaving me perched precariously on his lap. 'I'll hear what you've all got to say tonight, but I think you need to get it straight that there is no question of me leaving Phee behind. Isn't that right, Phee?'

What did he want me to say? Yes, sir; no, sir; three bags full, sir? I could only stomach so much of this before I snapped. 'That's right, Yves; I'm staying with you.'

'See.' Yves smiled at the Seer as if to say, what could he do? The little woman couldn't live without him.

'We'll settle that later.' The Seer was not going to surrender his ace so easily. He must have realized that once Yves got me away, his hold over both of us would be immeasurably weakened. 'For now we need to discuss business. Phoenix, you go and doll yourself up for the meeting while your soulfinder and I discuss terms.'

Mentally waving a single finger in his direction, I got up. 'Can I use something from the Community wardrobe again?'

'Of course. And look out evening wear for Yves while you're there. There's a white dinner jacket that will do.'

Out of the corner of my eye, I caught Dragon and Unicorn exchange a look. No male had ever been allowed to wear what was recognized as the Seer's colour.

'OK. Later.'

Yves gave me a brief pat, acting as if he'd forgotten me even before I left the room. I was tempted to stick my tongue out at him from behind the Seer's back but couldn't risk anyone else noticing my rebellion while Yves worked so hard to project the image of bossy male. But, really, he'd better not be getting ideas; he was enjoying this far too much for my liking.

Chapter 19

I tried to lose myself in the business of sorting through the clothes in the Seer's stores. Some of the dresses made Karla's choice at the boutique look restrained. I'd not seen so much diamanté and sequins on anyone other than a pantomime dame. Finally, I found a gown I could live with—a soft apricot chiffon over a satin slip. It had a classic halter neckline, gathered under the bust, and then flowed to end just above my knee. Looking at myself in the mirror, I decided the colour flattered my tan and that the choice of little kitten-heel shoes showed off my legs, making them more attractive than they normally appeared in my clumsy trainers. I accessorized the outfit with another diamond necklace—this one more delicate, with the stones in flower settings so it looked as if I had a priceless daisy chain around my throat.

For Yves, I found a white dinner jacket and black trousers designed by Paul Smith—or at least an excellent fake, you can never tell in the Seer's storeroom. I didn't yet know Yves's size for certain so held them up to me trying to remember where his waist came in relation to my body.

'Don't think they suit you.'

I dropped the trousers on the rug. Unicorn had entered silently behind me and was watching me in the mirror, his eyes cold with loathing. He pinched the bridge of his prominent nose, struggling to contain his temper.

'Oh, I don't know: I think the dinner jacket will finish off my look nicely.' I held it up on its padded hanger for his inspection. 'White was never my colour before, but now . . . well, maybe I've changed my mind.'

He moved forward smoothly and plucked it from my hand and hung it back on the rail behind me. 'Just because you are paired with the Seer's latest toy, don't think that that means you are going to take over his operation when he retires.'

As if I would want a role in this petty kingdom. 'That's so not my ambition, Unicorn: that's yours.' I picked up the trousers and hung them over the back of a chair. 'I just want to be happy and live somewhere without fear.'

My movement made my jewellery swing forward, the glitter catching his eye. He lifted the diamond necklace and let it fall. 'There's no such place out there for you and me, Phee, not with our gifts. To the rest of the world we are freaks and you either run the circus or obey the orders of the ringmaster.'

'I think you're wrong,' I said quietly, refusing to back up a step as he would expect. 'There are Savants who live a normal life. It doesn't have to be like this.'

His lips curled into a sneer. 'Says who? Your precious soul-finder? Look at him: he's quick to sell out his family, isn't he? At least we here in the Community are loyal to each other. I spit on him and his so-called normal life if this is what it means.'

I couldn't find an argument against him—not without revealing my hope that despite everything Yves would find some way to avoid damaging the Savant Net. It was unsettling to find that Unicorn really did believe in the Community and was loyal to it in his own way. But maybe I could understand when I imagined myself in his shoes: it was the only family any of us had known; what else had he to cling on to? I was so used to being afraid of him that I forgot he was also a teenage victim of the Seer, only he was dealing with the situation very differently from me.

I rubbed my arms to smooth the goosebumps that had risen on the bare skin. 'Still, you can't deny that it looks like the Seer is taken with Yves. Might make my life here a bit better if he values my soulfinder.'

Unicorn poked his index finger in my chest to emphasize each word. 'You will not take my place, Phoenix. I've given too much of my life to our father to let that happen now. I've spent years earning my place; I won't let a skinny slut step in and take over.'

I pushed his hand away. 'Hardly my choice, is it? If the Seer wants Yves at his side, then that's his business.'

'The Seer doesn't trust him enough for that. And he knows exactly how soft you are—unreliable when it comes to the tough decisions. He'll still need me and Dragon for the real work.'

'Then you've nothing to fear from us.'

Unicorn closed the distance between us and gripped my shoulders, fingers pressing into flesh to leave little half-moons from his nails. 'Make sure I don't. If your soulfinder gets in my way, I'll send him to an early grave. He'll be about a hundred of course—but that should only take me minutes. He won't like it but I'll enjoy every one of them. I'll laugh as you kiss the wrinkled, toothless old man goodbye.'

'I hate you,' I whispered, looking down at the toecaps of his black boots planted right by the tips of my little shoes. I couldn't let him see the terror in my eyes at the thought of him turning his gift on Yves.

We heard footsteps in the corridor outside. He forced my

head to his shoulder, hand gripping my hair painfully, a mockery of a brotherly embrace. 'I'm glad you feel like that, Phee. Now we know exactly where we stand, don't we?'

I said nothing.

'Don't we?' His hand twisted, hair pulling at the roots.

'Yes,' I choked.

'Phee, are you OK?' Yves had entered to catch the tail end of our exchange.

Unicorn pushed me away with a warning look. 'Yeah, she's fine. We were just having some brother and sister quality time, weren't we, sis?'

I nodded, rubbing the back of my scalp.

'So I'll let you two get ready then. We leave in fifteen minutes—that's what I came to tell you, Phee.' He brushed past Yves with a smirk.

'What was that about?' Yves glared at Unicorn as he walked away.

'The usual. Threats, punishment, intimidation.' I rubbed my shoulders, attempting to regain control over my emotions. I couldn't let Unicorn reduce me to a quivering wreck; he'd done that too often in the past and I had to find strength to stand up to him. 'Just promise me you'll keep away from him. He's very powerful.'

'Sure. I don't foresee us spending Thanksgiving with your family, sweetheart.' Yves stripped off his top and took the shirt I had found for him off its hanger.

'If they *are* my family. I'm still hoping that my mum had another boyfriend.' I passed him the trousers. 'I'm not sure these will fit.'

'Turn your back unless you want an eyeful of my shorts,' he teased.

I smiled wanly and occupied myself rummaging in a box of ties to find him a white bow.

'Have I told you yet how pretty you look? I really like you in that colour.'

'Thanks.'

'The necklace is just right.' He was trying to cheer me up and it was working, like a little sunshine after Unicorn's frost.

I turned back to him, holding out the tie. 'Shame all the jewellery's stolen, huh?'

'Right. But perhaps I'll get you one made just like it when we get to the US.'

'Sky mentioned you were obscenely rich.'

He shrugged. 'Embarrassing, but true. At least we don't have to worry about how we're going to pay for your college fees. I'll float you a loan.'

I closed my eyes briefly as this tantalizing dream hovered between us. I hadn't challenged his assumption that I'd go with him as I simply did not believe it would happen. 'I could go to college? But I don't have any qualifications.'

He scooped up my hair and planted a kiss on the nape of my neck. 'First, you can get your high school certificate with some intensive tutoring from a very gifted teacher.' He pressed another on my bare shoulder blade. 'That'll be free as he'll only ask for kisses in repayment.' He brushed his lips over the other shoulder, smoothing away the hurt.

'I guess this tutor you have in mind is about fifty, over-weight, with a comb-over? Hmm, yeah that'll be interesting.'

'Ha-ha.' He punished me for my teasing by kissing my jaw. 'He is almost eighteen and left high school with A grades in all subjects and in the top percentile.'

'Sounds really geeky. Not sure I'd want to kiss him.'

'Not so. I know for a fact you love kissing this particular schol-ar. He prefers that term to "geek"—so much more attractive.'

'But he has to go to college himself. He can't fool around teaching someone who's never had any formal education.' I slid my arms around him, coming in close for a hug. Yves had the ability to expel the last shivery aftermath of an unpleasant encounter with my so-called relative.

'It will be absolutely his pleasure. And he'll find you a school too—near him—so while he's out studying *geo-whatsit*, as the subject henceforth shall be known, you can also have your own life.'

'Hmm, sounds like a dream come true.'

'Just sit back and watch me make it happen.'

But we had the little matter of the Savant Net he had betrayed and the meeting with the Seer's criminal collaborators to deal with. 'Yves . . .'

He put a finger to my lips. 'Shh. Not now. Trust, remember?'

He was asking more from me than anyone ever had. I did not put my faith in another person easily. But this was Yves. I nodded and swallowed, trying for a bright smile. 'OK, gorgeous, let's go wow the crowds with our debonair air.'

He chuckled. '*Debonair* air? Ugh.'

'Yeah well, I'm not at my most eloquent just at the moment.'

'You know, I was thinking you should major in literature at college. How does that sound?'

'Years to do nothing but read books? Sign me up.'

He hugged me to his side and took a breath. 'Hold that thought. Let's go face the music.'

I had expected to be marched straight into a business meeting or dinner much as I had last time I met the Seer's international contacts, but the information Yves had passed them had put them in the mood to celebrate and we were to start the evening at a private jazz club in Soho. The delegation from the Community consisted of the Seer, Dragon, and Unicorn as well as Yves and me. Kasia was not visible but that didn't mean she wasn't lodged somewhere close by to monitor proceedings. All the top Savants would have their own communications expert—they'd be stupid not to and none of them struck me as being foolish.

Our taxi left us on the pavement in Frith Street facing the black doors and lit interior of The Knowledge. Once an eighteenth-century house, the inside had been completely ripped out and excavated into the cellars to provide a cavernous space for the musicians' stage and audience seated around little tables. Only the row of sash windows on the first and second floor had been left to show its origins as a much older building. The crowds of fashionably dressed customers going in and out attested to the fact that it was one of London's hotspots—and it was about to become a lot hotter with a delegation of the Savant world's crime lords on the premises.

The Seer brushed an imaginary speck from his white lapel. 'This is in your honour,' he said with a fleeting grin at Yves.

'I'm impressed.' Yves scanned the busy street of thriving bars and venues. 'I've always wanted to go to The Knowledge—any jazz fan has it on the top of their list when visiting London. How did you know I love music?'

The Seer began walking. 'You'd be surprised what we've learned about you, Yves, over the years. You live quietly according to my American colleague, but not everything can be hidden from interested parties.' He paused on the threshold. 'But then you know that, because you've been watching us, haven't you?'

Yves squeezed my hand. 'I guess some have. Not me, though. I've been in high school for the last four years, studying hard. No time for spying.'

'And very clever you are too, by all accounts.' The Seer gestured impatiently for us to follow. 'Having plenty of brawn at my disposal, I need more brains in my operation; you'll be a welcome addition and I think you'll find there is far more scope for your talents when not fettered by the Savant Net's foolish taboos.'

Like morality and decency.

Behind his back, Unicorn and Dragon glared at me, but, really, it was hardly my fault if the Seer labelled them as nothing but useful muscle.

The plaintive strains of a saxophone drifted out from the auditorium. The Seer entered with us following like a cloak rippling at his heels. The room was full but the Savants had reserved the best spot, right in front of the stage. They were all there—each of the world's crime syndicates represented as they had been in the hotel. Every table had a little candle in a red holder; in the dim lighting, the flames looked to me like demon eyes crouching at the rim of each table to peer malevolently at us. I had a sudden desire to turn tail and run—run for my life. Yves increased his grip, sensing my hesitation.

'It'll be OK,' he whispered.

Our entry coincided with the last notes of 'Cry Me a River' and the audience broke into a scattering of applause. The Seer smiled, liking the coincidence that made it appear that they were greeting him. 'Jim' New York stood up and waved us over. I could see the other leading members of the group—Moscow, Beijing, Sydney and the rest—seated close at hand. This wasn't going to be a time for a private discussion; we were here on show, proof that the Seer had tamed him a Benedict.

Jim shook hands with the Seer then clapped Yves on the shoulder. 'Good to meet you. I'm New York. Read a lot about you, of course, but never thought to see this day.' He caught sight of me in Yves's shadow. 'But then if I had a little lady like that to protect, I'd rethink my life plan too.' He hooked my arm and pulled me into the circle of light by the table, acting as if we were old friends. 'You look lovely, Miss London. Take a seat.'

There were only four chairs at the table, leaving Unicorn and Dragon to scramble for places as near as they could. A waiter arrived with a bottle of champagne and proceeded to pour us all a glass. While pretending to join in the toast, I left mine untouched. Yves kept my hand in his, hidden below the table top, providing much needed comfort as he chatted easily with Jim about the baseball season. Not required for anything but decoration, I examined the room we were in, spying out exit routes should we have to make a rapid departure. Only when I scoped out the nearest emergency door with its green-lit sign of a running man did I turn my attention to the musicians. My fingers gripped Yves's convulsively. The saxophone player was a small blonde girl. The heavy eye make-up, black-rimmed glasses and the vampire-red lipstick did not hide her identity from one who had spent the last few days sharing her bedroom. Sky. Hope mixed with horror as I searched for Zed, guessing he would not have let his soulfinder walk into this situation alone. I finally identified him as the heavily bearded drummer in the flowery shirt and, yes, socks and sandals. I bit my tongue, repressing the absurd desire to laugh at his fashion sacrifice for our cause.

But what did this all mean? If they were here, then so were the other Benedicts. And they either had to know that Yves had betrayed them, or he had been playing false all along and gone against the Seer. I shut my eyes, head spinning. If that turned out to be the case, then I would be forced to hurt someone he loved. I just couldn't . . . wouldn't . . . unless . . . I realized that the Seer's command had not forbidden me to turn his order on myself. Yves loved me—he'd said so only hours ago. I would do something to myself before I touched one of his family.

'All right, my dear?' The Seer feigned concern when he saw my pained expression but I could tell I was putting him on the alert by my response. I tried to master my reactions. I didn't know for certain what had brought the Benedicts here. Yves had sworn he wouldn't trip any of the triggers the Seer had set in my mind. They could have other sources of information that I didn't know about. No need to go overboard on the strength of suspicion alone.

'Um . . . yes, thank you. I was just thinking about the song. It always reminds me of my mother's death.'

Overhearing my remark, Jim shook his head. 'Oh, we can't have that—no sad thoughts tonight. Let's ask them to play something you like. What'll it be?'

I thought quickly, dredging through the songs I knew to find a suitable one. 'How about "I Put a Spell on You"?' I'd heard it as background music in a café recently and the title had stuck as bizarrely appropriate to Savant powers.

Jim clicked his fingers and ordered the waiter to pass on his request. The musicians paused in their preparations for their next number and quickly conferred. Another message was sent backstage while the pianist—I didn't recognize him—tinkled away with a medley of songs. From behind a curtain at the rear, a shapely older woman in a tight red dress and silk turban stepped up to the microphone to sing. I now wished I'd chosen something without words because it took me only a second to realize that Yves's mum, Karla, had been thrust into the lime-light by my selection. She was almost unrecognizable, thanks to tinted glasses and heavy diva costume jewellery. And, boy, could she sing! No one would suspect her of being planted there by Victor as she sounded like a professional—her voice deep and sultry.

I wasn't sure if Yves had even realized he was surrounded by his family as his attention appeared to be fixed on our hosts.

Surely he had to recognize his own mother's voice? But if he did, he gave no sign.

'Um . . . Yves . . .' I whispered. I wanted him to pay attention to me so I could let my expression do the talking when I didn't dare risk the words.

He gave me a brash smile, so different from his usual open expression. 'Not now, honey.'

That was no answer. I still didn't know if he knew. I subsided and listened in on their conversation for a few minutes. Jim was trying to lure Yves to his organization, talking in veiled terms about the drug-running operation he had established with other members of the loose confederacy of criminal-minded Savants. I could sense the Seer getting increasingly hot under the collar as he was sidelined.

'London is a big market,' he interrupted suddenly. 'I have plans for Yves to help establish a route into the capital. His computer expertise will be invaluable in getting around Customs and Excise checks.'

Jim waved a dismissive hand. 'Those fools? We've got talented carriers who can persuade their way past anyone with their powers.'

'But how much more reliable to have a software system that clears any cargo under our name? If it comes up as already checked then you've no need of such tools.' The Seer sipped his champagne and wrinkled his nose. 'Bit dry for my taste.' He signalled for another bottle to be brought to the table, specifying another vintage—a none-too-subtle sign that he was taking back command of our little party. 'What do you think, Yves?'

Yves looked as if he would very much prefer not to be put on the spot. 'Both ideas have merit,' he replied diplomatically. 'You can't always rely on technology though. A government might take it into their head to do a spot check. And there are always the sniffer dogs to catch out a carrier.'

Jim gave a dark chuckle. 'Damned dogs. Haven't yet found someone who can persuade them to sniff the other way—mind powers only work on humans.'

The Seer's eyes slid to me. 'What about you, Phoenix: can you control animals?' He turned back to Jim. 'My girl here does this very clever thing where she can stop your brain for a few seconds.'

Jim raised his glass to me.

'No reason why it shouldn't work on dogs. What do you think?'

'Er . . . I've never tried.' I felt sickened—bad enough being a thief but now the Seer was plotting to use me as some kind of drugs mule. 'I guess it will need some more thought. Excuse me. I'm just going to freshen up.' If Yves wasn't going to let me warn him, I would see if I could find out what was happening so I was prepared for whatever came next. He kept hold of my hand, reluctant to let me go, but I tugged free. 'Won't be long.'

I headed for the toilets, aware that Unicorn had got up from his table and was tailing me. I kept my eyes peeled for other Benedicts but, if they were undercover, I didn't spot them. Giving Unicorn a sour smile, I entered the Ladies and stood gazing into the mirror for a full five minutes, hoping that either Sky or Karla would take the hint and come to let me in on what they were doing there. I also wanted a chance to plead Yves's case—that was if he had betrayed them for my sake—and to find out what their plan was, because surely they had one, and they had had no opportunity to share it with us as we had been monitored ever since Yves joined the Community. With so many different parties in the dark about what the other side had in mind, we were liable to end up with one hell of a mess.

But no one came in.

Chapter 20

Unicorn was still on watch when I emerged, patting my hair in place as if I had spent the time checking out my appearance, as he would expect from classic girl behaviour. With him standing, arms folded, in front of the toilets, it was no wonder I had been alone. I swallowed the remark I longed to make about creeps haunting the Ladies and walked swiftly back to my table. I noticed that Karla had retired, leaving the band playing some tunes I didn't recognize, Sky back on sax, eyes locked on the drummer as she wove with the beat. I didn't know how they could keep the music so loose and easy when everything was heading for disaster.

'OK?' Yves murmured.

'Hmm.' I was wound way too tight. No! I wanted to shout: don't you know your family is in the club and we are surrounded by a bunch of merciless killers out to make a fast buck from other people's misery? 'Everything's lovely, thank you.'

Yves stroked my arm and smiled reassuringly.

His gesture was premature. Before I knew it, the crisis was upon us. A man at the next table checked his mobile then came to Jim's side. He bent over and whispered in his ear.

New York's eyebrows shot up. 'You're sure?'

The man nodded and showed him a text.

Yves tapped the back of my wrist, a warning, but of what, I had no idea. Be ready, he seemed to be saying.

Jim turned to Yves. 'Well, Benedict, we seem to be having a little difficulty with that information you gave us.'

Yves swirled the champagne in his glass. 'What kind of problem? If you did what I said, then there should be no issue.'

'And what did you say?' Jim reached inside his jacket—for a terrible moment I thought he had gone for a gun, but instead he pulled out a BlackBerry.

'I told you not to copy it from my original.'

'Too late for that: we've all been given the files. And somehow, since I last looked, some of the names have changed.'

Yves nodded as if this was all to be expected.

'Your information now suggests that Donald Duck and Mickey Mouse are leading members of the Savant Net.' Jim's tone was far from amused. 'And somehow their names have replaced those of the genuine contacts I checked off this afternoon.'

Yves shrugged. 'Did you print off the list?'

Jim tugged his bow tie loose, anger making his neck bulge with tension. 'No, of course not. But you know that, don't you? You'd put a protection on the file so we couldn't do anything but read it on screen.'

Yves pushed his glass aside. 'I can change that for you, no problem. Just a question of adjusting the permissions.'

All around us I was aware that other Savants were receiving whispered messages or texts.

'Tolstoy! Rasputin!' spluttered Mr Moscow, throwing his smart phone on the table. His heavies gathered at his shoulder, hands in deep pockets or feeling under the side of their jackets for their weapons. 'This is an insult!'

'Very funny: Crocodile Dundee and Kylie Minogue!' Mr Sydney shoved his chair back and grabbed Yves by the scruff of the neck. 'What's your game, mate?'

Heart in my throat, I saw that the commotion at the front of the club was attracting the attention of other patrons, and a number of the wise ones got up to leave. Waiters moved into position, poised to break up an altercation—but they didn't look like any bar staff I'd ever seen before, too watchful and unsurprised by the crisis down front. Without seeing any sign of Yves's older brother, I was beginning to suspect that we were surrounded by Victor's police friends. Even the band had taken note of the drama, grinding to a halt as the Savants clustered around our table.

Yves was playing it cool. 'It's no game,' he spoke loudly in the silence. 'I warned you not to copy from the memory stick. As soon as it is moved off my stick, the self-destruct begins.' Yves shook off Sydney's hand, backing away from the table so that I was behind him. 'Look, you don't expect me to leave sensitive information lying around begging to be posted on Wikileaks, do you? I thought you'd have better security protocols than that.' He sounded disdainful of their technical know-how. 'The information, if copied from my original, gradually corrupts—in a culturally sensitive manner, of course. I like the recipient to realize it's happening. I'm not trying to hide what I've done.'

Jim yanked Yves back into his seat. 'So, after this amusing display of your technical wizardry, you can send us the information again? Without the time-corruption?'

'Sure. I'll just need five minutes with a decent computer.' Yves looked innocently round as if expecting one to appear in front of him in the middle of the night club.

But the Seer was not pleased to have his protégé spring this on them all in public with no warning. He wasn't buying the line Yves was trying to sell. 'Phoenix, go and join your brothers.'

'What? Why?' I hated having the spotlight put on me, feeling the interest of the Savants swing in my direction.

Yves showed the first signs of failing confidence. 'She stays here.'

'She goes.' The Seer gestured to Dragon to take me out of the centre of the gathering. 'I think you will concentrate better knowing she is being looked after by her family.' He gave Yves a humourless smile. 'I am beginning to wonder, Mr Benedict, if you have any more surprises in store for us. Remember, Phoenix has something she must do if you have betrayed us, so think carefully before you reply.'

'I've done nothing. I told you not to copy the information. Your own actions caused this.'

'But you must have realized that we could only use your data if we could distribute it to interested parties.'

'But you never asked me to enable that function, did you?'

Oh my God, that was it! My uncertainty lifted as swiftly as a helium balloon. Yves had got round his loyalty to his family and his promise to me by allowing others to make the decision that caused the corruption. Literally, they had caused their own betrayal. My relief was overwhelming.

Sensing the unfavourable direction of the conversation, Dragon bent my arm up behind my back, stopping me from making any rash move but keeping us both within earshot. I glanced desperately to see what Victor's team were doing, but they were maintaining their distance. I wondered if they had the whole place bugged; perhaps they were hoping that the Savants would incriminate themselves further? New York had already discussed drug shipments: wasn't that enough? Or maybe they were waiting for Yves to give them some kind of signal. Come on, Victor, I urged silently, end this before Yves gets hurt!

Jim studied Yves, his expression perplexed. 'Where exactly do your loyalties lie, Mr Benedict?'

The Seer gestured to Unicorn to approach. 'I think that much is apparent—with his soulfinder.'

Jim circled Yves's neck with his hands, pinning him back in his seat. 'But the thing I don't know is what else he put on that memory stick. If he planted one virus, I'm wondering if there are more that we've spread into our own systems. We were stupid not to consider this in our gold-rush moment for the information.'

'I agree. I'm afraid we all quite lost our heads.' The Seer's remorseful tone was chilling. 'Unicorn, remind Mr Benedict here of what he stands to lose if he double-crosses us.'

Unicorn removed one leather glove and flexed his fingers. 'How much shall I take?'

'A year or two should do it.'

Yves struggled against Jim's stranglehold. 'What are you doing?'

I shoved against Dragon. 'Don't you dare touch him!'

The Seer turned his pale blue eyes on me. 'It's not him that he cares about, my dear. I wonder, if you age a soulfinder, does that break the link with their counterpart? After all, the legend claims you are linked by birth.'

'No! Please!' I screamed, fighting hard against Dragon's grip as Unicorn swung towards me. Events were spinning out of control and had turned into a nightmare: he looked so eager to get started on his latest task—that's how much he must hate me. 'Please, don't!'

Shouting for Victor, Yves shoved Jim's hands away and tried to break through the crowd to reach me, but the other Savants held him back. Desperate, I grabbed for Unicorn's mental pattern, managing to freeze him for a couple of seconds, but he knew my power well and was fighting it even before I put it in place. Dragon succumbed for only an instant before shrugging off my attack.

'Stupid—now you've got us angry!' he growled, dragging me towards Unicorn. 'A couple of years won't be enough.'

Just then, the table beside us burst into flame; the red candles erupted like miniature volcanoes. Dragon swore and lurched away, almost yanking my arm out of its socket. A fire alarm shrieked and the sprinklers sprang into action. People ran towards us, shouting—from the sudden appearance of weaponry, waiters and patrons alike were revealed as law-enforcement agents. Missiles whistled overhead, thrown in response by the Savants' bodyguards.

Dragon dived beneath a table, taking me with him.

'Police! Police!' Shouts from all directions. 'Put down your weapons. Raise your hands where we can see them.'

'Phee!' Yves bellowed above the noise. 'Where are you?'

'Yves!' I screamed.

Dragon shoved a hand over my mouth. Unicorn joined us, slithering along on his belly.

Yves!

'We take her?' asked Dragon curtly.

Through the forest of legs, we could all see the white figure of the Seer and the other Savants surrounded by armed officers. No one was touching them; they must have been briefed about this group's powers, but the policemen were not moving forward. The counter-attack had stopped; three chairs and several glasses hovered above our heads, spinning slowly like rocks in an asteroid field. Why weren't the Savants fighting back? In the midst of the officers, Mr Benedict stood holding hands with his wife, eyes closed as they concentrated, oddly still as around them confusion reigned. Dipping into their minds, I could see the couple were holding some kind of protective wall to hem in the group, holding the missiles back. One man, Sydney I think, crumpled—a dart in his neck. A chair fell to the floor at the same moment, released from his mind. The police were using tranquillizer guns—brilliant! I felt a flicker of hope.

'Time to go.' Unicorn replaced his glove. 'I think we need something more obvious than my ageing power to get their cooperation. I don't want to pass out and find myself in a high-security prison.'

Dragon pulled a gun from a holster under his jacket and shoved it under my chin.

Yves! I called frantically.

Where are you?

Our temporary shelter of the table lifted off the ground and flipped towards the stage. Out of the corner of my eye, I could see Sky, crouched behind the piano, directing it with her finger like an orchestra conductor. Positioned to protect her back, Zed lobbed a champagne bottle telepathically towards Dragon, making it swerve to come up on his blind side, but Unicorn saw it in time to pull his brother out of its path. Dragon blasted it with a flick of his wrist, contents spraying the officers hunkered down behind the bar. He wasted no time dragging me towards the exit.

'Put down your guns!' ordered the officer in charge, spotting the three of us outside the police cordon.

Unicorn kicked open the emergency exit. 'If you follow, she dies.'

Dragon pushed the officers guarding the back door out of our path with a wave of power. They smashed into the wall and slid down like puppets with their strings cut.

Stall them! Yves begged frantically. I could feel him trying to get through the ring of policemen but they had orders to hold everyone in position and not touch them—no exceptions.

I tried—it doesn't work on them. They break it too quickly.

Then we were in an ugly alleyway at the back of the club—nothing but wheelie bins and drifts of fast food wrappers. The police—if they were there—were keeping out of sight.

'Car,' Dragon said tersely.

'Yeah, give her to me. You get one.' Taking over possession of the handgun, Unicorn pressed his handgun to my temple as Dragon passed me over. He then strode out on to the street, eyes on a black BMW that had just set down its passengers outside a restaurant. As the driver accelerated away, Dragon stepped out and held up his hands. It was as if the car hit an invisible brick wall. I could see the tension in Dragon's face as he stopped the powerful engine in its tracks. He then pointed a finger at the chauffeur.

'Out!'

The driver did not need to be asked twice. He scrambled out, leaving the door swinging.

Dragon opened the rear so I could be bundled in. Unicorn practically fell on top of me, gun trapped between us, so for a gut-wrenching moment I thought it might go off accidentally.

'There they are! The car!' I could hear voices—Victor's among them.

'Go!' snapped Unicorn.

Now behind the wheel, Dragon put his foot down and pulled away with a screech of tyres. Turning the corner, he gave a crow of triumph.

'That was fricking easy!' he laughed.

Unicorn sat up, safe in the knowledge that no one was going to shoot while I was in the car. 'Yeah, sweet. We made a good team back there.'

Dragon took a sharp left through a red light, causing a double-decker to plough into railings. He hooted with glee. 'Where to?'

'Back to the Community.' Unicorn had ripped strips from the hem of my chiffon overskirt and was busy tying my hands and ankles. 'I say we take what we need, tell the others to split and make a new rendezvous in four days' time—once the dust has settled.'

The car lurched. 'What? We're taking over?'

Unicorn rubbed his temples. 'Of course not. We remain loyal. We have to—I'm sure we have to. But while the Seer is away, he'd want his stuff looked after.'

Dragon was quick to catch on. 'Yeah, and if he doesn't get free for a long time then at least he knows we are honouring his wishes, living as he lived, waiting to welcome him back a hero.'

'Yeah, something like that.'

'Poor old Dad.' Dragon began to snicker—his amusement spreading to his brother. 'He won't like jail. No fancy ladies to keep him happy.'

'They'll have to put him in a cell on his own—won't have one big enough otherwise.'

'Get this, though: I wouldn't put it past him to *persuade* his way out in no time. We had better send him a lawyer—show our good intentions.' Dragon's suggestion sobered them both up.

'You're right—he must see that we did all that we could—and believe it too.'

Sirens echoed behind us. Dragon glanced in the mirror and deliberately took a turning that led to the river, away from our true destination. Heading over Tower Bridge, he then tried to lose the tail in the backstreets of Bermondsey.

Where are you? Yves was desperate.

South of the river. Heading back to the Community eventually. But you can't tell the others where that is, remember? I'd prefer to be held hostage than lose my link to my soulfinder.

Phee . . .

Promise!

Yes, OK. I'll think of something else. Stay alive.

'I think we need to swap cars.' Dragon slowed outside a bikers' pub, seeing two leather-clad heavies lounging on their saddles.

241

'Can you take them out?' Unicorn asked, tying a third piece of chiffon around my mouth as a gag.

'No need. Let's see if they'll do swapsies.' He snickered at his childish language as he pulled up abruptly and leapt out. 'Hey, guys, want a new BMW? It's hot but it smokes on the road.'

The bikers looked at each other, unable to believe their ears.

'Just need to use your bikes for the night.'

Unicorn pulled me out of the car, gun hidden by my skirt.

'What's wrong with her?' the bigger of the two men asked. He had to realize I was hardly there by choice.

Unicorn sighed. 'Bikers with a conscience—who would've thought?' He dug the barrel into my ribs. 'Your choice, Phee: either freeze them or we kill them.'

I nodded, signalling I understood. I quickly reached for the two men's minds and stopped time for them. Dragon shoved them off their seats and swung on the nearest bike. A helicopter circled overhead, spotlight dancing over the rooftops.

'Hurry, they're on to the car.' Dragon kicked his bike into life.

'What do we do with her?' Unicorn held me up by a punishing grip on my upper arm.

'Either dispose of her or keep her as a bargaining chip.'

Thinking quickly, Unicorn took his decision. 'She's probably already told them where we're going, so I suppose she might still be useful as a hostage till we get our stuff from the Community.' He cut the ties on my ankles, pulled my bound arms over his neck so I was draped on his back, then settled us both on the bike. He revved the engine. 'Let's go.'

The bikes surged away, leaving the two former owners sprawled by the open doors of the BMW.

Chapter 21

There was no sign of pursuit when we arrived back at the estate. Everything seemed weirdly normal as news had not yet filtered back that the Seer had been caught. Dragon banged a hammer against the rusting climbing frame in the playground—our rudimentary alarm system.

'Everyone get out!' he shouted, as heads popped out of doors all over the complex. 'Check the usual place for your instructions in three days' time.' This meant that a small ad would be placed in the window of a newsagent's on the Mile End Road. A postcard advertising cleaning services, listing a non-functioning mobile number and an address, was the means by which we knew where we were supposed to head next after evacuating an old hide-out.

Community members were well trained. I could hear doors banging throughout the building as they picked up their already-packed bags and headed for the exits, leaving the usually locked gates yawning open. Tony peered out of his basement door and ducked back in quickly before my brothers noticed. Then I realized I could smell smoke.

'The building's on fire.' Dragon scanned the rooftops. 'Up

there.' He pointed to the ridge.

Unicorn unlooped my arms from around his neck and dropped me to my feet. I crouched down, shoulders screaming after the last twenty minutes of abuse as we had raced through the backstreets of the City. I was freezing even though it was a warm summer night. Perhaps they would leave me here. That would be nice.

But no luck. My brothers must have been discussing what next telepathically, for I was thrown over Dragon's shoulder as they raced upstairs.

'Do you think anyone else would have got to the stuff first?' Dragon panted.

'Nah. They wouldn't dare.' Unicorn pushed past a group of the Seer's women who were descending with a rapid click-click of heels.

'What's going on?' one asked, grabbing his sleeve. 'There's a fire up there. Can't you do something?'

He ripped free. 'Later. Just get out.' His tone told them not to press for more information and they obediently made way for us and then carried on down the stairs. I could see a few concerned looks cast at me as I dangled over Dragon's back, but no one was going to ask. We didn't do that kind of thing in the Community.

Reaching the fifth floor, Unicorn drew out a bunch of keys. 'What do you reckon: just the small stuff?'

Dumping me down like an unwanted suitcase, Dragon leant against the wall to regain his breath. 'Yeah, no time to take the rest. The jewellery and the money should be enough to set up a new operation somewhere.'

Phee, watch out! I'm smoking them out. Yves can't have been able to see that I was tied up and could do nothing about his warning.

I'm trapped. Top floor.

The Seer's apartment erupted in a sudden flare. The rooftop fire had spread down a level.

'What the—!' Dragon yelled.

'It's her man—he's here.' Unicorn kicked open the door, releasing a belch of black fumes. 'He's burning the place out from the top down.'

Tell them not to go in. It's wild fire—fast and hungry.

I used my bound hands to rip the gag free. 'You mustn't enter,' I shouted, clawing the back of Dragon's jacket as he prepared to make a mad dash for the strong box. 'It's not a normal blaze—it's already out of control.'

Dragon pushed me away. 'Your soulfinder did this, didn't he? He's after the money.'

'And he's not getting it.' Unicorn took off his shirt, made a mask of the material and passed it to his brother.

Throwing the cloth over his face, Dragon didn't wait—he launched into the burning room, disappearing into the smoke.

'You're both mad! Let's get out of here while we still can!' I tried to move past Unicorn to get to the stairs before the fire did.

'You're not going anywhere.' Unicorn drew his gun. 'Your soulfinder's messed up everything for us. He's not getting you too.'

Dragon staggered back out carrying the strong box from the storeroom, hands red with burns. 'Kill the bitch,' he said succinctly.

I took the only path left to me, running towards my old room at the far end of the walkway. A gun went off, a bullet hole appearing on the wall by my head. A cloud of smoke billowed between us, partially hiding me from sight. Another shot and I felt my leg give out from under me. White pain. A spear of lightning in my leg.

'She's down. Let's go,' Dragon said, coughing hard.

I came to a halt face-down on the concrete, bound hands caught awkwardly beneath me. I'd taken a bullet in my thigh. Unicorn was right. I wasn't going anywhere.

I must have passed out momentarily. Calloused hands were slapping my cheek.

'Phee, you need to wake up.' It wasn't Yves as I'd hoped but Tony who crouched over me, his newly whitened hair flopping over his forehead. We were lying in a little clear space, the smoke seeming to curl away from us as if directed to leave us alone.

'Tony?'

'Yes, *dashur*. We are in big trouble. Stairwell is on fire.'

'What are you doing up here?'

'Saw them bring you up and thought I'd follow.' He un-knotted the binding on my wrists and helped me sit up. He used the same cloth to tie around my wound, though it was soon splotched red. I was losing a lot of blood. The pain lanced through me like glass spikes hammered into my flesh.

Phee, where are you? Yves was still looking for me.

Still on the top floor.

He swore. *I didn't know. You went silent.*

I passed out. I'm well and truly trapped, Yves. Tony's with me.

Your brothers were supposed to run out when the fire started, not run into the building!

That would be the reaction of normal people. They aren't. What was that your brother said about your plans not taking other minds into account?

While I was talking to Yves, Tony had been looking for an escape route.

'There's a way down—the drainpipe.' He pointed over the edge of the balcony. 'Looks solid.'

246

'Go for it.' I didn't bother to move. No way was I going to be able to climb to the ground with a bullet in my leg.

Tony hovered. 'You should've left when I told you, Phee.'

'Yeah, maybe I should've. But I wouldn't've met my soul-finder, would I?'

'I hope he was worth it.' He patted my shoulder awkwardly, then tugged off my necklace and pocketed it. 'I'm sorry, *dashur*.'

'So am I.'

He swung on to the parapet. 'Perhaps the firemen will come soon.'

Tears pooled in my eyes. 'Perhaps.' *Tony's coming down*, I told Yves. *Help him if you can.*

The wiry Albanian thief had compensated for his injuries by developing strength in his good side, and it was this that came to his aid now. Clinging on one-handed like a monkey, he slung his belt round the pipe and slid out of sight. I had to see that he got there safely. Pulling myself up to the wall, I watched his head disappear.

Phee, down here! Yves had spotted me. I found him standing in the centre of the playground, a lonely figure in front of the burning housing estate. *You next.*

He was expecting me to follow Tony.

I can't. I'm wounded. Got shot in the leg. The limb in question was shaking. I leant heavily against the wall wondering vaguely what would get me first—blood loss or smoke. My lack of concern told me that I was lightheaded. The idea of passing out again seemed quite welcome.

Then I'm coming up for you.

No way. *Is Tony down?*

Yves looked towards the foot of the building. *Yes. He's running. Do you want me to stop him?*

No, let him go. And don't you even think of coming up. You couldn't bring me out that way and we'd only both die.

But I started the fire—this is my fault! He was tearing himself up about something he couldn't now help. It would have been a good plan if it had worked, making us all flee the building.

It's not your fault my brothers are psychos.

I can't stand here and just watch! There has to be something I can do.

And then, suddenly, he wasn't alone: his family arrived, sprinting into the playground through the open gate that led on to the street. I felt a huge wave of relief. At least they'd stop him doing something stupid. They gathered around him, burying him under their hugs. I sank against the parapet, pleased that the last thing I would see would be Yves surrounded by those that loved him.

You are not to give up, Phee! Yves ordered me. *We're getting you down from there.*

I love you.

No sappy stuff. That was Xav, joining our conversation. *We need you to get up onto the edge.*

We're going to float you down, Phoenix. Mr Benedict's voice was reassuring.

I wiped my eyes. My vision was beginning to blur. I could see the Benedicts and Sky surrounding Yves, arms on each other's shoulders.

Wake up, Phee, we have a plan. Sky's light tone brushed my mind. *Zed's going to channel everyone's telekinetic power. We should have enough to get you down from there.*

Get up on the parapet, love. You'll have to help us help you. Yves sounded confident again.

How am I going to help you?

You are going to jump.

Ha.

You are.

Have you done this before?

Yeah, with fruit. That was Xav.

And why am I not reassured?

Get on the ledge, Phoenix. That was Victor, flexing his persuasive powers.

Tell your brother to cut it out. I'd had enough of men messing with my mind. *I'll do this of my own free will or not at all.*

The wail of the fire engines brought me new hope. Perhaps I would wait for a ladder?

Phee, you don't have time. I know fire—this one's almost onto you. I'm keeping the smoke back but even I can't stop flames once I let them loose. Yves was running short of patience with me; if I didn't act, he'd do something stupid like try climbing up to fetch me himself.

OK, OK. I gritted my teeth and pulled myself up on to the ledge. A shaft of pain shot through my body. Black dots whirled across my vision—faintness or specks of ash, I couldn't tell which.

We'll catch you, honey, whispered Karla, her hands to her mouth to stop a scream.

Oh God, oh God: was I really going to launch myself off the edge and trust them to do their bit? I didn't doubt they would try, but what if they failed?

I dangled my legs over the edge, ignoring the teeth-grinding agony. *About those fruit, Xav: do you always catch them?*

Every time, he promised, totally serious for once.

I pushed off.

And fell rapidly towards the ground.

Yves!

Then my descent changed direction. I could feel myself being propelled away from the building, as if a J-shaped slide had appeared under me. But surely I was going too fast?

Hold on! Yves warned.

To what? I screamed.

I shot forward and into his arms. He took a tumble, breaking my fall with me landing on top of him.

'To me,' he said, out of breath.

I could hear Xav laughing. 'It worked! It actually worked! I don't believe it!'

'I'm not letting go of you,' I vowed, before passing out for a second time.

Chapter 22

I woke up in a hospital bed believing, in a confused fashion, that I had a watermelon for a leg—a throbbing, swollen one.

'I feel terrible,' I murmured to no one in particular.

'You don't look terrible; you look wonderful.'

I cracked open my eyelids to find Yves sitting close by the bedside, his hand wrapped around mine where it rested on the cover. Sunlight poured in through the window behind him, making the white sheets on the bed glow. I could hear the growl of traffic outside, voices in the corridor beyond, but my room was peaceful. Multicoloured balloons floated above every table and ledge, the Benedicts' celebration of my survival determinedly invading the clinical hospital room.

'Why do I not believe you?'

'You should because it's true. You're alive and my stupid fire didn't get you so to me that's wonderful.'

'You're an easy guy to please.' I ran my tongue over my dry lips. He reached for a cup with a straw and held it so I could sip. I made a further examination of my body and realized I had a drip in the back of my left hand and a thick bandage around my right thigh. 'The bullet?'

'Out. You should make a good recovery. Xav's promised to help reduce the scarring but it'll always be there, I'm afraid.' He scowled at the tiled floor. 'I'm sorry about the fire, Phee. That's the second time I've done that to you.' Darling Yves: he appeared genuinely worried that I would hold him to blame.

'Stop it. You can't feel guilty for doing what you thought would work. My brothers are mental—you can't predict how they react to stuff like that.'

He squeezed my hand. 'I . . . er . . . have some bad news about them.'

My heart fluttered. 'What kind of bad news?'

'We don't think they got out. The fire services found two bodies on the stairs.'

'I . . . see.'

'They'd like to test your DNA because . . . well, they weren't easy to recognize once the blaze was put out. And, as their closest relative who is cooperating with the authorities, Victor wondered if . . . ?'

'Of course.' I swallowed, not sure what I felt. They'd left me for dead but I couldn't rejoice that they'd fallen victim to the fire. No one deserved to die that way. 'Tell him I will.' I didn't want to think about this and there was so much I didn't know. 'You had better fill me in on the rest.'

Yves released my hand and brushed his fingertips over my cheek. 'We've got the ringleaders locked up. Most of them are awaiting deportation as their crimes were committed abroad, but the Seer is being charged with multiple counts of theft and murder.'

I closed my eyes. 'That's good. But how . . . ?'

'That program I put in the memory stick? It also carried a little extra to ferry out key files to interested parties. As soon as they were stupid enough to copy it over to their machines— against my express instructions, remember—my digital scout went looking for selected terms. Law enforcement agencies around the globe suddenly began receiving the most incriminating information on illegal shipments and many other things. The Seer had boasted online about the disappearance of one Mitch Bannister; did you know him?'

I remembered Tony telling me about Mitch being ordered to kill himself. 'Yes. He's buried in Epping Forest, I think.'

'That's only one body that they'll be busy exhuming; there are others over the years. And we now know the Seer's real name. Want to know what it is?'

I nodded.

'Kevin Smith. How boring can you get? No wonder he invented a new name for himself.'

It helped a little to know the Seer was an ordinary person along with the rest of us, like checking under the bed to see that the monster really wasn't there. But the traces of his domination still remained in the traps he'd set for us in my head. 'And how did your family find us both times—at the club and at the Community?'

'I didn't tell them, you needn't worry about that. Do you remember I mentioned that I was counting on them to do their part?'

'Yes.'

'As I hoped, Zed foresaw us at the club—or you, at any rate. He can't see me usually as the family tie gets in the way of his future sense. Fortunately, they assumed I'd be with you. They didn't know why we were there but it was enough for Victor to set up the operation. The American and British law-enforcement agencies had been watching the group for some time, so it was only a matter of putting into action what they had been planning, with the tranquillizers and everything. The biggest problem was finding musicians at such short notice— we couldn't risk exposing real artists to that kind of volatile situation—which was why my family and a few friends stepped into the breach.'

'I thought they were amazing. No one looked at them twice—they played so professionally. Your mum and Sky—just wow!'

He smiled. 'Yeah, they were good, weren't they? Dad and Zed were having conniptions letting them stand on the front line, of course, but it worked out OK.'

'Did your family know you hadn't betrayed them?'

Yves shrugged. 'They never would've doubted me.'

'But I did.' That thought was not nice to acknowledge.

'Come on, Phee: give yourself a break. You threw yourself off that ledge for me. I think we can say you trust me when it counts.' Yves kicked back in his chair and put his feet up on the end of the bed. 'I kept you in the dark on purpose so you're not to blame. I didn't want the Seer worming the secret out of you.'

I wasn't completely innocent myself: I still hadn't told him about my attempt to steal the stick from him on the London Eye. Even so, I felt stupid not guessing what he was up to, but that was something I could fret about later: there were still things I had to know. 'And the flats—how did your family arrive in time if you didn't tell them where to go?'

'The files did that job for me. When I got your message, I'd jumped in the first taxi I could find, leaving the others high and dry. Victor knew where the Seer had been working recently—he made an educated guess that your brothers would come back for their stash. He's got good instincts when it comes to bad guys.'

I fell silent, thinking over what he had told me. None of the Seer's red lines had been crossed; I didn't have to do anything to punish us. We'd been incredibly lucky; we'd skimmed past the Seer's mind-traps like skiers in an Olympic downhill slalom, clipping but not taking out any of the flags.

'Tired?' Yves reached out to smooth my hair away from my face.

'No, just . . . just finding it hard to believe it's all over. It is, isn't it?'

'Almost.' His eyes twinkled mischievously. 'I've got a present for you—and a question, but I think we should wait until you're feeling stronger.'

I groaned. 'You can't do that—tempt me with a present then snatch it away.'

He laughed, a wonderful bubble of sound. 'You're right. Here it is then.' He dropped it on my stomach: a little red booklet.

I flipped to the back page. 'My passport!'

'You are now official.'

'Where did you get the photo?' It was me as I had looked at the club, including the daisy necklace.

'That club was bristling with cameras. I just took a screen capture of you looking sombre, a bit of Photoshop magic and there you are. The Brits were more than happy to rush it through for us as we are pretty much their favourite people right now.'

I glanced out of the window. For him to have been able to do all this, I must have been out for longer than I thought. 'What day is it?'

'You slept through most of yesterday—in surgery and then post-op. You surfaced a couple of times but I doubt you'll remember.'

So long? My brothers had been dead for almost two days and the ashes of the fire would be cool. Had everyone else got out? I knew the answer without asking. Yes, Yves would have confessed if there had been more casualties. Only those stupid enough to head into the burning block had been caught. But with no Seer and no Dragon and Unicorn, the Community was finished, the members scattered. We'd never regroup now—that's if the justice system could keep hold of someone as manipulative as the Seer. That was a problem for tomorrow; for the moment, the others were free. Tony had probably already hocked the necklace and begun his new life somewhere away from the authorities. I too was facing a fresh beginning.

'And what was the question you had for me?'

Yves leant over my pillow and kissed me softly. 'Now that really does have to wait. You are under doctor's orders to rest and I have to tell everyone that you're awake and not too mad at us for that stunt we pulled on you.'

'Not mad, but I am convinced you're all crazy.'

'You might well be right.'

I didn't want him to leave just yet. 'But I'll rest easier if you ask me your question now. I hate waiting.'

'OK, but remember you wanted this.' Then, to my utter shock, he went down on one knee, right there by the bedside. 'Marry me, Phee.'

'What!'

'I know it's far sooner than either of us planned to get hitched, but it'll make getting you into the States so much easier if you go as my wife.'

I clutched my chest, heart still pounding. 'Crumbs, you know how to surprise a girl.' I gave a choking laugh. My brain was finally catching up with what he had just said. 'You want me to marry you so I can get a visa?'

He shot me an offended look. 'No! That's a side benefit that kind of brought it all forward. I want you to marry me because I love you—just that.'

'But we're only going to be eighteen in a couple of weeks. How can we possibly be ready to marry?'

'You don't want to marry me?'

'It's not you.' Oh damn, he looked hurt. 'I'm just not the kind of girl who gets married.'

He folded his arms. 'Why not? It's entirely legal and would solve a truckload of problems Stateside.'

'Oh, Yves.' I bit my lip. Who was I fooling? We'd already decided to be together for ever by our actions over the last few days. Marriage made perfect sense and I wasn't so foolish as to turn down the one whom I loved more than life itself.

Except . . .

'How many high school girls are married?'

He shrugged. 'Not many—if any. But you are one of a kind already, so why not?' He leaned closer. 'We can have it as our guilty secret if you like. We are both good at keeping quiet when we have to be.'

I liked the sound of that: turning up at a school with what appeared to be a scandalous background when really I had become a respectable married woman. 'OK.'

He looked puzzled. 'OK what?'

'Yes, Yves Benedict, I will marry you.'

He sprang up and joined me on the bed, noses together, taking care not to touch my injury. 'That, Phoenix Corrigan, has made my day.' His lips pressed gently against mine to seal the deal.

Somebody cleared their throat behind us. 'Now, now, none of that.'

I peeked round Yves's shoulders to find his entire family and Sky clustered in the doorway. It was Mr Benedict who had spoken but he didn't look that upset to catch us in this way.

Zed looped his arm around Sky. 'See, I told you she'd be fine.'

Xav tugged Yves off me and handed me the call button. 'You'll be needing this, Phee, when my irritating little squirt of a brother bothers you again. Just press and the nurses will come running. One of them looks like a pro-wrestler, so she'll make short work of him.'

Yves cuffed Xav in the stomach. 'I don't bother her. I'm going to marry her.'

As Karla squealed with delight, Xav and Zed groaned.

'You said the "M" word,' Victor said with despair. 'There will be no stopping our mother now.' He approached my bedside. 'Phoenix, I am very, very sorry for all you are about to endure at the hands of our parent.' He bent closer and whispered in my ear. 'She means well.'

Too late, Yves realized his tactical error. 'Just a small ceremony—tomorrow. So Phee can come back with us as soon as possible.'

'But that won't give us time to get Trace, Uriel and Will over!' wailed Karla, looking at Yves as if he had just shot her favourite puppy.

'Phee won't be up to a big event for some time yet, Mom.' Yves tried to dig his way out but we all knew it was hopeless. 'Tell my mom, Phee.'

I grinned, refusing to be drawn into the discussion. 'I'm sure your mum knows best, Yves.'

Karla beamed at me then shook her finger at her son. 'I knew I liked that girl, Yves. You treat her right or you'll have me to answer to.'

I couldn't stop a yawn, even though I was more happy than I'd ever been. I was fighting tiredness and the dull pain from my leg. Mother-radar fully functioning, Karla was on to me in a second.

'Out, out, all of you!' she fussed. 'Phoenix needs her rest if she is going to be a bride so soon.' She beamed at me. 'And so young! Same age I was when your father hurried me to the altar.'

Saul looked a little embarrassed by the memory.

Xav laughed. 'Cradle-snatcher,' he teased his dad.

Karla landed a kiss on her husband's mouth. 'We snatched

each other. Now, everyone out of here.'

Obediently, the Benedicts filed from the room. Yves looked as though he'd prefer to stay but his mother hooked him by the elbow to continue their 'discussion' in the corridor out of earshot. I fell asleep smiling.

chapter 23

Karla was persuaded to settle for a small civil ceremony in London to complete my visa requirements on the promise that Yves gave me a proper church wedding a month later in their home town of Wrickenridge, Colorado. The argument that clinched it—a rather brilliant one on my part, Yves acknowledged—was that no bride would want to hobble down the aisle. Sky was to be my bridesmaid, and Xav, Yves's best man, and his other brothers, ushers.

I immediately took to the little town in the Rockies where the Benedicts lived, falling in love with the scenery and the people within five minutes of arriving. Even though we were technically married, Karla insisted that Yves and I live apart until after the 'proper' wedding, which was why I took up residence with Sky and her parents, Sally and Simon, for a few weeks in their Gothic clapboard house. Sally in particular was curious about me, sensing that my English background was unorthodox to say the least, but somehow Sky managed to keep them from asking too many questions. I think her secret was distraction: every time Sally embarked on an interrogation, Sky would ask her opinion on the wedding dress or the flower arrangements. I was going to have to learn how to manage mothers now I was gaining a formidable in-law to compensate for my glaring lack of relatives.

In this little interval of peace between the events in London and our wedding, I began to learn there was more to soulfinders than even my mother's fairytales had promised. Though not in the same house, Yves and I were almost continually together through our telepathic link. This was not to say that we were chatting the whole time, just that we were aware of the other, like a mental holding of hands. My world had shifted on its axis, the magnetic poles flipped, because now I was never lonely. And, when combined, our gifts showed signs of blooming as Sky had described with her and Zed. I discovered I could use my mental freeze to act as a kind of fire break so Yves did not have to worry much about losing his cool (something I made him do all too frequently, I'm afraid—a new life had not completely reformed the old Phoenix). We were really more complete together than apart.

The night before our big day, Sky came up to the guest room to announce that I had some visitors. Quickly brushing my hair, I went downstairs with barely a trace of a limp to find all the Benedict brothers waiting for me in the lounge. They were quite a sight, including the three whom I had only just met: Trace, the burly cop from Denver whose looks were softened by his intelligent brown eyes; Uriel the thoughtful and intuitive academic with a mane of light brown hair; Will, the most laid-back, every boy's buddy and every girl's heart-throb. I looked to Yves, wondering what had brought them all out in force like this.

'Scared I was going to do a runner?' I joked.

Yves pulled me to a seat beside him. 'Too late, Mrs Benedict: we are already married.'

'Only technically, according to your mother. So why are you

here? Not that I don't like seeing you all, of course,' I corrected myself rapidly, not wanting to offend so many brothers-in-law.

Victor cleared his throat. 'We have some good news and some bad news. Which do you want to hear first?'

My pulse spiked. 'Always the bad news. Don't tell me, the minister has chicken pox?'

Victor smiled slightly and shook his head. He glanced at Trace but his older brother nodded at him to be the messenger. 'The two men known as Dragon and Unicorn?'

'Yes, my brothers. They died in the fire, didn't they?'

Yves brushed my thigh, not liking the memories. I know he still carried the burden of feeling partly responsible for their deaths.

'They weren't—your brothers, I mean. The DNA test came back a negative on any family tie.'

I gaped.

'Also, they weren't brothers to each other. This made us curious and we checked a sample taken from Kevin Smith, known to you as the Seer. He is not the father of any of you. In fact, we very much suspect from other indications of the state of his health that he is infertile, though even a criminal is allowed his medical privacy so I cannot confirm this.'

'What do you mean . . . ? All those women . . . ?'

'Quite. I think we can assume they were purely decorative. He liked the fantasy of being father to their children without acknowledging that he was making it up. He probably even persuaded some of them that it was true, maybe even himself.'

I wrapped my arms around myself, deeply shaken. I'd only just reconciled myself to the notion I came from such bad stock, and now I had to revisit the entire matter. 'He wasn't my father.'

'No.'

'So who was?'

'That only your mother knew.'

'A man . . . in Greece, she said.'

Trace got up to examine me closely as if he was about to file a report on a suspect. 'Seems plausible to me: you have the colouring—dark hair, olive skin, five-four. Mediterranean.'

'OK, yes, I can believe in that, then. She didn't lie to me after all.' I turned to Yves, smiling through tears. 'I thought she had.'

He rubbed away a droplet as it tracked down my cheek. 'It didn't matter either way, Phee.'

Trace returned to his seat. 'You may wonder why we are all present to hear the news.'

I hadn't been, but he was right. It was a bit odd to have such a private moment shared before so many. 'You're nosy?'

He laughed, a deep rumble in his broad chest. 'Yeah, that too. But we realized at dinner that you have no father.'

'Um . . . yes, well, we've just established that, haven't we?'

'No one to walk you down the aisle.'

Ah. Now I understood.

'So we thought we'd give you a choice if you want to take it. Any one of us would be deeply honoured to be chosen.'

Yves grinned at his brothers, incredibly proud of all of them at the moment.

Sky bounced on Zed's lap where she had been perched. 'That is so sweet, guys! I don't know how she is going to choose.'

Nor did I. Trace, Victor, Uriel, Will . . .

Xav shook his head. 'Not me, I'm afraid. I'd better stick to that ring thing I have to do.'

So not Xav. That left Zed. Five amazing guys all queuing up to let me hold their arm tomorrow.

'Dad would offer too,' Uriel mentioned, 'but we told him this was our deal. He has to stop Mom crying over everyone.'

'Toughest assignment,' murmured Will.

I turned to Yves. 'Would you mind very much if I stole something—or some things—from you?'

His eyes crinkled in laughter lines. 'My pleasure. What is it this time—phone, wallet, not the ring, surely?' He patted his pocket.

I poked him. 'No, of course not. I want to steal all your ushers. I want five stand-in fathers to give me away to make up for the fact I keep losing mine.'

Zed high-fived Sky. 'See, I told you the wedding looked odd when I foresaw it yesterday.'

Delighted by the compromise, Yves kissed me until I was breathless. 'Take them please. They wouldn't allow me to live if I refused.'

So that was how they come to be still talking about our wedding in Wrickenridge: about the poor minister jumping out of his skin as five gruff voices answered when he asked who was giving away this woman, the wedding photos with the bride's side strangely outweighing the groom's even though I'm an orphan, the bizarre goings-on with fruit at the reception.

Yet they don't know the really scandalous secret: that the bride and groom are both accomplished thieves. My claim to that title is already well established—though from now on I plan to keep my stealing on the right side of the law. Yves has now joined me in the Robin Hood Hall of Fame for, as he pointed out as he drove us away from the reception, he had stolen me out from under the noses of some of the toughest criminals in the world, and he was not planning on handing me back. Ever.

About the author

Joss Stirling lives in Oxford and has always been fascinated by the idea that life is more than what we see on the surface. She was born in East London but it has changed so much thanks to the Olympics 2012 that she decided it would be fun to return to the area for *Stealing Phoenix*.

You can visit her website on www.jossstirling.com